Drive!

"Go on home and get plenty of rest. It might be an idea to pray a little, too. Because this drive ain't the worst thing you got to put up with. The worst thing's me. I been hazed into it against my will. I don't take kindly to being pushed into doing something I got my doubts about. So I'm feeling pretty damn mean, and I'm gonna stay that way until this whole damn thing is done. So watch out. You got a summer ahead you'll remember to your dying day."

From THE COWBOYS by William Dale Jennings

"A refreshingly different picture of the West . . . sad, hilarious, heartwarming."

—**Publishers' Weekly**

Warner Bros.
A Kinney Leisure Service
presents

JOHN WAYNE

in
A Mark Rydell Film

THE COWBOYS

Co-Starring
ROSCOE LEE BROWNE
BRUCE DERN
COLLEEN DEWHURST as Kate

PANAVISION® TECHNICOLOR®

Music by
John Williams

Screenplay by
Irving Ravetch & Harriet Frank, Jr.
and William Dale Jennings

Produced and Directed by
Mark Rydell

The Cowboys

William Dale Jennings

A NATIONAL GENERAL COMPANY

RLI: $\dfrac{\text{VLM 6 (VLR 5–6)}}{\text{IL 10-up}}$

THE COWBOYS
A Bantam Book

PRINTING HISTORY
Stein & Day edition published September 1971
Bantam edition published February 1972

Map on pp. viii-ix was redesigned from map by Rafael Palacios from
The Frontier Years by Mark H. Brown and William R. Felton. Copy-
right © 1955 by Mark H. Brown and William R. Felton. Reprinted
by permission of Holt, Rinehart & Winston, Inc.

Cover photograph by Bob Willoughby from Lee Gross

Published simultaneously in the United States and Canada

Bantam Books are published by Bantam Books, Inc., a National
General company. Its trade-mark, consisting of the words "Bantam
Books" and the portrayal of a bantam, is registered in the United
States Patent Office and in other countries. Marca Registrada.
Bantam Books, Inc., 666 Fifth Avenue, New York, N.Y. 10019.

PRINTED IN THE UNITED STATES OF AMERICA

This book is dedicated to
RAMON F. ADAMS

It might be an idea for the reader to go to the back of the book and read the glossary first. You'll understand everything that's going on without it, but you'll have a great deal more fun these next few hours if you bone up on the West a bit. The Western language is so rich and full of crazy comparisons and double meanings that those few pages at the end may open doors for you instead of only close a book.

WJD

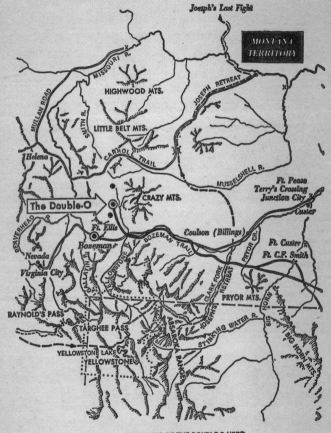

THE DRIVE OF THE DOUBLE-O HERD
SUMMER AND FALL 1877

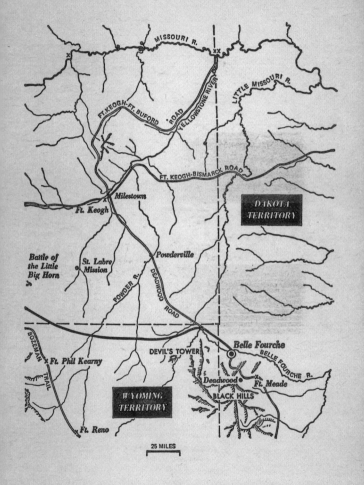

MISSOURI R.

LITTLE MISSOURI R.

FT. KEOGH–FT. BUFORD ROAD

YELLOWSTONE RIVER

FT. KEOGH–BISMARCK ROAD

DAKOTA TERRITORY

Milestown

Ft. Keogh

Powderville

Battle of the Little Big Horn

St. Labre Mission

POWDER R.

DEADWOOD ROAD

BOZEMAN TRAIL

Ft. Phil Kearny

DEVIL'S TOWER

Belle Fourche

BELLE FOURCHE R.

Deadwood

Ft. Meade

BLACK HILLS

WYOMING TERRITORY

Ft. Reno

25 MILES

The Cowboys

1

Wil Andersen's ranch house was made of logs, with clay between. It was big, comfortable, and well put together. It had a long covered porch, glass in several windows, and floors in all the rooms. Wil and Annie were pleased when guests were impressed; both remembered well the tent they'd lived in when they first settled on the land.

Wil himself was big and well put together. At fifty-five, he had become handsome in a rugged, weather-beaten way. He sat on the top step of the porch braiding rawhide into a rope. He wore good boots, a silver buckle on his belt, and a five-year-old hat that looked like he couldn't have bought it before last fall.

At the sound of horses riding hard, Wil looked up, squinted at the approaching dust cloud, and went back to his plaiting. When the riders didn't slack up coming in the gate, he laid the rope aside, stood up, and drew his gun almost casually.

The first of the three riders began talking as they jumped down. Then they saw the gun. All of them stopped dead and stood in the settling dust. They were in their early twenties, lean and male. Smiley was a hair shorter than the other two, and less afraid to talk.

"What's the matter, Mr. Andersen?"

The gun kept pointing through Wil's answer: "When a man rides right up on me and then gets off on the far side, I draw. I don't give a damn if you are my hands, I draw."

1

The words "I'm sorry" were not in use on this spread. Smiley took off his hat, whacked the dust out of it against his thigh, and stood with it in his hands. The other two followed suit. Wil glanced at the lines across their foreheads where they'd pulled their hats down tight going at a gallop. He slipped his gun back in without touching either side of the holster.

"All right, what's the big news?"

Smiley swallowed and said one word: "Gold."

"Where?"

"Ruby River."

"You mean there's another strike at Alder Gulch? I thought that was all played out years ago."

"No, sir, this is a new one about eighteen–nineteen miles up the Ruby. Almost to the Beaverhead."

"Ain't no gold up there."

The tall red-headed fellow surprised himself and everyone else by bursting in.

"But we just seen a whole fruitjar full in Bozeman! Oh, Mr. Andersen, it's happening all over again, and maybe even bigger this time!"

Wil looked at him quietly. Red-headed Howdy blinked, blushed, and looked at the ground.

"Boys, there might be two or three jarfuls up there, but that's all."

Smiley shook his head. "That ain't what they're saying in Bozeman, sir! Everybody's lighting out! The town's empty as a bone orchard. And from what we hear, they's gonna be rich men coming down from the Ruby River!"

Wil squinted at him. He looked at the other two and shifted his weight to the other foot. His voice was low and even: "Boys, in sixty-two and -three, one hell of a lot of people with gold colic got to the gulch too late. It was all staked out. So they spread out and prospected every stream and hill inside of fifty miles. They went as far north as Helena, and south clear down to the Targhee Pass. None of them came back with enough dust for a souvenir. Boys, the chances of finding gold on the Ruby River are mighty, mighty slim."

The three young men shifted their positions; two looked at the ground, one at the far mountains. Wil shrugged. "But I might set a few head aside just in case this rumor starts a rush. Prospectors like their beef, at any price."

Unable to look up, Smiley said to the ground, "Well, the fact is, Mr. Andersen, me and the boys kind of thought we'd like to snoop around up there for a couple weeks and just sort of take a look-see."

"Oh?"

Smiley began to take short peeks at him to see how he was taking it. "The way we figure, it ain't quite time for the roundup yet, and you're just wasting good food on us without much work to do. So we thought we'd like to take off up there just to sort of satisfy our curiosity, and then git right back down here as soon as you need us."

". . . If you don't strike it rich."

The other two peeked at him hopefully, and Smiley grinned his glowing grin. "We know we ain't coming back rich, Mr. Andersen. But damn if we ain't just real curious. I swear it'd take a whole carload of genuine gold to keep us away from your roundup and the drive. After all, we ain't missed a one in three years now."

"And if you're still real curious after a couple weeks, I suppose I'll just have to mosey on down to Bozeman and pick me out some more hands, huh?"

"Oh, sir, as far as that goes, I swear you won't never have no trouble finding good hands to replace us. The Double-O's got a real fine name all over the territory, and as long as you got Charlie Nightlinger running your chuck wagon, you won't never want for good hands aplenty."

"But didn't you say Bozeman was like a bone orchard? Hardly nobody left in town?"

Smiley licked his lips and said, "Well, it ain't that empty. I mean, they's people there."

"Who? Women and children? But I guess I could go on a roundup and a drive if I had *enough* women and children. Maybe one or two for each cow. Maybe fifteen hundred?"

He turned his back on them and started up the steps.

Smiley swallowed and said, "Then—hm—it's all right with you, Mr. Andersen?"

Wil half-turned. "All right?"

"I mean, honestly, you won't be needing us for the next couple weeks, will you now?"

"No, I hadn't planned on making you sweat until we started rounding up the horses. Now it looks like that's what *I'll* be doing. I thought I was all set and ready to go; now it looks like I'll be starting from scratch right at the time of year there ain't a good man to be had."

Smiley shook his head. "No, Mr. Andersen, you got no cause to worry. I just know we'll be right back here standing on this very spot in exactly two weeks to the minute! It's a promise."

"If something *else* don't come up that you get real curious about."

Smiley swallowed. "Now, look yere, Mr. Andersen, if they's gonna be any hard feelings, we—"

"Hard feelings? Why should there be hard feelings? You boys know damned well I'll have to ride all over the territory trying to find good hands this time of year. That means I'll be starting the beef roundup in the middle of the summer, and ending the drive in snow. And that's just what I'll do if I have to do it all myself, because this beef's *got* to go to market. Hard feelings? Why, if I wasn't such a believer in sparing the rod, I'd bash your damn empty heads together."

"But it ain't like we're leaving the Double-O, Mr. Andersen!"

"What do you mean you ain't leaving? What the hell do you call going up to Ruby River?"

Smiley was beginning to frown. "But we're coming back! Ain't we, boys?"

The other two showed how uncertain they were about the whole thing by coming out with real strong yeses and sures.

Wil snorted: "If nothing better comes along. I was taught that when a man puts in with an outfit, he stays with it until the last cow's drove to market."

"And that's exactly what we're gonna do! You watch and see! But in between now and starting the roundup, we just *gotta* take a little peek at them findings. What if it turns out to be a bigger strike than Alder Gulch?"

"What the hell good'd that do me? I ain't no prospector!"

Smiley brayed: "If we strike it rich, we'll come back here and buy them critters off you ourselfs! Now, what do you say to that, sir, huh?"

"I say you're all three grown men and old enough to abide by the decisions you make. It's all up to you."

One of the other two said, "Smiley, I don't think we ought to. I just as soon stay."

Smiley turned to the third man. "What about you, Howdy? You willing to let the whole thing drop— *and never know?*"

Howdy shrugged and looked off at the horizon. "You two decide. I'll go along with whatever you boys want."

Smiley looked like he was about to cry. "Mr. Andersen, we leave it up to you. Say the word, and we'll stay and forget the whole thing."

Wil Andersen turned again and started for the door.

"Mr. Andersen, sir, we just can't decide ourselfs!"

The big man turned around. His eyes were ice. His jaw muscles rippled. He spoke quietly. "You got nothing to decide. I don't want you."

The three young men stared at him. Wil glared back.

"Pick up your gear and get off my spread. And don't set foot in here again. I'll come out shooting if you do."

As Wil opened the door and stepped inside, Smiley said, "Mr. Andersen?" The door closed.

The three stood numbly for several moments; there was about them the terrible air of those who have been wronged and cannot plead their cause. Then Smiley set off for the bunkhouse. They made up their saddle rolls in silence, mounted, and walked their horses down the road toward Bozeman. None of them looked back.

Annie Andersen stood back from the window with folded arms and watched them go. Her handsome face seemed to be remembering.

Wil walked around the big room aimlessly. His hands were fists in his coat pockets. He went over to the kitchen pump, gulped a cup of water, and wiped his mouth on his sleeve. He sat at the big table and said, "Got any coffee?" When Annie set the steaming cup before him, the words finally came.

"Dammit, I liked them boys! I liked them a lot, and they failed me. I don't give a damn if they did change their minds. Even if it was only for two seconds, they failed the spread and you and me. And two seconds is all it takes to lose everything."

The two graves up on the hill seemed to burn through the room's thick walls.

"Annie, how could I ever feel easy around them again? God Almighty, woman, that herd's everything we got in the world! You know how many long, hard years it took us to build it. And, Annie, if I can get it to Belle Fourche in one piece, there'll be real comfort around here for the rest of our lives! How could I risk all that with a bunch of feather-brained young fools that might leave me and the herd way out in the middle of nowhere? No, Annie, I'd rather tighten my belt and risk a bad winter."

She looked at him across the room. Her eyes fairly crackled. "You don't mean wait till next year! Wil, if next winter is just a hair worse than this last one, we stand to lose our yearlings again."

"I know that."

"And the *Almanac* says—"

"I know what the *Almanac* says."

"What's more, you wouldn't be fit to live with. I can just see you pacing back and forth out there in front of the thermometer all winter long. And not eating. Most men get nice and fat during the winter, but you get so skinny it scares me."

Wil smiled to himself. She was always whittling big issues down to trivia. He sat turning the cup around and around between his rough hands. After a while he said, "I was wrong, wasn't I?" His voice was soft and low, but what he said was a cry.

She came to him and stood behind his chair with a hand on each of his shoulders. "Sure you were." She thought a moment, then sighed. "The thing is, Wil, you just don't know how to handle young fellers when you like them."

2

Bozeman was a little better than thirty-five miles from the Double-O. It was a small, shabby town of some two dozen buildings, and fairly sad even when it prospered. Its loyalest citizens had to admit that Bozeman was the sort of place that you had to pass through to get somewhere else, and now it looked as if whole hordes had done just that. Both of its streets were filled with the rubbish of travelers. The air seemed to echo with the word "Good-bye," called out by many voices, and the few people to be seen looked definitely left behind.

Each time Wil rode into town, he stopped first at Mrs. Bowen's Hotel and Dining Room. There she set before him a ridiculously large meal at pre-rush prices. And the last thing he did before heading home was look in on Anse at the Golden Eagle Saloon. But where that had once been the rousing finale to an eventful day, it was now dismal.

Wil hesitated at the door. He went on in only when he realized that Anse must see him through the cut glass. He wanted a drink, but not in a dark, deserted hall. It was the time of afternoon that the Golden Eagle should have been thundering. Instead, the plain, long room was empty except for Anse, on the sober side of the bar. The crack in the big mirror behind him throbbed like a nerve. Wil's boots echoed across the floor. Touching glasses vibrated. A bottle and glass were waiting for him by the time he hooked a heel around the brass rail.

They both stood for a long while without saying a word. Wil leaned on one elbow and Anse on two as they looked out through the painted window at the town.

A dog trotted quickly from place to place, as if it had lost something. A solitary chicken pecked around outside the boarded-up feed-and-grain store. Two women stood talking with folded arms and shawls drawn tight. There was nothing else but the wind blowing a piece of crumpled paper.

Wil took a deep breath and sighed through his nose. "Anse, I've stopped every man on the street for two weeks now, and nobody wants a job. They say they're either already spoke for or off to the Ruby. I sure must of made a name for myself as one mean old son of a bitch."

Anse's voice was surprisingly deep. It seemed to be piped up from some nearby well.

"Now, Wil, that ain't so. They ain't a man in

Montana territory that wouldn't be proud to work on the Double-O. The thing is, you just let yourself get caught between times."

"Let?"

Their eyes met.

"Let. Go on and get mad if you want to, but Smiley and the Boys was good boys. Maybe kind of easy to lead, but that's better than having nobody but top screws in your outfit. And I can tell you right here and now that the onliest thing in the world that could make them quit on you was gold. Their worst fault was they was a little greedy, just like the rest of us."

Wil slapped the bar with the flat of his hand. "Gawdammit, Anse, I'm as greedy as the next man, but you don't see me going around promising to do business with old friends and walking out on them right in the middle of it."

"Middle?"

"I planned on starting the roundup this week. Now, Anse, do you honestly think they'd of come back in time?"

Anse scratched an armpit and squinted up at the high ceiling. "Hmm, no. As I recolleck, you was gone *all summer* during the Alder Gulch stampede."

"Anse, that wasn't the same."

"You come back so thin you couldn't keep your pants up!"

"Anse, you're the only man I ever knew that talked better sense drunk than dry. Have a drink and sober up."

The big man beamed and reached himself a glass. "There's one thing to be said for you, Wil. Nobody could ever accuse you of a lot of sweet talk."

Wil watched the brown liquid rise in the glass, and sighed: "The fact is, if I don't find myself some hands real soon, I'm gonna be in trouble."

"Oh, come on, Wil. You'll make out the exact same way all the rest of us poor humans does—on tick."

Wil's eyes went wide. "Credit? Me? Anse, I never

did live on my jawbone, and I never will. Anyhow, Annie and me ain't gonna starve. That's not what I'm talking about. Take a look at this."

Wil pulled a letter out of the breast pocket of his shirt and laid it on the bar. Anse unfolded it and put on the frown that goes along with lip-reading.

It was from John Tingle in Belle Fourche. After a single sentence about the weather, he got right down to business. The government was hurting for beef to feed the Indians on the reservations. The public was in such a great big uproar about what they'd heard of starving and disease among the tribes that a cattle man could pretty well name his own price. You could count on today's asking price of four to five cents a pound to just about double.

Anse looked up at Wil and blinked several times. Wil nodded and tapped the letter on the bar. "I *expected* to get maybe eighteen thousand dollars for my beef this year. If he's right, I'll come home with thirty-six. That's more money than I ever dreamed I'd make."

Anse stared at him for a long moment, then suddenly downed his drink and poured another. When he spoke, his deep voice was soft with wonder. "And you kicked Smiley and the boys off your spread because they hurt your feelings! Wil, I ought to throw you outta here. This here's a saloon, not a insane asylum."

Wil waved his remarks away. "Aw, they didn't hurt my feelings! They scared me. All of a sudden I saw everything I own in the hands of a bunch of crazy young hoodlums that might skedaddle on me right in the middle of the drive! You know yourself how young fellers are having themselves whims all the time. And there's nothing in the world that can change their minds but time or . . ." Wil looked away and added, "Or hot lead."

Anse looked embarrassed. He knew all about Wil's sons.

"And it's getting late for me, Anse. I can't risk

everything I own with a bunch of wild youngsters. I'd rather give up the Indian beef and wait a year and get just the going price. It would be more than enough for Annie and me."

He looked out of the window, and his eyes stared back in time. His jaw muscles rippled, and he said softly, "But for all these years of hell, I would like to get us that thirty-six thousand dollars. *Just to know I could.*"

Suddenly Anse broke into his thoughts and said an idiotic thing. But he said it softly, like a devil tempting. "Then, Wil, it looks to me like the only thing you got left to do is come on and ankle over to Miss Fanny Zook's with me 'fore school lets out."

"What for?"

"My friend, she's got some pupils that'll honestly open up your eyes!"

Wil glared at him. "What the hell are you talking about?"

"The girls are young and go clear down to eight. But the boys are all thirteen, fourteen, fifteen. The oldest boy's almost as big as a man, and there's not a one that don't ride real good or can't rope a jackrabbit in a high wind."

"Anse, I just don't get what you're driving at!"

"Wil, you know as well as I do, lots of cattlemen use young fellers on their drives—and they work out real well."

"Maybe poking and punching cows onto boxcars, but not out on the range! Anse, this is man's work!"

Anse tapped the edge of the bar to emphasize his words. "But, Wil, boys is easier to handle than growed men! They ain't so cod-proud and set in their ways. They won't be off drinking and fighting and fornicating every time you come in smelling distance of a honky-tonk town."

Suddenly the big man looked down at his hands and blushed deep red. Word for word, he'd just described exactly what both Wil's boys had done.

Wil didn't seem to notice. He snapped up the

discussion without a moment's pause. "Anse, it's four hundred miles from my spread to Belle Fourche. That trail don't miss an inch of mean country, wild rivers, and long stretches where there's nothing to drink but the sweat off your brow. For every soldier at Fort Smith, there's a dozen outlaws and wild Injuns out there. Don't forget what happened to our fine Mr. Custer just last year. And on top of all that, you stand there and expect me to play nanny to a bunch of little tiny baby boys?"

Wil had been playing with his full glass. Now he tossed it down in one long swallow. Anse refilled it and poured himself another. Together they looked at the ceiling and drank thoughtfully.

When they brought their heads and glasses down, there were three men standing just inside the door. Their appearance was so silent that Wil looked first at their feet. They were white, but all three wore moccasins. Wil turned away and studied his empty glass.

Anse inspected the trio as they padded toward the bar. They were sorry-looking specimens, greasy and filthy as buffalo skinners, and dressed in an almost clownish mixture of clothes to keep out the Montana winter. The tallest looked stupid and dirty, the young one with the oddly new-looking Stetson looked depraved and dirty, and the little long-haired one looked good and dirty. Leading them to the bar, he said, "You Wil Andersen?"

Wil didn't look up. Anse asked, "What you want with Wil Andersen?"

"We hear tell he's looking for hands, Mister Bar Dog."

Anse's nostrils quivered. There was nothing wrong with running a saloon. It was the way the little viper said it.

Without looking up, Wil said, "I got all the hands I need."

Six eyes focused on him. The long-haired one said, "But the man down at the stable said you was in there not twenty minutes ago looking for cowhands, any size, any shape, any age."

Wil neither answered nor looked at him. The cocky little man waited a moment, with eyes flashing. He shifted his weight to the other foot, put his hands on his hips, and began talking louder than a man should only a couple feet away.

"Mister, you mean to say you found cowhands in Bozeman right in the middle of a gold strike?"

He smiled over his shoulder at his companions. His teeth were brilliant white.

"Must have got himself some drunk Injuns."

Still smiling, Long Hair looked up at Wil and began tapping the big man's arm for emphasis as he spoke.

"Tell you what, old friend, I'll make you a real good deal. Me and my partners here'll go on your drive with you, and we won't ask a cent of pay!"

Wil looked thoughtfully down at the forefinger tapping his arm. The young man continued enthusiastically.

"Honest fact is, we'd take mighty kindly to a couple months of your Charlie Nightlinger's chuck. Hear tell he's real good with the pots and pans, and we ain't had a real meal all winter long. Now, if that ain't the best offer you had all year, I don't know what is!"

With a toss of the head, he whipped a strand of hair back over his shoulder. Then his eyes settled fondly on the bottle in front of Wil.

"Now, old friend, we'd be mighty obliged to seal the bargain with a small libation."

Anse whacked the cork into the bottle with the palm of his hand. It was a familiar gesture.

The short man's smile vanished. Then suddenly he turned to Wil Andersen with a generous smile, as if nothing had happened. "Well, what do you say, old friend? When do we start?"

Wil spoke to his glass. "I got all the hands I need right now."

Long Hair refused to let go the smile. "But we're gonna work for free!"

Wil looked him up and down with quiet eyes. "Son, I accept the value a man sets on himself. Nobody gets nothing worth having free!"

Long Hair's smile vanished. It left eyes that glittered like broken glass.

Wil took in all three of them. "I do need hands. Only not that bad."

Long Hair couldn't seem to believe his ears. His eyes were blank with rage. He shouted up at the taller man: "*What did you just say, old coot?*"

Wil looked down at him quietly. His gray gaze was cool as a cougar's. He spoke quietly. "I'd feel safer with the drunk Indians."

Long Hair controlled his rage for only a moment. He whipped out his gun. His friends drew, too. They all stood ready, with feet apart.

They looked mighty dangerous. But nothing happened. The cool gray gaze never wavered.

Wil heard Anse moving behind him. He stepped aside. The three young gunmen found themselves looking into the black eyes of a double-barreled shotgun lying across the bar. It would take in all three of them with one blast.

Long Hair was the last to put his gun away. He glared up at Wil a moment, then suddenly showed all his fine teeth in a glowing smile. "I feel like I just had a real close call, and I don't mean that old shotgun, neither. I almost tied in with a man that's *too damn old to know when he's lucky*. He ain't for me, no, sir!"

Then came the surprise. Wil Andersen stepped back in front of the shotgun and poked his forefinger in Long Hair's chest. The force of the jab made the smaller man step back to keep his balance. For an instant he looked surprised; then he looked at the floor and gave a little shrug, as if he were smiling at himself.

Wil said, "Get out of Bozeman. Right now."

Long Hair held up both palms and moved them

as if he were patting an invisible wall. The smile was only on one side of his mouth. He turned and took a step toward the door, then turned back and made that take-it-easy gesture again, still with the tight, wry little smile.

The two men at the bar watched in fascination as Long Hair began an elaborate stroll toward the door. It was the very slow, lazy, I-don't-care stroll of a young boy who does care—very much. His partners followed uncertainly.

Long Hair flipped his golden mane over his shoulders with the backs of both hands. He stopped beside a cuspidor and carefully spit on the floor beside it. He ran his forefinger across a tabletop, then, imitating Wil's gesture, pushed a chair over with a single jab.

At the door, Long Hair let the others go first; then he turned back to the two men at the bar and made that same take-it-easy gesture one last time before going out. He closed the door behind him with elaborate care.

Wil and Anse looked at each other. Wil said, "My God, what was that all about?" Anse shrugged. Wil grunted thoughtfully: "It was almost too easy."

He looked up when Anse said, "By grab, I got to load this thing one of these days. Keeps slipping my mind."

Wil smiled for the first time in days. "Let's see your Colt." Anse slid it across the bar. Wil broke it and shook his head. He began loading it.

"I'm putting just five beans in the wheel, Anse. My old dad used to say you ain't losing nothing by keeping one chamber empty for the hammer. And if you can't do the job in five shots, you sure better get the hell out of the way."

Anse wasn't paying any attention. "Say, Wil, you know what's safer than drunk Indians?" Wil looked up. "A round dozen of Miss Zook's schoolboys!"

"It's plain to see you never had any boys of your

own. You ought to know, my two was in trouble every minute of the night and day. And I was rough on them. Nobody can say I wasn't."

Anse mumbled, "There's a difference between being only rough and really being tough. Lots of parents just yells."

"I was tough on them, too." He slid the Colt back across the bar. "There you are. Five beans in the wheel, and if them stinking three ever comes in here again, I'd advise you to draw, fire, and ask questions later. They'll be looking for trouble."

Anse was taking off his apron. 'Wil, I think I'm gonna close up for a spell and meander over and see Miss Fanny home from school. Ever since all the able-bodied bucks has left for Ruby River, I been able to drop in on her almost every day without having to stand in line. She may not be the prettiest gal that ever drew breath, but she's sure got spirit. And a figger! Come on along."

"Now, what kind of a fool brings along a friend when he goes calling?"

Anse was pasting down his hair with saliva in front of the mirror. "A scared one. I tell you, she's got *spirit*! She may look like a Monkey Ward wife sent on approval, but she carries herself like the Queen of Sheba. And underneath, she's one of the nicest little old gals that ever drew breath. Come on, Wil. I want you to take a squint at the only female I ever wanted to propose to."

Anse turned and stared at Wil as if somebody else had said that. He added in a sort of panic, *"But I ain't going to!"* He walked to the door, putting on his short coat, brushing it, and saying, "Not me, not at my age, no, sir!" Wil shook his head in silence, and Anse boomed, "Now, you stop that!"

3

The schoolhouse was a big square room with a pot-
bellied stove in the middle, long movable benches,
and cruelly large windows so that the students could
see what they were missing. There was a steel en-
graving of George Washington by an artist who had
evidently allowed him to remove his wooden den-
tures while posing. Except for a blackboard and the
students, all the rest was Miss Fanny Zook.

She was little more than twenty-two, pleasant as
good news, and ugly as sin. There was indeed something regal about her. She seemed to be hostess to
the world, and anxious to demonstrate that you didn't
need lineage to be a real lady.

Wil watched the way she assigned various tasks to
each little group around the room so that she'd be
free to chat with her visitors. He was fascinated.
Anse was awed, and the students were devoted—especially the older boys. She was calmly undermining
a whole generation that would never again look on
beauty as important. These boys would all look for
spirit in a woman and find few to measure up to
Miss Fanny Zook.

Wil's gaze moved from boy to boy. They were
studying him. Their eyes dropped as he looked at
each face. They were a grave bunch. Not a one
looked like he knew the first thing about giggling.
They might laugh on occasion, but nobody seemed
familiar with the function of smiling. He nodded.
This was all to the good. He'd never felt easy around
a carefree boy, a boy that put his trust in the good-

ness of living and believed that justice was always done.

What's more, he'd seen five horses grazing in the meadow and five saddles on the fence. Riding to school was rare. They must come a long way.

He tried to picture these boys at work on the range. The tall, lean one with the high cheekbones and auburn hair fit in right off. That boy could ride. You could tell from the way he straddled the bench. And something else. He might never invent anything like Mr. Bell's telephone, but he'd be deathly stubborn about getting done what he had to do.

There was a little blond German-looking boy beside him staring out the window with a quiet passion in his eyes. He was like a wolf in a cage, remembering. This must be the Schwartz boy, the one that got himself crippled in a fall. He'd be of no use.

Nor would the great big fat one beside him. He beamed around him as if the whole world were a pumpkin pie. And the smallest wasn't even old enough to remember to button his fly.

But the short little muscular fellow at the end of the bench seemed to radiate maleness. He was that special breed of boy that comes out of the cradle not a large baby but a little man. He sat with his legs spread wide, as if crossing them would be a discomfort to his virility. Wil nodded to himself. He knew the position.

Most of the rest were just plain unlikely. The one with the glasses might make a farmer. One stuttered. That let him out right there. And the inward-turning boy drawing flowers on his slate. Lord, no.

Miss Zook was explaining something to the girls floridly for the benefit of her guests. The girls were aware of them, too. One said loudly for the men to hear, "That's the way it is in our Monkey Ward catalog. It says, 'Each one of these stoves *is* built to last.' Not *are*." Miss Fanny nodded. "That is correct. The verb agrees with the subject, and the subject is *is*. You can't go wrong studying your *Montgomery*

Ward catalog. Their grammar is generally quite acceptable. Now, let's get to work, young ladies."

Then she seemed to read Wil's mind about the boys. She said, "Shall we show our guests how mature our understanding is, boys? Charles?" Three of them looked up, and she narrowed it down to, "Charles Honeycutt, would you please favor us with a reading from today's English assignment? The opening stanza, please."

The tall boy with the auburn hair unstraddled the bench and stood up, frowning at his book. Finding the place, he nailed it down with a finger, cleared his throat, and read with slow caution. "Hail to thee blith uh blithe spirit." He squinted, unbelieving, at Miss Zook, and finished the line as a question: "Bird thou never weren't?" His alarmingly high, cracked voice echoed around the room.

Wil groaned as the whole drive evaporated before his eyes. He said aloud, "Oh, my God, their voices ain't even changed yet!" He jammed on his hat and strode out, cursing by both note and rhyme.

Wil got home just as Annie was lighting the lamps. It was good to see the orange windows appear in the dark. He ate a light supper and went right to bed. After what seemed hours, Annie followed. The fireplace made the whole house alive and shadows dance.

He reached for her. Annie was surprised and pleased. Had he murmured, "Fanny!" she'd still have been pleased but not surprised. Miss Zook's figure was an inspiration to most men in this part of the country. Annie returned his love with zest and strength. Again Wil suspected that it was merest chance that Annie had turned out to be his wife and not the most famous woman of pleasure in all the world. It was a flattering thought.

They slept very late. It was almost six before Annie stirred, and only then because of the quiet sounds outside. She shook Wil. He moved quickly to the

front window with his Sharps cocked and his finger
on the trigger. She followed with hers.

They stopped abruptly and stared.

Twelve boys sat quietly on the porch steps, their
backs to the door. Their horses were lined along the
fence, and their guns stuck out at all angles.

4

They hurried back to their clothes on either side
of the bed. Wil muttered angrily, "I could kill that
Anse. You know what he did, don't you? He went and
told them schoolboys I was out to Miss Zook's looking
for hands. And he knows damn well there isn't a boy
in the territory wouldn't give his left one to go on
a drive. Why, they must of been riding half the night
to get here this early! And ditching school, every
mother's son of them! Annie, what in hell am I gonna
tell 'em after they come all this way? 'Anse was talking through his hat, so just turn around and go on
home'? Make a big pot of coffee. That's the least we
can do."

His gunbelt was part of his clothes. He started to
buckle it on, then changed his mind.

"Well, I guess there's no getting around going out
there. I don't know what I'm gonna say. They're setting
out there serious as a pow-wow of hundred-year-old
chiefs. Well, here goes their first big heartbreak. At
least they'll go home a little older."

Wil opened the door. They all scrambled down to
the ground and stood facing him with their hats in
their hands. Most looked shabby and a little lost in
their oversize hand-me-downs. Wil hitched up his

pants and said, "Morning, boys." They murmured back out of a hush. Wil pushed his shirt deeper inside his pants, then stood several moments, hands on hips, looking at the sky. He cleared his throat and said, "Looks like we're gonna have a pretty dry summer." The boys glanced out there to see what prompted the remark, then quickly back. Nobody said anything.

A soft snorting came from out behind the corral. He knew it was Crazy Alice complaining in the breaking pen, but it did give him something to do to walk to the end of the porch and take a look. That done, he had to turn around and come back to the waiting boys. They stood motionless as a picture, and Crazy Alice had never stopped moving since she was foaled. The two facts and the idea came as naturally as the sun rising. It was so good he almost smiled. Everything was solved.

Wil slid everything but his thumbs in his front pockets and said, "I guess you heard I'm needing hands for my roundup and the drive later on this summer. I need help bad, but not so bad I want to leave a line of graves all along the trail. This is my biggest drive, and I'm set on getting both man and beast to Belle Fourche and back in one piece. No accidents this time."

He scratched his side. All the boys watched steadily.

" 'Course, a man always says that. This time'll be different, but it never is. A drive's never no Sunday-school picnic. First, you're dealing with the dumbest, orneriest critter on God's green earth. A cow's nothing but a lot of trouble tied up in a leather bag. To get him where you're going, you go without food and sleep, you bake in the sun, soak in the rain, and freeze all night. You ease rattlers out of your soogans, coax ticks out of your hide, and pray to God no buffalo stampede don't sweep up the herd and the horses, and leave you jellified under a bush fifty miles away."

The boys watched his big hand as it checked his buttons, rubbed his jaw, and hid back in his pocket.

"But it takes one hell of a lot more than just grit.

You got to be able to ride any horse in any situation. The men on my drive this year'll have eight or nine horses apiece in their string—besides their own individual horse they came on. Each one of them's pretty good for what he was trained for, but there ain't a horse living that don't have his bad side, and you may be the waddy to bring it out. I don't care what Miss Fanny Zook says, the horse ain't no more noble than you are. So what I want's a man that can take good care of every horse in his string but never let a one of them forget who's in the saddle.

"Now, it just so happens I got a real pesky little filly out back name of Crazy Alice. I know nobody ever takes a filly on a drive, but just the same, if there's anybody here that can stay on her ten seconds by the watch, I just *might* keep him in mind when I get around to hiring."

Very pleased with himself, he went inside to get his watch from the bureau drawer. When he came back out, they were all sitting on the top rail that's called the opera house. He'd hoped there'd be more hesitation.

It took Wil a while to saddle the little brockled filly. Once she stepped on his foot. He swore softly and said, "Ain't no mystery why nobody takes a mare on drives." He continued saying offensive things to her in a soothing voice until she was saddled, cinched up, and stood tied to the snubbing post in the middle of the breaking pen.

That done, Wil crawled up to join them, took out his big, thick watch, and said, "There she is, boys. Silly as a lickered-up squaw, but she's the test you got to take. Just remember, there ain't a horse that can't be rode or a man that can't be throwed. Go to it."

There was a long silence as the boys sat looking at the proud and restless filly. Wil would have been startled to know that the spirited little horse reminded most of them of Miss Fanny Zook. It was a fact with implications.

"Come on. Who's first?"

"Oh, I am, sir."

The tallest boy, with the high cheekbones and auburn hair, jumped down to the ground and walked toward Crazy Alice. From the way his body moved in his clothes, there was no question of who'd be in the saddle. Softly, steadily talking his breaking patter, he untied the reins, took them in his teeth, and stood a moment on the near side. Then he reached out, grabbed Alice's ear, and twisted it almost off. She braced her feet and froze in pain, and the boy mounted quickly but without haste.

By the time the ear stopped hurting, Crazy Alice discovered that something had happened she'd never intended to allow. She had a rider. She thought it over. Then she arched her back and rose straight up into the air, as if raised by wires. Sometime later she came back down to earth with a tooth-loosening jolt, arched her back again, and went back up to join the chicken hawks.

Crazy Alice repeated this whole routine monotonously every two seconds while the needle-pointed hand of Wil's big watch crept slowly toward the numeral two. The boy's face looked gravely shocked, yet he never once touched the horn. During the last couple of seconds, he managed to take his hat off and hold it high. Everybody clapped and yelled.

Wil frowned and roared, "Time!" and that sassy young pup yelled back between jolts, "I'll stick till she slows down a mite, sir!" When she paused for breath some five seconds later, the boy swung down with grace, looped the reins over her head, snubbed her at the post, and faced Wil Andersen.

He said, "My name's Charlie Honeycutt. Most everybody calls me Slim. I'm the oldest."

Wil blinked at this announcement and blinked again when Slim turned to the little fellow with broad shoulders and said, "Homer, you go next." It was an order.

The miniature man jumped down and strode toward Crazy Alice as if he were going to eat her in-

stead of ride her. It was a long stretch getting his foot
up in the stirrup. When he did, Crazy Alice pulled
away and showed the whites of her eyes. Homer came
right with her, letting the momentum carry him up
into the saddle. Alice was deeply irritated. This hurt
her pride as much as the twisting had hurt her ear.
Then, on top of that, this abbreviated man in the
saddle raked both heels along her ribs and invited her
to take flight with a ripple of high-voiced but rich profanity.

The little filly started making dust around the corral,
as if she had an important appointment with her tail.
Homer's strong little body clenched her like a vice.
He never stopped scratching. She jolted the breath out
of him with each jump, but he stuck his time and a
little over, then jumped down and dragged her over
to the post by main force. Crazy Alice stood stunned
and tired as the boy faced Wil Andersen and announced, "I'm Homer Bickerdyke. Everybody calls me
Shorty. I'm fifteen and two months."

Wil Andersen's face was calm, and his arms folded,
but his lids quivered slightly, as if he didn't know
whether to laugh or cry. His plan was going all wrong,
but these boys were a delight to his soul. He wanted
to hug the wonderful little bastards, and laugh and
shout right along with them. Instead he sucked a
tooth.

Both Slim and Shorty helped the fat boy mount.
After a while the one with the glasses and the stut-
terer joined in, and they finally got Fats up on the
leather throne. Once there, he sat grinning foolishly,
but the man knew he was scared stiff and respected
him for it. The boy had a ring on his little finger and
a fat man's delicacy in the way he held the reins.
His clothes were well sewn and interesting; they said,
"Somebody loves me." But none of that mattered to
him now. He had a terrifying duty, and he must carry
it out as best he could. He flew no banners.

Crazy Alice was pretty winded. She seemed to sag
in the middle under all this weight. But she had a

duty, too, and she'd do her damnedest. She see-sawed from front to hind legs, presumably hoping to snap the fat boy's neck. During the eight seconds that he lasted, his head did seem to trail behind his body farther than it should. But the higher he rose, the heavier he thudded back down into the saddle. His weight was like a huge mallet. Alice shuddered each time they came down to earth together. Then suddenly the saddle was empty.

Wil's eyes went wide. He stared anxiously into the dust and almost smiled when it cleared. Fats was sitting there on the ground grinning a beaming, golden grin. The ordeal was over, and he'd stuck eight seconds longer than he thought he would. The boys helped him to his feet. He brushed himself off, looked up at Wil Andersen, smiled, and said, "Gol-*ly*!"

Everybody laughed and clapped except Wil. He bit his lip. Slim took a breath and called out, "Charlie Schwartz!" and watched with a special sort of interest as the thin little blond boy crawled down and started to limp toward the snubbing post. Wil knew that Slim hadn't called him until he knew Alice was good and tired. That meant he was afraid for his little friend. Chances were he'd end up worse than a cripple this time. Wil called out, "Hold on there, boy! You sure you want to try?"

The little fellow glared up at Wil. "Sure I'm sure."

"Well, I don't generally hire . . ."

The boy's eyes went blank with anger. Wil swallowed hard.

"Hire what, Mr. Andersen?"

"Truth is, you look a little peaked to me, son."

The boy had approximately twice Wil's pride. He said, "Try me, Mr. Andersen. I'll show you how peaked rides."

"Your folks know you come out here today?"

"Try me!"

"I don't want to have to take you home in the wagon."

The boy's voice was high, but it rippled with a man's

anger. "Sure, I got a bad leg. But in the saddle I'm as much a man as anybody! *Just try me!*"

Wil was taken back. He shrugged helplessly. The boy pulled his hat down firmly with both hands, whipped the reins off the post, and flung them over the horse's head. He had to jump to grab the horn, then swing into the saddle. His feet rammed into the shortened stirrups, his heels dug in sharply, and he leaned forward to yell in Alice's ears. As if shocked out of her fatigue, Alice reared high and began to outdo herself.

Wil felt a certain dark satisfaction. At last one of these cocky little buggers was going to get himself dusted. And he was a little glad it would be this one. He'd never been able to abide infirmity.

Crazy Alice seemed to try to shake herself to pieces. She followed no pattern this time. Every kick and twist was improvised. She seemed out to kill.

The boy rode with the serene dignity of a little prince. With one hand held high and the other easy on the reins, he let Alice do anything she would, and almost seemed to smile. And she did go through every trick in the book except a complete somersault. Yet that ganted boy stuck for ten, then fifteen, then twenty seconds without pulling leather. He'd have ridden her to her knees if Wil hadn't shouted, "I'm not calling time again! Get down from there! You want to wear that poor damn horse out?"

The boy yelled back, "Yep, I guess she does look a little peaked!" He let go and landed neatly on both feet. He faced Wil Andersen through his pale gold hair. "I'm Charlie Schwartz, and I can ride anything on legs."

Wil pinched his septum and looked away as if he weren't the least impressed.

There was a sharp tapping on the window behind them. Wil looked over his shoulder and climbed down. Jumping was for an age gone by. Annie had lots of hot coffee ready, and some good-smelling raisin bread. Wil crammed a piece in his mouth and stood chewing

thoughtfully. He glanced at Annie. She was going
about her business with a funny little half-smile on
her face. He barked, "If there's anything I can't stand,
it's a knowing woman!" and stalked out of the house.

Annie returned to the window to watch with folded
arms and a cup of coffee.

The boy with the glasses seemed more concerned
about them than himself. He sunned his moccasins between six and seven. The impact chipped a tooth and
dented his pride. He handed his glasses to Slim and
strode back to the picket post with clenched fists. He
declared, "No grass-eating, feather-headed filly's gonna
throw *me*!" in a high, clear voice. Wil didn't approve
of second chances, but the boy's anger impressed him.

It impressed everybody except Alice. No sooner had
he settled in the saddle than she threw him on the
count of one.

In the silence, somebody behind them laughed. They
all looked around.

During the noise of Crazy Alice's performance, a
stranger had ridden up. He was darkly Mexican, handsome, perhaps fifteen years old—and scornfully amused
at the rider in the dust.

While Wil and the others sat fascinated with the
dark angel's face, little Charlie Schwartz jumped down
on the outside of the corral and limped over to the
stranger with a hand extended. He said, "Howdy,"
and the young stranger leaned down to shake. Charlie
clenched his hand and pulled. The dark boy fell hard.
While he was getting up, young Charlie said, "Up
here, we don't laugh at other people's bad luck." Then
he hit him in the stomach.

The stranger looked more outraged than hurt. His
stare was murderous as he lunged. The smaller boy
was no match for him, but managed to keep twisting
away. In moments, Wil and Slim were peeling them
apart. Wil was interested to see that the Mexican boy
stood almost a head taller than the little Schwartz
fellow.

Wil said, "Charlie, pick on somebody your own

size." Then his strange resentment for infirmity rose, and he added, "Or do you only start fights when there's somebody around to stop them?"

Slim lashed out instantly, "No, sir, he don't."

Wil looked down at the dark boy. "Around here, we don't laugh unless we can do better. That's a lot of rope you got there. Can you use it?"

He was looking at a real *riata;* it was again as long as their northern ropes, and so stiff it stayed in a perfectly round coil.

"I will show you."

Wil put a hand on his shoulder and called out to the rest of the boys, "There's coffee. You can have it on the porch. We'll finish up here later."

The smallest of the lot was hurrying up on short, bowed legs. His pants were half-open again. He said, "Mr. Andersen, I'd like to take my turn before we eat."

Wil looked down at him gruffly. "Who said anything about eating?"

The boy put his hands on his hips and thought; then he squinted up at Wil from behind freckles and asked uncertainly, "My nose?"

Wil snorted, and Slim spoke up: "Sir, I know the horse is getting tireder and tireder, but the boys is getting smaller and smaller."

Wil said, "Yes, I been noticing that. All right." And he climbed back up the fence. Everybody followed.

By now Crazy Alice was sick and tired of the whole thing, but she gave the rest of the job applicants a ride for their money. Heads snapped back and forth, teeth jarred, hats flew, and the bigger boys stood around close to catch their cometing little friends. Yet almost all of them came within a second or two of staying their time. One spent the last counts with his arms locked desperately around Alice's neck; the two that ate grass came up with only bruises but nothing broken.

When the short one with the freckles had ridden, he strode from the corral beating the dust out of his hat and saying, "Okay, we can eat now." Wil wanted to swat him like a fly.

"Señor."

Wil looked up.

"You would like to see me use the rope?"

"Oh, sure. Go right ahead. Let's see what you can do."

The dark boy rode into the breaking pen and whacked Crazy Alice on the rump until she was running full speed. Then in five throws he roped each of her legs in turn, and dropped the last almost lovingly around her neck. Having performed, he bowed a little in the saddle and said with a touch of condescension, "My compliments."

In the silence, young Charlie Schwartz said, "My ass."

The performer recoiled his rope carefully, then whirled and flung it hard at his little blond tormentor. It whipped around his ankles and dragged him to the ground with a thud. Then the handsome rider backed his horse around the pen, dragging Charlie in the dust.

Wil yelled, "All right, that's enough of that!"

He was a moment late. Charlie Schwartz had been fumbling at his belt. Now he drew a knife, slashed the rope off his ankles, and stood waiting with the blade ready.

The dark boy's eyes went wide with rage. That rope had been precious. He flung himself off his horse and lunged forward bare-handed.

Wil caught him around the waist in the crook of one arm and warded Charlie off with the other foot. The dark one struggled wildly, but Wil held him tight. When he had a chance, he said something in the boy's ear. It took all the struggle out of him. Wil put him down.

"When?"

"Right now. Go put your gear in the bunkhouse."

"How much you pay?"

"Twenty-five dollars for the summer."

"I will stay. But—." He pointed a finger at Wil. "No more will you touch me, *sabe?*"

Wil pointed back at him and smiled dangerously. "And never again will you point a finger at me, *sabe?*"

The boy shrugged and walked his horse toward the bunkhouse. Twelve pairs of eyes looked at him with deep resentment. He seemed to enjoy it.

Wil turned to Charlie Schwartz. "I ain't partial to knives. Don't ever pull one on my spread again."

The instant he said it, he wished he hadn't. That last damned word turned the whole threat into a promise. These younkers wouldn't *be* back on his spread again, dammit!

The boy's reply didn't help, either. He said, "I don't wait around for somebody to stop my fights, Mr. Andersen."

This Charlie Schwartz was smart as a whip. Wil wished he'd never laid eyes on him. This whole thing was getting out of hand. He didn't realize how much until later, when he and Annie were having supper before the fire.

"Why the dark one, Wil?"

"He's good. He'll earn his keep whether we go on the drive or not."

"He's a loner. That's trouble."

"Annie, the wilder the colt, the better the horse."

She gave that little tiny shrug of hers and said into her plate, "If he lives," then looked startled and laid a hand on Wil's in silent apology.

They ate heartily. They talked. It had been good to hear boys' voices around the place again.

5

The Schwartzes drove up first. They must have been on the road for hours. The wagon held man and wife, five robust children, and young Charlie looking more peaked than ever. But not so pale. His face was flushed with anger and embarrassment. He refused to look at Wil Andersen, and the man refused to look at the boy.

While Wil's face had set at the sight of the family coming into the yard, Annie's glowed. All at once she was the lady of the house, warm, friendly, generous. The Schwartzes tried not to stare at the real glass windows, wood floors, and ceiling that showed few signs of leaking. Annie fetched her cider for the children, coffee for the adults, and cookies for all. She was careful to serve young Charlie coffee, too. While the other children watched in envy and surprise, the boy vowed in his heart to love this woman forever. Wil saw and made a note to bring her something extra nice from Belle Fourche.

When the froth of the occasion was skimmed, Mrs. Schwartz said, "Charlie, take the children outside and play." It was plain that the visit was her idea. Young Charlie didn't move. His father said, "Charlie, you heard what your mother said. Take the young ones outside and get right back in here. We got to talk." When his wife's eyes went wide, he said, "This whole thing's about him. He's got a right to hear what's said."

The woman sipped her coffee without answering. She was a small, thin little woman, and tense as a clenched fist. Annie was especially kind to her.

When the children had gone, Annie said, "My but he's grown! Last time I saw Charlie he was just a little tyke, no bigger than a minute. Now here he is a man!" Wil smiled to himself at what a shrewd wife he'd married, but Mrs. Schwartz's eyes burned with irritation. She started to answer, but Aaron jumped in. He was the man. He had to speak first. What happened after that was out of his hands.

"He looks older than he is, Mrs. Andersen. Charlie's only fourteen."

Mrs. Schwartz added immediately, "*Just* fourteen, and never very strong."

Annie said, "But of course he's a little peaked! He's just at that age! Mercy, he's a growing boy!"

Mrs. Schwartz looked at her hard. "Annie, he's never in his life been in the best of health."

It was clear that nobody was going to mention the limp.

Wil recrossed his legs and said, "Oh, anybody can see that."

Man and wife looked at him. The door opened and closed. Young Charlie took his seat and his cup of coffee. His mother plucked it from his hands. "Time enough for that when you're growed." Annie immediately poured him cider and pushed the whole plate of cookies near his hand. Mrs. Schwartz frowned. Apparently sweets were dangerous, too.

Wil said, "What I can't understand is how you even let him ride. A boy that peaked could get throwed by a porch swing."

Man, wife, and boy looked at him. Then the boy looked down and smiled at the floor between his feet. Aaron Schwartz cleared his throat so deep it sounded like a growl. "Oh, I don't know, Wil. Seems to me the boy rides pretty good."

"But not good enough."

The boy looked up sharply. The smile was gone. "I rode better than anybody there! I stuck twice my ten!"

Wil looked at him coldly. "Son, it's a hundred times easier to ride a bad horse for ten seconds than a good one for ten days."

"But you said you'd take on anybody that could stay on Crazy Alice for a count of ten!"

"I did not." He turned to the boy's father. "Aaron, I guess Charlie here didn't hear me right, because I wasn't talking straight the other day. I wasn't man enough to come right out and tell them I wasn't hiring no bunch of green schoolboys for my drive. So I said if any of them could ride that horse, I'd sure keep 'em in mind the next time I did any hiring. I thought Crazy Alice'd bounce 'em all off on their bottoms; then I wouldn't have to hurt nobody's feelings myself. And I deserved what happened. Almost every single one of them boys rode his time. I can tell you, I was the most surprised man in the whole damn—sorry, ma'am—in the whole *dang* territory."

Aaron frowned at him. "What's so surprising about that? That boy sitting there's been riding since he was six. He broke his own horse himself! The blue roan out there, she's the one! Why, Charlie's more at home on a horse than he is at home!"

His wife looked at him icily.

"You know what that boy does, Wil? That crazy young honyock you see sitting there reads his lessons riding back from school, and by the time he gets home he's got 'em done! You ever heard of such a crazy dang—sorry, ma'am—crazy *damn* thing in all your life?"

His wife looked at him in gray anger. "Yes, whenever you open your mouth."

Aaron looked blankly at Wil. "What'd I say?"

Annie quickly poured more coffee. Wil said, "Oh, now, friend, I saw right away he's born to the saddle. He stayed on that silly filly longer'n any of the boys twice his size. But even if I changed my mind and decided to take on a passel of boys between hay and grass, I'd have to think twice about this one. Like your missus says, he's peaked."

The boy glared at his mother as if she were a titted Judas, then turned to Wil Andersen. "But you hired that bean-eater! He's the same age as I am."

"Just for the branding, boy. The way it looks, I ain't marketing no beef this year. Ask your dad if he'll hire me at his lumber mill."

"Ask him what he can do, Charlie. And while you're at it, ask your mother if she's satisfied." He turned to Wil. "I told her you wouldn't hire no bunch of boys on no drive, but oh, no, she had to get her back arched up and come all the way out here and have it out face to face."

Mrs. Schwartz sat looking into her cup.

"But don't let her looks fool you none, Wil. She may sit there looking like a hobbled heifer, but wait till we get back in that wagon and head for home. It'll be forty miles of nothing but screaming."

Wil laughed and winked at Aaron. "I hear tell you can spare the old rod and spoil the wife, too, my friend!"

Aaron roared, Mrs. Schwartz glared, young Charlie looked puzzled, and Annie cried, "Why, *Wil Andersen!* What's got into you?"

During the noise, two more wagons drove up.

In an hour there were seven altogether, thirty horses and fifty-three children sprung from twenty-four parents. The yard swarmed with piercing play, except for the older boys, who tended to stick together, talk solemnly, and threaten one another darkly. Inside the house, women of all ages were talking, shouting, laughing, and whispering, and some cried now and then off in a corner. Admiring the glass windows and wooden floors, they helped Annie lay out the guest food they'd brought, supplemented by everything she had in the house. It was largely pies, cakes, buns, and cookies; an honest-to-goodness meal for this many would have taken days. Annie brought screams of delight as she set a couple girls to rolling the doughnuts in sugar, an unheard-of extravagance to most. And she quickly whipped up thick sugar syrup for the pies and buns, and put a big bowl of honey for dipping in the middle of the table. After all those winter months of meat and potatoes, they'd all be ravenous for something sweet. Annie freely made an event of it, and the women were hysterically glad to get together with their kind.

Wil took the twelve men out into the cool shadows of the barn. They lounged and sprawled, and passed the brown stone jug around with a slow casualness belied by the length of the swigs they took. Very soon they were all in the perfect mood for long and thorough deliberation. This was a serious thing. It might take hours, thank God.

Wil upset a good many by coming directly to the point. He folded his arms and said, "I guess everybody knows I ain't going on no drive this year." It was the one statement they hadn't come prepared for. It took the pro and con out of the whole shooting works. There went the long and thorough deliberation.

"I know that meddling Anse must of said different. He means well, but he wasn't speaking for me."

Nobody said anything. Dutch Bickerdyke lifted the jug. You could hear the whiskey making a distant think-thunk sound inside.

Wil went on, compelled by the silence. "Still and all, I didn't want to call him a liar in front of the children, and turn them around and send them clear back home for nothing. So I did something kind of yellow. I decided to let Crazy Alice settle the whole question of hiring. Well, she settled it, all right. Now nobody'd use her to do anything but eat grass. Yep, them gritty young sprouts of yours surprised the living daylights out of her *and* me!"

Dry little old Reeves Wrisley said, "You're plumb out of touch with boys these days, Wil, or you'd of knew better. What you should of done is just say *All of you git on home* and be shed of the whole thing."

"Aw, Reeves, how could I do a thing like that! They'd come a long way! It—it was a kind of a compliment. You see, I know I got a name for being too hard on boys. When I say hello to one on the street, he generally backs away. And when I was in the school the other day, they kept peeking at me like I was a ten-foot rattler. Now and again it sticks in a man's craw. Then all of a sudden here they were coming clear out to my spread and looking at me the way boys do when there's something they just got to have."

Fred Honeycutt laughed. "I got eleven, and not a day goes by one of them don't look at me like that!"

"Then you know what I mean! What's a man to do!"

"Do? Why, boot 'em in the ass! The littler ones, that is. Slim's getting a little big to boot no more. What he needs is somebody to really put the fear of God

in him when he gets out of line. That's why my ears
perked up when he said you was hiring boys for your
drive. The first thing I thought was: Son, you'll come
back a man if you go on a drive with Wil Andersen!"

"Aw, Fred, any drive'd do that!"

Then they were all talking at once, and the jug was
going around faster. Wil blinked at what he heard.
It sounded like they'd all gotten together in Bozeman
and decided that nobody but Wil Andersen was the
man to take over the higher education of their sons.
Some were a little less enthusiastic than the rest, but
they were all willing. Tall Ben Conway said if it was a
matter of money, he'd be willing to pay his boy's way.

After his dozenth pull on the jug, Wil shook his
head and came right to the point: "Oh, I don't doubt
with plenty of help and a sharp eye watching over
them, your boys could get the herd to Belle Fourche.
It wouldn't be easy, but it wouldn't be impossible,
neither. But what I can't understand is how you're
all so ready to trust your sons to me when you know
how mine turned out."

There was a pause, and someone said quietly, "Wil,
old friend, that could have happened to any father
on earth. I think it's kind of proud of you to think
it was all your fault and none of theirs. It means you'd
of took all the credit if they'd turned out good, and
you know yourself that don't make sense. Boys are
people. They ain't clay. No matter how hard you try,
when everything's said and done, they shape themselves."

"But I was too hard on them! That's what drove
them away from home! It's my nature to be just as
hard on everybody else as I am on myself. And it
don't figger. I'm no fit man to handle young fellers.
I always thought I was, but now I ain't so sure. I seem
to break boys, same as I break a horse."

Jim's father pointed with his pipe. "That's exactly
the reason why I'd trust my boy to you. I don't want
his first boss to be lovable, for Gawd's sake! I want
Jim to learn to be not just a good cowman but a good

man, too. And it's discipline that does it. If he turns out bad, I'll know it wasn't your fault but his. And if he's good, Wil, I know you'll bring him back better."

The boys themselves were out at the breaking pen on the opera seat. They were silent and glum. After Charlie Schwartz had told them, "He don't want us, Alice or no Alice," they just sat and contemplated black futures.

The dark boy rode by. He always seemed to be smiling to himself. Somebody said, soft but clear, "Bean-eater!" He turned back and stopped before them. They were above him, and numbering twelve to one, but he didn't seem to care. He was good-looking as the Devil himself, and twice as confident.

He said, "I am fifteen. When I was nine, I shoot my father. Perhaps you think I lie. I do not care."

Charlie Schwartz said, "I believe you. That's just about exactly what you'd do."

The dark one looked at him a long moment, then rode on.

The women were sipping camomile and talking about birth and death, and what a sweet little *unmarried* thing Miss Fanny was. Mrs. Schwartz moved among them trying to work up feeling against the use of children on a drive. The word didn't set well. Mrs. Bickerdyke said, "My youngest boy's hardly nine, but, mercy, he's no *child!*" Mrs. Schwartz went out on the porch and stood for ages with her arms folded.

Wil stood up and began to move around in a sort of desperation. He said, "Dammit, I can't say that I take to what you boys are doing here today. Look, I'm getting to an age where a man smells a little sour and he's kind of tired a good deal of the time. That's when friendship means more to him than it ever did before, and he gets a lump in his throat when folks say a good thing about him that he don't expect. But it ain't fair! Them sons of yours is too much of a damn re-

sponsibility! This drive smells of trouble, and if even
one of them boys came back banged up, I'd never be
able to face a one of you again. Or myself. I buried
two already. *I just couldn't face failing another time.*"

That embarrassed everybody, including Wil. Frog
Lapeer got up, stretched, and said, "Well, it's up to
you, old friend. We didn't come out here to help you
make up your mind. We just wanted you to know that
whatever you finally decide to do, we're with you.
Now, let's get at them eats. I'm hungrier than a wood-
pecker with a headache."

Six dozen people ate heartily, talking between bites
and smiling during them. The boys ate in silence, looking blessed. Dry little Reeves Wrisley had murmured
to his son in the glasses, "It's all right, boy," and the
news had gone around like wildfire. The whole thing
was completely settled, and there'd be nothing but
glory from here on in.

Wil, feeling he'd turned them down too brutally,
couldn't look at the boys at first. But when he did,
and saw their quiet, beaming faces, his heart sank.
What the Goddamn hell was going on here anyway!

Tall young Honeycutt waited until he could catch
Mr. Andersen alone, then he swallowed, coughed, and
looked at his boots.

"What is it, Slim?"

"Uh, Mr. Andersen, sir, do you really want me on
your drive?"

"If I went on one, and if I decided to hire boys,
yes, I think I'd want you."

"Very much, sir?"

"More than most."

"Well, hm, if that's the case, there's something I got
to tell you. I can't go unless you take Charlie Schwartz,
too."

"Ain't that kind of a threat, boy?"

"No, sir. The thing is, he's a good man, and I don't
think you know that yet."

"He's peaked, and I can't abide peaked people."

"He's smart, and sharp as a tack. He's worth all the

rest of us put together." There was a pause. "So, if you don't mind, sir, I wouldn't want to go without him. He's my friend."

Young Charlie Schwartz was standing twenty feet away with his arms folded and looking at them steadily. He'd never looked skinnier and less engaging, but there was pride written all over him.

Wil looked him up and down and spoke out across the distance between them: "What if your friend here's wrong about you?"

"Just wrap me up in a tarp like you would anybody else."

"I think I can keep the lot of you from getting yourselfs killed, but what if you turn out to be no use to me?"

"Mr. Andersen, I don't mind your low opinion of me. I know I limp. But that just means I'll have to prove myself a little more than the rest. Like I had to do with that greaser of yours. He may be the prettiest thing that ever warmed a saddle, and mighty tricky with a rope, but he ain't the one you're gonna turn to when the chips is down."

"I'll turn to you?"

"No, sir. Slim, then me."

Wil sighed helplessly and tried to assert himself: "Well, just remember you won't get no special privileges. When there's a stampede in the middle of the night, them critters ain't gonna run around you just because you're peaked."

"All I want's an even break, Mr. Andersen."

"I always give a man an even break."

"Except when you latch onto a word like *peaked*."

". . . Fair enough, boy. You won't hear it again."

There was a strange relish on the man's face as he watched the two boys walk to their horses. Then suddenly he was thunderstruck. Those little bastards had tricked him into talking as if he were hiring them! He wanted to go and straighten them out once and for all, but couldn't bring himself to run after them.

Everybody was saying good-bye in the early afternoon. Mrs. Schwartz had been fairly quiet the whole day long. Now, with time run out, she couldn't hold it in any longer. Standing on the top step of the porch, she turned to Wil. Her voice rose clearly over all the talk.

"I just want to know one thing, Wil Andersen. *What makes you think you can take care of ours when you did so bad with both your own?*"

Everything stopped. Annie looked slapped. The others looked stunned, and Aaron Schwartz blushed red as a beet. Wil dug his thumbs in his belt, looked the little woman coldly in the eye, and said, "Because I promise right here and now *not to love them like my own.*"

After a moment Aaron bent down to his wife and growled, "You satisfied?"

The line of wagons made golden dust against the sun. The sound of hoof and harness and voices came back over the prairie long after there was only dust to see. It would be dark before any of them got home, but there'd be a full moon tonight.

Annie put her arm around his waist. "Feel better, now that you've decided?"

"Decided?" He stared at her, then said, "That's right, I did. *But when?*"

6

The die cast, Wil went right to work. Before the week was out, he went back into Bozeman and stood in the schoolhouse door with his hat in his hand. Miss Zook's eyes fluttered over him.

"Miss Zook, if you don't mind, I'd like to talk to the boys after school lets out. I kindly thought this would be a good place to do it while they're here together."

"Why, certainly, Mr. Andersen! Do come in and sit yourself down." She consulted the little gold watch hanging on her firm bosom. "We'll be just a bit, and then the entire institution's yours!"

Wil stepped inside, and the girls stared at him again as if they'd never seen a man before. Wil Andersen was simply beautiful, no matter how terribly old he might be. The sight of him sent little waves of panic through their young bodies. It wasn't a nice feeling like in books, but it was real like in life.

The boys looked at him with much the same excitement. The only difference lay in them saying, *"I'm like him, thank God!"* and the girls saying deliciously, *"Thank heaven, I'm not!"* Yet all alike became vibrant at the sight of this mature and towering male.

There was a clatter of hooves outside, and the bean-eater pushed open the door. He jarred the scholastic atmosphere with his loud announcement: "Mrs. Andersen says you want me."

Wil answered in a low, church tone: "Sit here by me and take your hat off indoors."

The bean-eater obeyed and looked around him. He'd never been in a school before. He looked at everything carefully. That is, everything but the girls; that would have interrupted their minute study of him. Half of them had fallen completely in love with his handsomeness and forgotten Wil Andersen completely.

The dark one didn't look at the boys until last, then one by one he took them in with his faintly smiling scorn. Meeting Charlie Schwartz's gaze, he held up his middle finger behind his hat and smiled quietly. Wil saw the blond boy redden in anger, saw the dark boy's raised hat and smile and guessed about the finger. He glared and pointed at him. A rustle of satisfaction passed through the boys' side of the room, and the handsome one submerged in floor-staring embarrassment.

Miss Zook asked if perhaps the whole school might stay and listen to his plans for the great roundup and the drive. It would be most instructive, and she was sure every single one of the young ladies would consider it a great privilege. They all mewed, "Please, Mr. Andersen, please?" Actually, she'd have preferred that they all go home so that she could bask in his maleness alone. Under all this beautiful roughness, you could see he was one of nature's gentlemen at heart. As if to prove it, Wil said he didn't think a lot of cow-talk would much interest the womenfolk, but Miss Zook stood there burning daylight with lyric pleas. He shrugged.

He stood up in front of the blackboard, shoved his shirt front farther down inside his pants, pointed a finger, squinted, and said, "*Now, you listen to me, you snot-nose, wet-pants, sugar-tit, greenhorn pee-wees. . . .*"

Within seconds there wasn't a female in fifty yards of the building, and those still in sight were high-tailing it like deer, with Miss Fanny in the lead. The boys thought it was the greatest moment of their entire lives but sat stony-faced.

Wil continued as if nothing had happened: "There's one thing I want to make clear right here at the start. I never did, and I still don't, want you little sons of bitches on my drive. You're here first because some . . . feckless bastards walked out on my drive."

He could see they didn't know what that meant, and he only remembered it as some high-toned word out of his school days that meant something pretty bad. So he fulfilled an ancient wish and wrote on the blackboard as he spoke. He slashed the word "feckless" savagely in chalk, and underlined it. The boys automatically copied it on their slates. Wil blinked helplessly and raised his voice to get their attention back.

"I say more feckless than any cowhands I ever knew. A man can't sink no lower than to walk out on his outfit, and don't you forget it. And second, I got wrangled into this by a bunch of feather-headed, well-meaning do-gooders that think they're all my friends. But as God is my witness, they're stampeding me into the worst calamity that ever hit the Double-O, and I stand here telling you one and all I don't expect to ride into Belle Fourche with a single head of beef. I don't even expect to get that far, and remember I said that."

He walked over to the side window, angrily arranging himself, and came back to stand with hands on hips. "So this is the way it's gonna be. I am a man, and you are boys. Not cowmen, no. Just cowboys, like the word says, and I'm gonna remind you of that fact every minute of every day, and all through the night and in your sleep when you get sleep. And if I tell one of you to stand on his head in the middle of a cloudburst, you're gonna stand on your Goddamn head in the middle of a cloudburst. And if some hollow-horn critter takes it into its mind to wander off and get lost and I tell you to go get him, you will go get him or not come back. Pound for pound, he's worth a hell of a lot more to me than any of you. And when you're the night-hawk, or on guard, if I catch just one of you once as much as yawning, so help me God I'll pack you off for home alone, no matter where we are. Prob'ly face down on your saddle with every bone in your body broke."

The boys were seeing far more than they heard. They watched the way Wil walked and how he used his hands. They admired the big silver buckle shining in the middle of his solid gut and the tooled-leather belt snug around his narrow waist. They felt the whole place shake when he strode across the room. The very resonance of his deep voice vibrated in their ears. Oh, here was a man. He must know just about everything there was to know. And he surely could do anything any other man could do. And the only way you could grow to be such a giant was by being tough with yourself and everybody else. So they sat and soaked up every one of his hard words and reveled in his roughness.

Wil hitched his pants and walked toward the other window, trying to choose from the thousand things he had to say.

"Next to me, you'll take orders from Charlie Nightlinger. There ain't no mystery why I pay him more than anybody else on my drive. He happens to be the best damn cook in the whole damn West. As you will see. The chuck wagon is *his* as long as he's with me. You as much as snitch one miserable crumb without asking, and you'll likely end up without a hand. You'll sure end up without a job. Don't backtalk him. That's worse than saying baaaaaa to a cattleman. Only a fool argues with a mule, a skunk, or a cook. He'll be your doctor, too, and stake-holder, banker, dentist, veter'narian, barber, father confessor, and he'll do whatever undertaking's necessary. But he'll lay down his own law when he gets here, and you sure as hell better listen. He speaks for me."

He cleared his throat, spit out the window, and came back as if he were just beginning. "Next, you'll respect and take care of your string. Besides your own individual horse that you ride in here on, you'll each have eight—maybe nine—of mine. There'll be no excuse for wearing any down, with that many in your string. Bake just one of them horses, and you'll be sorry you ever laid eyes on me. I'm like a horse. I ain't no good when I get heated up. Go easy on us. Horses is what a spread's built on. Without them, there wouldn't be ranches, or beef on the market.

"I've collected one of the best saddle bands in this part of the country. Took me years. You'll look at their feet before you get on and after you get off. You'll trim their hooves and shoe them when it's needed. Oh, I'll help. It's a man's job.

"And another thing. You may be a bunch of pea-picking hay-shakers, but I want *my* horses' tails kept

thin and short. Only farmers and dudes lets them
grow way long. So the first thing you're gonna do
after the horse roundup is pick your string and care
for them and *learn 'em*. You're gonna find out what
each horse does best, and you're gonna learn to
pick your own string out of a hundred others in a
storm on the blackest night. That understood?"

Like a wind shushing through young pines, the
boys murmured "yes sir yes sir."

Dry little Reeves Wrisley's boy with the glasses
said nothing. He was too fascinated discovering things
about this man. A family heirloom, his glasses magni-
fied things slightly. This made him look somewhat
bug-eyed to the world, but it made the world infinitely fascinating to him. It trained him to look at
details. He was the only one that really saw Wil
Andersen's hands. They were big, strong, and rough,
of course, but the nails were clean and all the same
length. The boy saw that these were hands that could
both kill and love, and had many, many skills. They
could shoot and rope and plait, tie wondrous knots,
help a mare to foal, and one stanch blood while the
other wrapped a bandage on. They were strong as
death, yet they were thinking hands as well. And it
must be good beyond imagining to have them touch
you fondly.

The boy seldom talked about such things to others.
They'd be hard to say and harder to understand. Yet
it was sad that his friends would never know what
it was to sit still and watch a bee inside a flower or
scrounge up to a drop of water on a blade of grass
and see the rainbow world hanging upside down.
These things set him a bit aside from his un-myopic
fellows, but the best part was, he didn't really know
it.

Wil slid his hands into his rear pockets, except for
thumbs, and paced and talked in a quiet sort of
desperation.

"You'll bring along your own rope, saddle, slicker,
and soogan. And just remember, it gets real cold out

there nights, even in the middle of the summer, so make that soogan a real Montana bedroll. And a good tarp to spread over it. Small size. The six by fourteen is for growed men. Or you can save money and stay warm by doubling up. Smiley and the boys only had one bedroll between them, because least one was always on duty. Don't fill your war bags with a lot of foolishness. That's just for your Fish and personal things and a razor just in case this drive lasts long enough for any of you to start shaving. And if it does, you'll *shave, by God!*"

Turning to the blackboard, he picked up a piece of chalk. "Might be an idea to show you where we're going. Here's the Crazy Mountains and the Shields, and here's the Double-O right in here. Take a good look at that brand. It's a pair of overlapping balls, which you may have, but none of you's earned as yet. The roundup will cover all of the upper Shields Valley, and the drive will come right down here to the Bozeman Trail, then strike out almost due east for four hundred tail-breaking miles to Belle Fourche where the train is. We'll come inside of twenty miles or so of where they had the Little Big Horn thing last year. So I guess you better bring along whatever firearms your folks can spare. 'Course, the minute I say that, I can picture every last one of you shooting himself in the foot every time he cleans the bore. But there's still bands of hostiles roaming around these plains, and more than enough rustlers to go around."

He put down the chalk and slapped his hands to get the dust off. "Show up at the Double-O the Monday after school lets out. I expect Eph Wormwood by the middle of the week to do my breaking. So the horse roundup comes first. And don't you believe that old crap about a bronc-buster having a strong back and a weak mind. You got a lot to learn from Eph, and you see you learn it. So you'll have only about a week or ten days to learn your strings before we start the calf roundup. And that's all the time I'll have to find out what job'll fit each one of you—if any."

He went over, picked up his hat, and put it on at
that special Wil Andersen angle.

"Go on home and get plenty of rest. It might be
an idea to pray a little, too. Because this drive ain't
the worst thing you got to put up with. The worst
thing's me. I been hazed into it against my will. I
don't take kindly to being pushed into doing something I got my doubts about. So I'm feeling pretty
damn mean, and I'm gonna stay that way until this
whole damn thing is done. So watch out. You got a
summer ahead you'll remember to your dying day."

He walked out without looking right or left. The
bean-eater had to run to keep up. Everybody else
just sat. They were deeply gratified at the big man's
hard, mean man-talk. It showed he didn't really think
them boys.

7

At dawn the Monday after school let out in June,
the yard began filling with boys and horses. The
horses' ears kept pricking up, because the boys talked
in whispers that they weren't used to. The new
hands wore brand-new store-bought pants, a variety
of shirts and vests, and real genuine knot-and-dip
bandannas around their necks. But what raised Wil's
eyebrows was all the uniformly new and cream-
colored Stetsons. There couldn't have been that many
in Stein's store in Bozeman. Some of them must have
ridden as far as Helena or Virginia City, or sent to
Miles Town, to get theirs.

Wil didn't hurry to go out to them. He dressed
methodically. "Maybe it won't turn out so bad after
all, Annie. They seem to be a pretty well-behaved

bunch of boys. All on their wagon manners!" She
patted his back reassuringly and set down his coffee
at the head of the table. He sipped it noisily, then
frowned. "I sure hope they all got fed before they
left home. Charlie Nightlinger's not showed up yet,
and I'm not going to have you feeding all them bottomless pits out there alone."

The idea of boys being hungry worried Annie. She
moved the iron skillet off the fire and went to the
front window, wiping her hands on her apron. Things
were very quiet out in the yard. Then she said, "Wil,"
in a funny, trembly tone that brought him at once.
He bent over with her and looked out. His mouth
opened.

Everybody had taken cover. They peeked up over
the edges of things. Pale young Charlie Schwartz
and the dark boy were facing each other forty feet
apart. Both were armed, and each waited for the
other to draw.

Wil charged out of the door roaring like a bull.
Charlie drew his gun, held it in both hands, squinted
down the barrel, and fired. The dark boy seemed too
fascinated to remember to draw. When he did, it
was too late. Wil was all over him.

His comments could be heard all the way to Miles
Town as he took their guns away from them. When
he stopped for breath, the dark one smiled at Charlie.
"*I* wouldn't have missed." And Charlie asked, "You
think *I* did? You think that's a fly on your ear?"

The handsome face went blank. He felt his ear
lobe. His fingers came away wet with a little smear
of blood. He frowned and said, "Yes, you missed.
You're not good enough to nick a man like that on
purpose."

Wil felt left out. He roared at the others: "Anybody else with firearms will go and put them on the
porch *right now*. I want everything that shoots."

The gallery came out of hiding. Wil stared as they
began covering the porch with a startling variety of
artillery. They might be from poor families, but they'd

come on good horses, and these were good guns. And there were at least two to a man. He said, "Good God Amighty, are we going on a drive, or another war between the states? Now, is this *all* you got? You hold out on me, and I'll boot you off my spread!" There was silence. "All right. I'm locking these up in the chuck wagon. I should leave them here. God knows the West ain't still *that* wild. But they're yours and ought to come along. Now, if any one of you wants his back for any reason whatever, sit down and write me a letter all about it and send it care of general delivery in Belle Fourche. You with the glasses, go find a tarp in the stable and cover up this iron. And you two gun sharks come here with me."

They followed him around the side of the house.

"All right, now, what's this all about?"

Neither answered.

"I said what the *hell* is this all about, wanting to *kill* each other?"

As if called, the one that stuttered came around the corner. He dug his thumbs in his front pockets and said, "It ain't for them to s-s-say, Mr. Andersen."

Wil looked at the tattler coldly. "Then you say."

"Well, *he* called Charlie Schwartz a d-d-damn honyock, and Charlie c-c-called him a d-d-damn bean-eater. Then *he* went baaaaaaaaaa! and that's when Charlie went for his g-g-gun."

Wil tried to look angry and judicious, and failed at both. The boys had edged around the corner to listen to his decision. He felt naked. Angry at being pushed, he abruptly changed the whole subject: "Anybody heard anything about Eph Wormwood down Bozeman way? He should be here by now. And that damn Charlie Nightlinger ain't showed up either. What's the *matter* with everybody these days! Nobody keeps promises anymore! Well, we're burning daylight. Mount up. We're gonna brush up on our rope throwing. You may need it to hang a couple hair-trigger Harrys around here."

He stopped the guilty pair venomously: "You two

can just sit there on the steps and play with yourselfs, for all I care. I ain't decided whether to run
you off my spread or set you to cleaning out the
privy."

They sat as far apart as the steps would allow.

By noon everybody in the outfit knew what a genius
Wil Andersen was with the rope. And he was aware
that the boys weren't bad themselves. He'd been
away from youngsters so long he hadn't realized
how young they started these days.

Annie tapped on the real glass window. Wil went
in and came back out with two plates, then two
more, and another two—endlessly. The boys sat on
the porch eating in silence and looking at the
mounded tarp as they chewed. Afterward Annie said
she thought they were dumping their plates under the
porch, they emptied them so fast. By the time she got
to the last boy in the first serving, the first boy in the
second was ready and waiting. She didn't mind the
cooking; it was what all this walking did to her feet.

It was the same thing all over again at supper. Wil
helped her, but her smile was drawn. She murmured,
"Are they growing, or just away from home?"

"If we were paying them in food, they'd owe us a
year's work already!"

Help arrived the next day. Just before noon,
Charlie Nightlinger came riding in with his personal
chuck box strapped to the other mule. The sight of
him stopped everybody in his tracks. The boys stared
as Mrs. Andersen ran down the road to meet him,
and shook and shook and shook his hand.

8

Charlie Nightlinger was black as the ace of spades, white-headed as a pigeon's favorite statue, and wrinkled as a whore's bedsheet. Nobody knew how old he was, but they all agreed he was the youngest old man that ever outworked everybody half his age. Nobody'd ever seen him out of breath, nor anything but out of sorts. His irritability was the pride of the prairie. When old Black Charlie started to cuss somebody out, waddies came running from all around and listened in a sort of reverent awe.

Even his victims stood in wonder at the completeness with which they were being minced. Only one of them ever succeeded in having the last word; that was the man who tried to hustle pencil and paper during old Charlie's introductory remarks so he could make notes; Charlie glared at him and said, "You done provoke me on purpose to steal my vocalabery!" and refused to say another word.

Yet old Charlie never lost dignity. In his most violent rage, he remained a king pronouncing exile. It was a marvelously controlled anger that made even his mildest sarcasms seem delivered from a throne.

While Annie Andersen welcomed him back, he nodded and listened and nodded and nodded. Then he asked, "Miz Andersen, either you decided to run off to Californy with me, or you's after my deep-dish apple-pie recipe again."

She laughed. "Charlie, you give me that recipe, and I'm yours forever!"

"I donno about that. You just may be different, but I ain't met a woman yet that was worth my deep-dish apple pie! I worked on it forty years, and it get better each time. Where the woman you can say that of, hm?"

Annie laughed and blushed and said, "Charlie, Charlie, if your hair wasn't white, I do declare you'd be getting us both in awful trouble the way you carry on!"

Young boys were gathering around from all directions. Black Charlie looked at them like varmints. When he saw Wil striding this way, he leaned closer and said, "But I got a hunch you *is* different. Like my recipe, you git better as the years roll by. I know you gets prettier with every wrinkle. Oh, it's a sin and a shame you ain't black!"

Annie laughed and laughed. Wil arrived, holding out his hand, but as they shook he said, "Where the hell you been, you black old son of a bitch?"

"Jes' taking my sweet time, you white one."

Annie laughed again.

"You're the only one that ever made Annie laugh like this. What you got that I ain't?"

"Among other things, a recipe for deep-dish apple pie. She say she run off with me if I give it to her. What you say to that, Mister Tired Old Husband, hm?"

"That's just fine! And I'll come, too! I sometimes think that pie of yours is the only reason I keep this miserable spread going."

Black Charlie started looking around at the wide-eyed boys and counting out loud.

"Kin I ast you folks something personal? What you two been doing all winter? I never seen nobody get up such a big family so fast."

Wil smiled sheepishly. "Them? Oh, they're only ours for the summer."

"And what you going to do with ten little bitty hen-wrangling younkers?"

"Charlie, there's twelve, I think, and Annie hasn't

left the kitchen since five-thirty day before yesterday morning!"

Black Charlie shook a finger at Annie. "I knew they was a reason you come running out here to meet me like I's the Host at the Last Supper!"

Annie covered her face with her hands and bent over laughing.

"You teaching school now, Miz Andersen?"

She looked up archly. "No, Wil is."

Black Charlie looked at Wil. Wil looked at the horizon.

"What kinda school? Wil Andersen, you knows you can't teach school and go on a roundup and drive all twonct!"

"I know I can't, Charlie, but it looks like I'm gonna try to. All this acre of boys—they're my new hands."

Black Charlie's eyes searched his face. He squinted at Wil and cocked his head suspiciously: "What happen to Smiley and the Boys?"

"Gold colic."

"Oh, Lord God, they didn't mosey up to Ruby River?"

"They moseyed up to Ruby River."

"Then you neen worry. They be back."

"Not on my spread. I kicked them off."

Charlie blinked in disbelief, then looked at Mrs. Andersen. "You married the proudest man I ever met up with, next to me. He went and kicked them boys off his spread when all he had to do was pat 'em on the butt and say good luck and sit back and listen for them to come whining at the door in less'n a week. They was good boys, Mr. Andersen. You ought allow a man just one mistake!"

"Now, Charlie, don't you start in on me! You know damn well there's more to being a bean-master than just good cooking. I pay you more than anybody else on the drive because I know that if we get flooded out, burned out, stampeded out, froze, beat, or Injuned out, there you'll be with food on the plate and coffee in the pot. You're the most dependable old son of a bitch I ever met, black, red, or white. Next to me."

"You gotta 'scuse his language, Miz Andersen. He think the drive already started."

"Listen to me, Charlie. How could I ever trust those boys again after they run out on me like they did? What's lower than walking out on your outfit?"

"Why, after that one big jackassical mistake, I'd say you could trust them boys more than anybody in the territory. They come back with they tails between their legs and turn out to be the best cowhands you ever had. And, now you lock the gate on them, I wouldn't be surprise if they turn out to be nothing but shiftless gunneys."

Mrs. Andersen said, "No, not Smiley and the boys. They may be young and high-spirited, but they're good boys."

She stopped suddenly and glanced at Wil in a sort of horror, as if she'd said these same words once before. For an instant both of them heard gunfire and saw fine young bodies falling. Wil tore his eyes away and started for the house.

"Come on in. Have a swallow of bug-juice and set for a spell. Smiley and the Boys is past history. What we got to worry about now is getting ready for the roundup. By the way, if that good-looking young bean-eater's took your bunk, kick his tail out. He's just a hair less sassy than he is good. And while we're cutting the dust, we got to get up a list of supplies. If there's any left in Bozeman after this gold rush."

"I already thought of that and ordered everything we need in Virginia City."

A small boy was walking with them. Black Charlie looked down at him dourly. "I mean, everything but the diapers."

Wil glared at him over his shoulder. Charlie laughed silently and said to Mrs. Andersen, "Oh, have I got something to ride him about now! He be ready to turn me inside out before this drive's over!"

"M-M-Mister Andersen, how c-c-come you let a nigger t-t-talk to you like that?"

Wil looked down at the would-be bantam walking beside him. "Because that coal-black son of a bitch is just as important on this drive as I am. Without food, you ain't got a drive. And you want to know something else, boy? I bet a dollar to a doughnut you get served last from now till we ride into Belle Fourche."

Black Charlie grunted: "You wrong, Mr. Andersen. Stuttering Bob here get served *first*. On a platter with a apple in his mouth."

The boy looked at him intently over his shoulder, moved closer to Wil Andersen, and said softly, "I d-d-don't think he really m-m-meant that, M-M-Mister Andersen. He l-l-looks to me like he's kind of a n-n-nice nigger."

"What the hell's nice about him?"

"Well, he just give me a nickname!"

Then Stuttering Bob broke into a run on his way to spread the epoch-making news.

"Charlie, this is going to be the most haywire drive either of us was ever on in all our born days."

Black Charlie nodded and said, "That just could be."

A shot came from behind the stable. Wil said, "My God, what now!" and started to sprint.

Tow-headed young Charlie Schwartz and the dark boy were again standing forty feet apart, and Charlie was squinting down the barrel of his gun. Again he held it in both hands and stood with legs apart. The other boy wasn't armed. He just stood there, then reached up to feel his right ear lobe. As Wil arrived, he looked at the blood on his fingers and started grinning. Wil said the only thing he could think of: "What's going on here?" The dark one ignored him and went to young Charlie, holding out his hand. They shook.

"All right, gawdammit, what the hell *is* this?"

Charlie handed over his gun. Wil broke it. Empty. There'd been only one bullet in the cylinder. The dark one was still grinning. "I say it is a miss when he nick my ear the other time, but he say he can do it again. So I say, you nick my right ear the same way you nick my left, and by God I'll . . ." He stopped and grinned at the ground.

"And you'll what?"

Both boys looked at the ground grinning. Black Charlie was walking up. He looked from one to the other. "Go on, say it. You cold in the feets, Mexican Joe?" The boys kept grinning at the ground. "Say it 'fore Miz Andersen gits here. You nick *this* one like you nick *that* one, and I kiss yer hind side. That what you said?"

Pale Charlie blushed, and the dark one laughed.

"Well, ain't you gonna?"

Young Charlie looked up grimly. "I'll put one between his ears if he tries."

Annie was just arriving. "If he tries what, Charlie Schwartz?"

Wil startled everybody by shouting: "Annie, you get back in the house. It ain't safe out here. And dammit, Charlie Nightlinger, you got to draw me up a list of supplies. And all the rest of you runts get back to work. This is private business between me and Mexican Joe and Charlie Schwartz."

When the field was empty, he turned back to the sheepish boys.

"I ought to kick your tails off my spread right now, and I would if I hadn't seen you two shake hands. I'm a weak-minded ninny to let you stay, but I guess I ought to allow a man at least one mistake. Maybe two to boys. But don't think you're getting away with something. From now on, when you make mistakes like little boys, I'm gonna whip your tails like little boys. And when I whip a boy, he stays whipped."

The dark one lifted his finger and looked straight up at the big man. His eyes glittered. "Nobody whip me."

Wil took the finger in his hand and bent it back. "I told you once before about this finger thing. I ain't partial to schoolboys teaching the teacher."

There was a dew of pain on his dark and handsome face, but the boy made no move to pull away. Wil let go.

"I'm gonna let you two off. But don't get it in your heads I'm easy to get around. Because from now on I don't know either one of you. And I don't care how you settle your differences, just don't chouse the outfit, hear? We got plenty trouble waiting for us out there. Just don't make none here."

The boys said quiet little yes-sirs to the ground. The man said, "Git," and they walked on side by side.

When they'd gone, and Wil was alone, he turned his back to the ranch, lifted his face to the sky, and demanded angrily of the firmament, "*Why?*"

9

Only one other outfit wintered its stock in the Shields River Valley. This was the X Bar X, owned by a man named Henderson Choate. Nobody knew much about him, except that he was called Tiny because he weighed over two hundred pounds, and that he'd spent the better part of ten years paying off the obligations of a partner who had skipped the country. That was all anybody needed to know. Wil had already sent asking when he'd favor the roundup. Choate answered that there was no hurry; he'd send his rep anytime Wil gave the word.

This was what Wil had hoped. He wanted plenty of time to round up the horses, brand the colts, break the three-and-a-half- and four-year-olds, and give the youngsters a chance to get good and acquainted with their strings. They had to try to learn to ride every one of their horses with that special granite ease of a seasoned horseman. It was the only way they'd have a chance to win that annual three-way duel between the man in the saddle, the stupid, perverse critters of the herd, and the stupid, perverse horse under him. They may have ridden since they were no taller than prairie grass, but this was no schoolboy game. This summer had to do with death and great fortune.

Now that Black Charlie was here, Wil assigned three of the smaller frying-size to help him get the chuck wagon in shape. Every inch of it had to be gone over and cleaned out, including the mice nests in the cupboard drawers, the jewelry chest, and the jockey box. The wheels had to be greased, canvas mended, the leather hammock underneath new-slung, split boards replaced, and the whole thing tar-caulked for river crossing. An absolutely thorough job, because this would be Home, and it would have gone through the better part of a thousand miles before it got back here to the barn.

Black Charlie was exacting. His little crew sighed at having to do something over and over until it was right. On the other hand, they got the full benefit of the chuck master's rhetoric. The white-headed black man's profanity was awesome and fascinating. More often than not, the words weren't bad at all, just extraordinary. Like the time he called Eph Wormwood "a rancid, left-handed old parallelogram." Eph had never heard the word in his life, but he'd have gone for his gun if his young hazer hadn't talked him out of it.

Black Charlie's magnificent damnations rolled out of him like scripture from a preacher, but with infinitely more inventiveness. Each boy picked up an expression here and there for his own personal repertoire, and soon each one's swearing began to take on an individuality—just as their new bandannas were beginning to knot and drape to express the man inside.

Nights in the bunkhouse, the wagon crew repeated to the others all of Black Charlie's innovations. The day after he said, "Girls, this here *vehicle*, it gotta be in tippy-damn-top condition or we ain't leaving!" everything on the Double-O began to get into tippy-damn-top condition. And that was exactly the condition the chuck wagon was in by the time the roundup began. Thereafter each of the wagon crew looked on it with the fondness of a good craftsman: *I gave it part of me.*

Wil had put off getting up the horses until he found out whether Eph was coming or not. Then word came that he and his hazer were in Bozeman tanking up royally at Anse's Golden Eagle. Report had it that Eph was so lickered up he couldn't hit the ground with his hat in three tries! Wil immediately gave the word and started rounding up the saddle band, one hundred of the finest horses in the territory. He sent the tall, slim Honeycutt boy off down the east side of the valley with Stuttering Bob, sallow young Charlie Schwartz, and the silent little fellow with the broad shoulders and the rolling walk, the one called Shorty. He took the others down the west side.

His orders were to simply haze the horses they came to, walk them to the middle of the valley and back to the spread. There was no hurry. Quite a few hadn't been broke yet. They'd been running wild out here for over three years, and had to be spooky as an elephant's bride. So take it easy. Don't make work of it. Just jiggle them on home.

The two groups put the better part of twenty miles between them, and fanned out toward the south. There was still a lot of snow on the slopes of the Crazy Mountains. The early spring winds still had ice in them. But the grass was greener than it would be again all summer, and now and again a gust of sweet south wind blew in their faces. This was a piece of luck. The horses wouldn't know they were coming until they were there.

Wil directed operations in his bunch without knowing that sallow Charlie Schwartz was doing the same in his. The boy hadn't taken over. Slim Honeycutt had invited it with a question: "Charlie, you think we ought to go on a piece, or start back?"

Young Charlie pointed out that the cows had been increasing as they went along, and that grazing horses don't mingle in with them on the range. It was likely that all of the horses were behind them by now, and those that weren't would follow the herd. Horses are a close-knit lot. Charlie Schwartz said, "Sure, turn back, but spread way far out so we won't miss any on the way."

Slim called out, "All right, you heard him, boys! Stuttering Bob, you take the east end. Shorty, take the west, and Charlie and I'll hold down the middle. Spread out least a quarter of a mile apart. Don't yell. Signal with your hands, and take it easy."

Half an hour later they were moving up the valley in a long line that broke and reformed again and again to coax the frisky horses ahead of them. Gradually a herd began to form. Horses grazing on the outer edges pricked up their ears and trotted toward the center to join the rest. Some few wanted none of it, but they were convinced with patience. As the herd came together, the riders drew in closer and rode easily in sight of one another.

Twice Charlie had Slim tell the stuttering wonder to slow down. Why the heck was he pushing way ahead of everybody?

The answer was human and all boy: "Guess I'm just hungry. Black Charlie said he's making sucama-growl today."

Young Charlie snapped back, "All I can say is, you better learn how to get hungry when you smell food, and not a minute before. When Mr. Andersen says there's no rush, mister, there's no rush."

They'd rounded up something like seventy. It was the biggest herd any of them had ever ridden. They were so busy easing them along that nobody saw what was going on behind them. Wil's bunch, with maybe fifty head, was coming up behind. He was pleased with Slim's riders doing better than his had, and he liked the way Slim was easing them just right. The boy knew what he was doing, and he was a leader, too.

Then Stuttering Bob whipped around to go after a skittering colt. Shooing it back, he saw the herd behind them and let out a spontaneous howl of greeting.

In an instant both herds were running fast. Charlie Schwartz's horse snorted and reared in the commotion. The unexpected movement brought one of the boy's boots out of the stirrup. A sudden lunge forward threw him completely out of the saddle. He jumped to his feet, grabbed his new hat, and faced the horses of the second herd. They were coming on fast in a solid pack.

Stuttering Bob and the quiet boy named Shorty made dust getting from in between. Slim wheeled and went back for Charlie. He rammed his spurs in, bent low with his face in the mane, and swore his horse faster. The second herd was closing in right behind him as he crossed the open space. Charlie was hopping for the closest edge, but he'd never make it. You don't limp through grass in chaps.

Slim bent lower as he neared the little running figure. He shouted and held out his hands. Eyes stared from all sides.

At top speed he swept the other boy up before him. Wil and everyone let out a cheer.

That was when Slim's cinch boke. Both boys, saddle and all, went over the other side into the path of the thundering horses.

Slim lay still under the saddle. Young Charlie was on his feet in an instant. He straddled his friend, faced the oncoming horses, and screamed, *"Get the*

*gawdamn hell out of here, you crazy gawdamn sons
of bitches!*" over and over and over.

It was the piercing, painful scream that only a
boy with an unchanged voice can make. The startled
horses parted like the Red Sea and continued to part
in panic as that terrible sound came at them like
cactus in the ear.

The last of them passed. Charlie turned to see about
Slim. The tall boy was getting to his feet, looking a
little stunned. Then he looked up and stared at a
new, worse threat.

Wil Andersen was riding up raging mad. He
leaned forward on his saddle horn and shouted
at Charlie furiously. "You lost your horse! The best
rider we got, and you did the worst thing a man can
do on the range! You got yourself threw! Don't you
know a man afoot's no man at all? He's no more use
than a horse is without a rider! By God, if you can't
stay in the saddle, you sure as hell can't stay on my
spread!"

Then he turned to Slim and shouted as if the boy
were a mile away: "And you, Mr. Galahad, just you
listen to me! You better get down on your knees
and pray God that cinch of yours really broke. Because if I find it's in one piece and only come loose,
I'm running your tail out of here today. If you don't
know how to saddle a horse proper, you don't belong
on the Double-O!"

He rode off like Jove constipated. The two boys
stood with the saddle between them. The broken
cinch was right out in plain sight.

Slim said, "I thought I was gonna like him."

10

The next night, just before sunset, Eph Wormwood and his hazer galloped in, booze-blind and firing at a whole prairie full of unverified pursuers. They stumbled into the bunkhouse, fell onto the two nearest bunks, and sank into the sleep of the dead. The boys observed them with wide eyes and noses: these two smelled as if liquor were the only liquid they'd come near for a year. Bright and early the next morning they were hard at work, as if broncs were the only thing for a hangover.

Eph Wormwood was a contract buster. He wore great woolly chaps, a black bandanna, and a perpetual scowl. His hazer was a young fellow of twenty or so with a face that nobody could ever remember. Paid by the head, Eph worked fast and broke seven or eight broomtails a day so he could move on to the next ranch and have his insides shook out all over again for another couple dollars.

When he finished with each horse, his hazer made shavetails of them to show they'd been broken. Wil had his boys watch this closely. They'd be pulling their own strings' tails short, and he wanted them to get the hang of it.

Eph never did get used to the boys watching him at work. He got grassed only twice, but both times he blamed it on "them kids. They make me plumb nervous. A growed man tends to understand your accidents, but kids just stare at you and think." Then he added quite seriously: "Keep an eye on them, Jake.

They just might be red savages dressed up like midgets."

Seeing that his brains were scrambled, the boys watched him from a more discreet distance after that. But they were still endlessly fascinated by a man who made his living by having his innards seriously disarranged a dozen times a day. When his hazer remarked that Eph had begun to spit blood again, the boys moved back in close. They heard of people getting themselves killed every day, but this one way of doing it was bizarre beyond belief.

Wil was pleased at the way they studied Eph so closely. So far, they were knuckling down pretty well. All of them could trim a hoof passably, and that talky little feller they called Horny Jim and his friend Shorty made quite a team at shoeing. They did a fairly grown-up job.

Another good thing. Like Horny Jim and Shorty, the boys were pairing off. Almost everybody had his special friend to look out for. That paid off in many ways. Like the day that feisty little Schwartz boy had straddled Slim and split the herd. But since the shootout, he and the bean-eater were close as prairie oysters. Only time would tell which pair of the three would turn out to be bunkies.

Yet the choosing match made Wil a little nervous. The boys had never been in on one before, and he knew how personal the whole thing could be. A string was usually kept together as long as a man was with the outfit; when he left, it was handed to the new man intact. But getting the strings together in the first place was usually done by a choosing match. Lined up according to seniority, each man chose his first horse, then his second, and so on down the line.

Even the oldest hands got tense about it. They might know all the rules of seniority on the spread, yet it was only human to have your heart set on some fine little cutting horse, a nice girl's name all picked out for him, and a prayer in your heart that nobody would choose him out from under you.

By now the boys had had time to look over the saddle band and pick the ideal string they'd each like to have. Comparing notes, they were befuddled to see their choices hopelessly overlapped. Because seniority this time had to go strictly by age, they looked at one another narrowly and thought in numbers instead of names: "He's fifteen and three months. He's fifteen and five. And that poor sucker's only fourteen and ten!"

There'd never been much levity around the bunk-house. Now things were positively hushed.

Annie and Black Charlie noticed first. Then Wil saw it and decided to get the thing over with even before Eph Wormwood had finished with the broncs. There wasn't a corral big enough for the whole band, so he split it up in three, called for the boys to bring their ropes and each one drag out his heart's desire.

Tall Slim came first. That was all right with Wil—although he was curious to know what string the bean-eater would have picked for his druthers. He was intrigued by the boy and his tangy combination of handsomeness, scorn, and skill. And by his touch of manly elegance that these Montana boys could never learn.

Wil watched him, standing aside, slapping his leg with that long, stiff riata of his. Then he became aware that all the rest were looking at him. He said, "All right. What are you waiting for? Slim? Start off!"

Then damn if that knuckle-headed younker didn't squint over at Wil and say, "It's all right by me, Mr. Andersen, if Charlie Schwartz goes first."

It was so juvenile that Wil shouted back: "This choosing match goes by seniority, gawdammit! It always has and always will. If you want to trade with your dear little friend later on, that's your business. But right now, it's your turn to choose, so get in there and choose!"

Slim looked at the ground, then went into the second pen. The horses started to mill nervously. Wil glanced around to see how Charlie Schwartz had taken their exchange of words. He was surprised to

see him standing beside the dark boy. They were so
close that when young Charlie turned his head to say
something to the bean-eater, the brims of their hats
brushed.

The horses ran along the fence of the round pen.
Slim stood at the empty center waiting. Suddenly he
threw, California style, without whirling. The rope
landed around the neck of a fine little brown rim-
rocker that had already proved he could climb steep
hills, come down sharp pitches, and travel rough
country with the best of them. He surely didn't look
like much, but he was all horse, from the ground up.
Wil was pleased to see eleven disappointed faces.
They were learning their horses.

The bean-eater was next. For his first, he picked a
handsome little nigger horse that everyone had ignored
because he was so handsome. Wil pursed his lips.
He'd only ridden that horse once but had the feeling
it might turn out to be one of the best cutting horses
in the band. The dark boy was taking a chance, but
a shrewd one. Wil nodded.

The boys' choices revealed a great deal about them.
Wil watched the whole thing closely. When they'd
done, he felt he knew them all better. Without help
from him, each boy had picked two horses of each
type that he would need: a couple circle and cutting
and roping horses, and, perhaps more important than
any, a good night-horse that he would value beyond
price. Then each one rounded out his string with a
couple mandatory broncs that he'd be teaching cow
work on the drive. Eph Wormwood had done only
the spectacular fraction that showed these wild crea-
tures they were no longer free. Most of their education would be up to the wisdom and patience of the
riders that followed old blood-spitting Eph.

Their pride in their strings promised much. Wil had
told them that, once chosen, a man's string was as
good as his as long as he stayed with the outfit. Not
even the boss could ride one without permission.

The twelfth boy's legs were so short they stuck out

somewhat to the side when he rode. There were no
stirrups short enough. He was the marvelously snub-
nose tyke that wore a red vest, a fetching grin, and his
pants unbuttoned in an almost fixed forgetfulness.
Asked why he had such a good nature, he answered
that he was still too little to win a fight. And when
Black Charlie was guessing the boy's age, he said,
"Lansakes, you look like you's hardly fimps. I bet you
don't know what fimps is, do you, boy?" The little
fellow grinned his grin, dug in a pocket of his California vest, and pulled out a pair of dice. He held up
two fives and said, "That's fimps. But I'm almost over
eleven!"

Black Charlie's remark went the rounds and by
morning the boy was known as Hardy Fimps. Soon
nobody could remember his real name and he was
overjoyed.

He might be last in the choosing match, but little
Fimps seemed completely pleased with his string. He
led them away as proudly as if he'd had first choice.
Wil watched the bunch of them going over their
horses, looking at hooves, and discussing points. It
wasn't a new sight. Even the oldest cowhand regarded
his string as something a little special, even if he'd
been through this a dozen times.

Wil relaxed cautiously. He didn't like overconfi-
dence. He stood watching Black Charlie's pink palms
patting some kind of magic into ordinary dough while
the Dutch oven heated. He asked, "Got any coffee?"
and Black Charlie said, "You know where it is. Nobody gonna wait on you."

Wil slurped the hot, black brew, then leaned against
the wagon. "I know they're all doing their dangdest
to do everything I tell 'em to, and they're all mighty
respectful and quiet. But I don't know. Sometimes I
get the feeling there's a terrible lot going on behind
them baby faces. They're still hardly more than names
and sizes to me, but I know damned well they have
arguments and fights to settle. But it must be all in
whispers out behind the barn, because I never see a
sign of anything going on."

" 'Course not! The boss is always the last man to know what's going on. These is all real, genuine boys, and they got their differences, just like any bunch of hands. You can be damn sure they's plenty going on behind your back and that's just where it belong. You'd lose all their respeck sticking your nose in their little pissy-ant doings."

"Well, there's one thing they damn sure agree on. Ain't a one doesn't think I'm the hardest man that ever lived."

"Yes, indeedy."

Wil looked at him, waited, and said, "Yes, indeedy what?"

"Well, ain't you? This come like some kind of a surprise? First time in all these years I ever guessed you give a good gawdamn. That's what always made you so great. You didn't never care what nobody thought."

"But this is different. These are boys."

"Careful now, friend. You treat boys like anything but men, and you're gonna end up with nothing but boys."

"Oh, I'll never let 'em forget who's boss—still . . ."

His voice drifted off, and he reached out for a pinch of dough on the edge of the flapboard. The tip of the butcher knife buried itself neatly between his thumb and forefinger. He jerked his hand away and examined it.

"That was a damn fool thing to do, you belly-cheating old chuckle-head! You could've cut my finger off!"

"I s'pose snitching food *ain't* a damn fool thing to do!"

The boy that wore glasses ran up, slowed down, and stood listening in awe.

"If you ain't the bloodthirstiest old feather-head! You know, you could of cut my whole thumb off!"

"You bet your fambly jewels I's bloodthirsty! Do you catch me going into your house and sidling up and snitching a pinch of something off your table? You bet your pale tail you don't! Your house is your house, and my house is my house!"

Charlie Nightlinger turned away from him in offended dignity and looked down at the boy. "Git outta
here. Can't you see Mr. Andersen and me's discussing
business?" Then back to Wil: "You oughtta be ashame
of yourself! Acting like you just wants to pass the time
of day, and here what you really wants is to trick me
right on my own premises!"

"Trick, hell! I wasn't even thinking what I was doing, and you nearly cut my hand off!"

"You just lissen to me, Mr. Blue in the Face! When
I gets riled enough to cut your whole gawdamn hand
off, you can be damn sure I won't miss and only slide
in between your fingers! I ain't practice with this
thing forty years for nothing, and *that* you can *believe!*"

His eyes fell on the rapt boy again. "Looky here,
Mr. Four Eyes, did I or didn't I not just tell you to
remove your ass from these premises?"

The boy swallowed. "Yes, sir, but I got something
to say to Mr. Andersen."

"Well, git in line. I ain't finish with him yet, and
when I is, I don't guess he'll be in much of a mood
to lissen to a lot of little-biddy chit-chat from the nurs-
ery end of this outfit. Why in the world you wearing
them things anyway?"

Wil's eyes went wide. "Charlie, you're changing the
subject! You nearly cut my arm off!"

"Glasses only makes your eyes worse. Sooner you
bust 'em, the better."

"Oh, no! They been in our fambly for years!"

"Now, if that isn't about as feather-headed as you
can get! If they was a crutch in the fambly, I guess
you'd limp, huh? Four Eyes, you's so dumb you'd play
poker with cow chips and refuse to burn your winnings
on a cold night. I bet you think saddle horn is something you blow and a horse fly is something you saddle
and a blow fly is something you button! I speck you
call a cow chip a critter fritter and a heifer an udder
mudder and a colt in the head what happen when
a young horse step in your hair."

The boy had listened rapt. When Black Charlie stopped for breath, he said, "Say that part about poker again, please?"

Charlie pointed at the boy with the butcher knife and said to Wil: "Man, where you find a tick that talk?"

Wil looked down at the newly christened boy and confided, "Nothing wrong with this nigger that a good clout over the head wouldn't cure. All right, Four Eyes, what's this big important news you got?"

The boy was obviously pleased at permission to speak at last. He stood up straight, swallowed, and said, "The barn's on fire."

Wil looked as if he were going to cry and bounded off.

The report was exaggerated. There was a ten-foot patch of smoking hay and a smoldering soogan that had been used to beat it out. Both tarp and quilts were now past use as bedding, but the barn itself was intact, only smoke-filled and entirely empty.

Wil bent over. A half-sack of Bull Durham lay abandoned in the burned hay. Beside it was a little charred book of thin cigarette papers known wryly to cowmen as their bible. He went to the door and saw a whole landscape of boys in the far distance extremely busy at a variety of unassigned chores.

He wiped his face with his bandanna, stood several moments, then threw his hat on the ground. He roared, "We're starting the roundup in the morning! *I've got to get this over!*"

11

Hardy Fimps was the only one that Wil could spare to ride to the X Bar X. He was to tell Mr. Choate that they were starting the roundup, and to send a rep just anytime. The boy felt gravely honored. There is something about being given a message to deliver. Hardy left with his Stetson pulled firmly down and a serious look on his face. His good-bye was a question and a hint: "Mr. Andersen, what if I run into Injuns?" Wil wasn't passing out any artillery. He looked seriously back at the boy and said, "Son, if you can't lick 'em, join 'em." The boy said, "Yes, sir," and rode off so small on his horse that he looked like more of a passenger than a rider.

The rest were startled out of their bedrolls at three A.M. by Black Charlie's howl: "Rise and shine or your ass is mine!" A sleepy voice in the darkness said, "That damn nigger can't tell time. It ain't even tomorrow yet!" Charlie's big voice replied, "The hell it ain't! I been up since yestiddy cooking this garbage. Come and get it 'fore I dumps it on the ground!"

The darkness was filled with small figures that grunted and bumped into one another rolling up their soogans. Then they stumbled off into the farther darkness, and minutes later returned to sit cross-legged on the ground around the fire with tin plates in their laps. Breakfast was beef, hot bread, and dried fruit washed down by the good strong coffee they'd seldom been allowed at home.

It was Eph Wormwood's last meal on the Double-O. He and his hazer ate way off away from the boys. When Wil brought over his money, he took it without thanks and sopped his bread in gravy. When his mouth was full, he said, "This is the last you'll be seeing of me, Wil Andersen." Wil looked startled. Eph explained. "I don't take to kids staring at me when I do my work. I guess you know kids is close to the powers of the earth. They can make things happen. I wouldn't go on this drive with you if you fanned me with feathers and fed me sweet ice every step of the way." Wil grunted and said, "Come spring, send word if you change your mind." Eph looked away chewing. "I won't."

Then Wil Andersen began taking off his belt. He said, "Eph, I seem to remember you fancying this buckle for a good many years. I want you to have it."

Then Eph Wormwood did a peculiar thing. His eyes went wide in a sort of terror. He practically ran to his horse and rode away. His hazer followed, kind of puzzled. Wil watched them go as he put the belt back on.

Slim was eating alone off to one side. Charlie Schwartz brought his plate over and sat down beside him.

"What's the matter, Slim?"

"Nothing."

"Come on."

"Well, shouldn't I be kind of took back at the way you threw in with that bean-eater? When your soogan burned in the barn, I just naturally thought you'd be my bunkie."

"He asked."

"Did I have to *ask*?"

"I wouldn't of thought so."

"You gonna keep on with him?"

"I guess."

"Well, I never thought you'd choose a stranger over me. And for sure not a bean-eater."

"Call him Cimarron."

"That ain't his name."

"It's his summer name. It means somebody that ran away."

"And that ain't all. It's a name for somebody wild and lawless and won't join in. It must have been gave to him. It's too good for him to take himself."

"He's not really like that, Slim."

"And I'll tell you something else, Charlie Schwartz. I happen to know he's got a desperado flag in his war bag."

"A what?"

"One of them red sashes the old cowboys wore when they wanted to show off and raise hell."

"Slim, I'll thank you not to talk him down. He's my friend."

"All right."

There was a thudding of many hooves in the morning darkness. The boys looked up startled as Hardy Fimps and Mr. Andersen came roaring right up to the chuck wagon with the whole damn saddle band. The hundred horses milled around and snorted and filled the end of the night with food-gritting dust.

Wil's voice yelled out, "Well, go ahead, boy! Say what I told you to!" and Hardy Fimps came out with a high, clear squeal: "Horses! Horses! Horses!" Somebody said, "Oh, is that what they are?" Nobody'd known Hardy had been appointed night hawk. Now, the way he carried on, you'd think the job was an honor. Didn't the silly little bastard know it was the *boy* of the outfit that got stuck with wrangling horses?

Slim helped Mr. Andersen and Fimps run a line around the saddle band. They hitched it to the chuck wagon, looped it on forked sticks, or gave it to somebody to hold. The hundred snorting horses let themselves be hemmed in by the slender line of the rope corral and stood waiting under protest for the hands to pick their first mount of the day.

Wil dismounted for a quick bite and swallow of coffee.

"Pick your rock-rimmer, girls! We're going far and wide today. And scrape your plates. You won't be eating again until it's this dark tonight. Or darker. Hustle it up."

Then he shouted angrily, "And for Gawd's sake, jingle your spurs after the night-hawk's brought in the horses! The last man to pick his horse is just burning daylight!"

Few could resist glancing dubiously up at the black sky and cold stars. Wil didn't seem to notice. He emptied his plate, put it on the flapboard, and finished his coffee.

Black Charlie boomed out loudly: "Do like he say, not like he do. They's a nice big tub of warm water right there in plain sight for wrenching your plates when you's done. If one more of you greenhorn sodbusters pass by the wreck pan and put his dirty plate on my cooking table, he better find some place else to eat tonight."

Wil muttered, "Plain sight, my left eyeball," and swung up on Sad Sarah. The cream-colored gelding nickered nervously as he mounted. Wil yelled out, "Hop to it, girls. Even the best horse has to have his kinks worked out when you start up in the morning."

Ropes flew, and the boys pulled out the best of their strings. Wil fumed impatiently, watching them saddle up, then finally went on ahead. They hurried after him on horses that protested with kicks, twists, and much shaking of the head.

The sky began to lighten as they rode north up the valley. Nobody talked. They jiggled along, bathing their faces in the cleansing wind and hearing the meadowlarks wake up. It was daylight when they came to the cozy little grove near Weeping Woman Creek. Wil drew up.

"The Old Woman and his wagon'll be right here tonight. This is our base camp for the roundup. Bring your critters in on that side of the creek. And for God's sake bring 'em in easy. Don't chouse them. They been living wild all winter, and they'll be a thousand times spookier than the horses was. They'll be hard enough to cut and brand without you stirring them up."

The boys looked away, impatient at the lecture and anxious to get going. Wil seemed reluctant to put them to the test.

"Walk slow and talk easy, and every time you see Stuttering Bob, shove a bandanna in his mouth if you can find one big enough. Where is he? In front when I'm talking to you, boy. Now, listen, mister. One more yip outta you, my knuckle-headed little friend, and I'll personally see you t-t-talk soprano the rest of your life."

Stuttering Bob smiled at the ground in sheepish good nature. In recent years he'd come to feel his stutter was a distinction, and, in a sort of awe, realized that his mistakes were seldom small; they had about them a glorious touch of catastrophe. For instance, who but he could trigger a great big horse stampede with just an ordinary yell? So Mr. Andersen was right. He must try to keep the lid on this dark talent, or they'd all go up in smoke. When you got right down to it, his stutter made him quite important.

A man was riding out of the little grove of trees. He must be the rep from the X Bar X because Hardy Fimps rode beside him, going bump-bump-bump in the saddle.

He was a dour-looking man of a weatherbeaten forty. Branding irons stuck out of his saddle pack. He looked at the boys and asked Wil if this was a round-up or planting time. "This one you sent to get me ain't even frying size."

Nobody laughed, including Wil. He said, "They can do the job, Jesse. They're as good as most, and better than some I know."

"I hear Smiley and his two bunkies got over their gold colic and headed north."

Wil sniffed and said nothing.

"And another little piece of news for you, Wil. We been noticing the calves is more ignorant this year than they ever been before. I must have seen a half a dozen with a fresh T Square brand on them tagging after our heifers."

The boys looked at Wil. He rimmed a nostril with his forefinger. "I thought the T Square boys decided not to winter their stock here anymore after that little talk we had last year."

"Well, Mr. Choate don't want no trouble. But he says he'd like to see a T Square heifer for every T Square calf, or know the reason why."

"And if there ain't one?"

"Well, it's like this, Wil. We got caught in the same bind you did with this gold thing up the Ruby. We're down to just half the hands we was counting on, and not a schoolhouse in a hundred miles that we could raid. So Mr. Choate says whatever you decide to do about these T Square fellers, he'll go along with you. But don't count on him for any more help than just me and two more boys he's sending later in the week."

Wil sniffed: "That kindly dumps it in my lap, and you can see my lap's pretty full right now. But we ain't gonna do any different this time than we ever did before. When a calf suckles one of my heifers, we're branding it with the Double-O, no matter what's on there already, theirs, yours, or God Amighty's. We ain't looking for trouble, but we sure as hell ain't giving away nothing we know is ours."

The boys stirred like a gust of wind moving over wheat.

The X Bar X man nodded. "It'll sure be a pleasure riding along with you, Wil. Mr. Choate kindly hoped you'd look at it that way. He was just a bit worried that—" His eyes swept over the boys. "That under the circumstances you might feel obliged to back down a bit."

"He should know me better than that, Jesse. If I was all alone and sick in the saddle and this whole damn valley was filled with T Square men, I'd keep what's mine."

Wil ended with a decisive sniff, and several of the boys sniffed with him. Then he got right down to the business of scattering his riders. He split up the boys in pairs and pointed out the rim of the territory they'd sweep today. The boys rode off as soon as assigned. Wil left the roughest part of the valley for himself and Jesse. Their dust soon settled into clean silence, and the meadowlarks started up again.

For several hours this part of the valley lay still.
Then a bull came plodding up over the ridge and
down this side. He stopped to graze, then moved on
when several cows followed him. He looked up. The
cows looked up, too. A dozen head were trotting this
way, with the irritation of cattle that haven't been
herded all winter long. They joined the bull and his
cows and were soon grazing. In a while, another
bunch came out of a little gully on the eastern slope.
By the middle of the morning there were several hundred grazing in the center of the valley. It was afternoon before the boys themselves began showing up
with reluctant strays to add to the day's gather.

When the sun got around to setting, there were
maybe five hundred head bedded down and grazing
quietly, all headed in the same direction. The chuck
wagon was over by the grove. The early boys were
gathering wood for the Old Woman, and fearfully
good smells were rushing the day's best message on
the wind.

Wil and the X Bar X man came in last. Looking
down into the pleasant valley, Jesse said, "Looks like
them youngsters of yours got everything under control."

Wil frowned. "Don't tempt fate by talking about it,
Jesse. Me, I've give up sunny thoughts for the summer."

12

At that time there were only two ranches in the valley: the Double-O and the X Bar X. The T Square
was so small it didn't really count, so there weren't
really many irons in the fire. Winters, all their cattle

mixed together on the unfenced range, and in the spring were rounded up. The new calves were branded with the mark of whatever heifer they suckled. At the same time, their ears were marked with the outfit's particular slits or notches, and the bull calves castrated, except for a few set aside to breed. When they were old enough, they'd be driven to market and sold as beef.

Wil's boys sweated generously helping Jesse work his calves for the X Bar X in addition to the Double-O. The ten days set aside for the roundup and branding were always twelve hours long plus two hours of guard at night, yet they never seemed to tire. In fact, Wil seemed to sense a certain jubilee at the end of each day's work. Nobody laughed, but there was plenty of exuberant talk as they ate around the fire. It would be a while yet before the first guard was set out and everybody else went to bed. Now they were filling their bellies and competing in accounts of the orneriest critter they'd had to cope with today. Now and again Wil and Jesse exchanged a glance. Looking from face to face, Wil noticed that each of them was already beginning to wear his hat with a difference.

The subject changed from critters when syrup-covered berry biscuits came out of the Dutch oven. With a full mouth, Weedy said, "The Old Woman sure can cook!"

Black Charlie slammed down the oven lid: "*Who said that?*"

There was an impressive silence as the black man's eyes searched each face. When he discovered Weedy's look, he said, "Just exactly who you calling Old Woman, little boy? Something you and all your nice li'l playmates better get straight right now. Nobody, understand, *nobody* call the Old Woman the Old Woman to his face, you hear? Look to me like they only two things them rosy lips of yours is good for, and neither one's talking. Now, finish up these *de-*licious biscuits, or I throw 'em out."

Jesse said, "Wil, you notice anything kind of funny today?"

"About what?"

"This T Square thing."

"Well, I saw maybe a dozen of my calves with their brand on."

"Anything else?"

Wil thought a moment. "Yes, there is. The whole damn day I didn't see one single sign of a T Square man, and I had a feeling I should."

"I thought you'd notice that. Not hide nor hair. In fact, they're so scarce you get the feeling they're watching everywhere you go."

Wil looked at him a long moment. Then young Charlie Schwartz's voice cut into his thoughts: "Hey, Four Eyes, bring out your guitar, and I'll teach you the prettiest little old song you ever heard."

Wil raised his voice, "I thought I told you boys not to load the wagon down with stuff that don't belong on a drive."

The Old Woman pointed a big spoon at him. "Mr. Andersen, if that little old guitar weighs more than seventeen and eleven-thirds ounces, I eat it without gravy!"

"Look at the room it takes! It's just too damn much trouble, Charlie, that's all."

"Mr. A., the day music's trouble around here, wave me good-bye."

Horny Jim leaned toward Weedy and murmured, "What kind of a man don't like music?"

Wil grunted to Jesse: "I'm just filling in here till they can find somebody that knows what he's doing."

The plucking sounded better than you'd have expected of a boy. The card players were quiet and listened as they played. Fimps' crap game was hushed, too.

The Old Woman, busy at tomorrow's sourdough, said, "Who that playing? It can't be Four Eyes. He ain't that smart."

"Yes, sir, it's me. I been playing on this since I was

littler'n it is. It's been in the family I don't know how
long."

"Like them glasses."

"Yes, sir. And this tune that Charlie's gonna teach
me's wrote down on paper. He's got the notes!"

"If he know so much, why don't he play it himself?"

Charlie Schwartz's voice answered: "You don't have
to be able to play to figure out the notes. It's only
arithmetic. I'll show you."

He picked his way between the bedrolls with a
little folder of music. It had some Italian's name at
the top and thousands of notes beneath. Black Charlie
held it at arm's length and said, "My Gawd." Everybody laughed.

"No, look. Anybody that can whistle, can count these
lines and spaces and figure out what the tune is. And
the numbers over here tell you how many counts you
got in each one of these spaces, so it's easy to tell
how long each one of these little note things lasts. It
ain't hard—especially if you've heard it."

"Oh, I can see that. Now, kindly explain to me how
you gets pretty music out of all them fly turds."

The boys laughed, and young Charlie picked his
way gravely back to Four Eyes and the guitar: "You
wait. I will. And it's the prettiest little old song you
ever heard. Somebody name of Vivaldi made it up.
I think he must of been a wop of some kind."

Wil lay on his soogans leaning on an elbow. Beside
him, Jesse used his saddle as a pillow. They stared
into the fire and watched the boys beyond. When Wil
spoke, it was quietly: "That gimpy one, he's a funny
boy. For somebody with the shortest temper in all
creation, he's quiet as a little pebble inside. And he's
got horse sense that goes way beyond his years. And
he's quick; don't take him no time to figure something
out. Only drawback is the fool kid's all the time trying
to prove he's as good as everybody else. I never could
'bide a sickly boy, but I sure got to give him his due.
If pride don't trip him up, he's gonna be somebody
around these parts someday."

The strumming had begun again. It was slow and hesitant. Young Charlie figured out the notes one at a time and passed them on to Four Eyes, who sniffed around the scale like a terrier until he found the right one. Then he locked it in, and it was his forever. It was slow and irritating, and the tune seemed to hold back, as if afraid of being born. But once a part of Four Eyes' hands, it rose from arithmetic to melody, and sang out sweet and bold and thoughtful as times remembered.

Later Wil lay on top of his bedroll and looked up at the sky. He'd set out the first guard, and the talk between bedrolls was slowing down. The herd had been restless. Now that they'd drawn closer together, quiet took them. But, like the outfit, they never really slept. They might rest, but night was nothing but a wait. They watched the riders that came and went, and listened to their sounds all down through the dark hours.

The two on guard circled the herd in opposite directions, walked their horses slowly, and gently eased night wanderers back to bed. At the far side of the herd, they met, consulted Wil's big watch, and discussed how many minutes to cheat this time by setting the hands ahead. Then they separated and went on their humming, crooning ways alone. Things were hushed out here, but something was always going on. Except for the third guard men, who were supposed to wake only the cook and always managed to wake Wil as well, he was reassured by the fact that the outfit never slept.

The boys seemed to take to all this as if it were in their blood. They were almost too unsurprised. Wil would have been more comfortable if he could see a little strain on their faces or hear complaint. Instead he saw little signs of a strange exuberance. The work was hard. Their tender tails must ache from all those hours in the saddle, and their ears must throb with his endless yelling. Yet when one of them tried to write a promised letter home, the only thing that any of them could suggest to say was, "*All we do is eat and herd cows.*"

Wil almost groaned. He had the uncomfortable feeling that all this accumulating zest was greater than his lungs, his anger, and his fear. They were taking the whole dangerous job in their strides! Kids rushing in where old men fear to tread. And what can you say? "Don't love this life that I love, too?"

Dammit, they should have crawled into their soogans too tired to take their boots off and been dead to the world the minute they closed their eyes. Yet half of them were still talking and horsing around. The Old Woman was probably right when he said, "They soogans fairly crackle when they rolls them up in the morning. 'Fore long they gonna have to break 'em over their knees to fold 'em!"

Great God in Heaven, they were like those giant suns you heard about in school that burn off terrible amounts of energy just to be burning.

Wil's heart sank. How could he show them that discipline is only learning how to take care of yourself—and not just some cranky old man's heavy hand? Was it possible to prepare them for all the natural disasters of this country, or would they have to blunder on like he had, and trust to luck? He hated the idea, yet how can you arm a bunch of young boys who think a wild ride with death's a great adventure!

They lay among snakes on the wildest frontier left on the continent and laughed in the darkness.

Wil groaned.

13

The day they buried the old man with the grizzled beard started off just like any other.

The Old Woman woke them up beating on a pan and yelling, "Grub piiiiiiiilel Come onl Ain't no Sundays west of Omahal" Nobody cared whether it was Sunday or not. It was the three A.M. that hurt. A young voice muttered, "Seems to me this outfit has mighty short nights." Somebody else went into it a little further: "A man don't need no bed in this outfit. All he needs is a lantern to find his horse by."

It was cold. They dressed under their soogans, dragged their warm boots out after them, and grunted them on.

It was while all the bodies wrestled into clothes under the blankets that Horny Jim usually began talking. The sight seemed to suggest a universal orgy to him. He elaborated on the idea until many of the boys stumbled off into the darkness too stimulated to irrigate the plain.

Neither Wil nor the Old Woman could bring themselves to object, because the boy spoke with a relish and rare knowledge far beyond his years. They could never understand how a fifteen-year-old in a tiny little town like Bozeman had amassed such a wealth of fact and fancy on fornication. He knew about bizarre contraceptions in New Guinea and what perfect hosts were the Esquimaux; he knew Old China intimately, and the names of certain streets in Paris, France. Once he got started, all you could do was go

on about your business fast or he'd make your world
and time stand still with fevered, writhing fantasies.

This morning Wil just had to interrupt. Something
the boy said made him think of Annie's flair with
hammer impact. He shouted, "Come on, dammit,
we're burning daylight!" A voice murmured, "He must
of said that a hundred dozen and thirteen times
since we started."

Today they'd finish the sweep of the north valley
and start cutting and branding. The going was rough
on the high slopes and down in the twisting little
gulches along the edges of the Little Belt mountain range. Wil had pushed the rim to the limit this
last day: nobody'd stop until he'd gone as far as he
could and worked every nook and cranny on his way
back. Now, in the rough country, pairs of riders got
split up and didn't see each other for hours. Now
and again a rider would get worried about his junior
partner and go off looking for him instead of the
strays.

Stuttering Bob was with Singing Fats today, but
he hadn't seen him since noon. They'd started high
on the boulder-thick slopes and couldn't see each
other even when their horses sounded close as lovers.
But now Bob stopped and couldn't hear a thing but
the wind and a thousand pounds of silence.

He decided to go to the top of this slope and get
a good look at the whole layout. Halfway up he
noticed something big, dark, and humped just on
the other side of the crest. Buffalo! It was the dearest
wish of his young life to shoot him a buffalo before
they were all wiped out by the professional hunters.
This would be a perfect excuse to get his rifle back
from Mr. Andersen.

He got down, made Lucy stay put by letting the
reins touch ground, and began a long, careful climb.
He went way to the side of where he'd seen the
critter, so it would have to go uphill to get away
from him. He meant to get a good close look, at
least. It was rough going. He went much farther than
he realized. Coming to the crest, he moved bent

over, then eased along on his belly when he finally reached the top.

He lifted his head a hair at a time. It should be about fifty yards to the west.

Then Stuttering Bob found himself looking at a house-sized mother grizzly with two cubs.

His first thought was academic: "I should of knew buffalo d-d-don't graze this high." As if he'd spoken aloud, she turned, looked straight at him, and froze. He whispered, "I think Mr. Andersen n-n-needs me."

Boy and bear both broke and ran at the same time. He went bounding down the great slope like a pebble ahead of an avalanche. She followed like a ten-ton boulder. A good eight feet from head to tail, she moved with startling swiftness for a beast so big. The boy heard her claws scrape rocks as she lumbered after him hardly twenty-five yards behind.

Going straight down the slope brought him no closer to his horse. The damn thing grazed obediently down there a quarter of a mile away. Even if he dared stop to whistle, he doubted if she'd come to him with a grizzly on his tail.

There were big boulders up ahead. He felt his only hope was to get lost among them and squeeze in some little place where she couldn't follow.

There was a beaten trail among the boulders. He followed it. It slowed him with its twists and turns. But the grunts behind him seemed farther back now. Then he heard a heifer bawl somewhere up ahead. It sounded like home.

Suddenly he was in a hidden coulee. At the far end were some Double-O heifers. In the middle was a fire. Two young men were holding down a calf, and an older one was branding it. They froze and looked at the boy.

The older man with the grizzled beard said, "What you want?"

Stuttering Bob pointed behind him and said, "They's a b-b-b-b—" Nothing came out so he tried grizzly: "That's a g-g-g-g-g—"

Then he noticed the design of the iron in the old man's hand. It was a T Square.

The boy said, "F-f-forget it," and walked quickly past them out the other end.

Once out of sight, he began running again. There was an awful scream back in there, and the bear's savage grunting growl. The heifers bellowed, and a young man's voice shouted, *"Dad!"* Then there were shots, lots of them, and too quick for aim. They must be point-blank.

By then the boy was out in the open. He whistled for his horse and lit out for camp as fast as it would go.

Wil stopped everything to go help bury the old man. The bear had crushed his skull. While it bit and clawed one son, the other went for the gun. He emptied the whole cylinder into her head before she let go of his brother and lumbered off to die beside her frightened cubs.

The Old Woman brought his whole medicine drawer and treated the wounds adeptly. Wil did everything he could for the living and the dead, as if they'd all been friends. Jesse kind of hung back, yet nobody said a word about the stolen calves.

Stuttering Bob was the hero of a thrilling adventure among his fellows. They all sat through a long, staccato recital of the whole story, roared when he came to the part where he said, "F-f-forget it," and hid their admiration with many jokes. He was justly proud of himself, and they were proud of him, too.

Wil Andersen was standing at the edge of their laughter. He had his hands in his back pockets and looked at Stuttering Bob with a peculiar venom. Meeting his eyes, the boy stopped talking. The others looked up.

"I guess you're pretty proud of yourself."

The boy shrugged, embarrassed.

"You think you really earned your grub today."

The boy didn't know what he was expected to say.

He tilted his head and squinted up at the man. "Well, hm, I *d-d-did* catch them rustlers."

"Rustlers? Those weren't no rustlers. That was an old man you got killed, and that boy of his is clawed up for life. You brought the T Square to a dead stop. That's what you did today, Mr. Stuttering Bob."

"But they was stealing our calves!"

"Many a spread's been started on borrowed calves and working ahead of the roundup. It don't call for killing. Hard words maybe, but not killing. All you do is just change the brand back to what it should be. I remember when we killed the calves so they wouldn't slow down the drive. Or just give them away. Real rustlers won't take 'em. That's why they give 'em the hot-foot. But I guess all a honyock farmboy knows about the range is what he gets out of Wild West stories. Hang a rustler and be a hero. Well, Mister Man, I can tell you you weren't no hero today. You lost your partner. You left the round-up. You went buffalo hunting. And you got an old man killed just as sure as if you'd pointed a gun at his head and pulled the trigger. How's that make you feel?"

Many eyes looked at him blankly.

"B-b-but I t-t-tried to t-t-tell 'em!"

"The *hell* you did."

"Honest, M-M-Mr. Andersen, I really d-d-did!"

"Not after you seen the T Square brand."

"I c-c-couldn't g-g-get the words out!"

"You could if you wanted to, gawdammit! You just didn't want to bad enough."

The boy stared at him. It was the craziest idea he'd ever heard of. All he could say was, "I t-t-tried! I d-d-did!"

"Boy, I just said you didn't want to. Not clear inside. You didn't feel anything for those people. They weren't no different from that buffalo you wanted to kill just for the sake of killing it. That's why you stutter. You think you're so almighty important!"

"N-n-no, s-s-sir, I t-t-tried!"

"Trying's not enough. That's all stuttering is. Trying without delivering. I don't give a good gawdamn how hard you tried, you got an old man *killed*, you hear?"

The boy seemed near tears. "Ain't m-m-my fault I s-s-stutter!" The other boys looked away.

"The hell it ain't! You can stop anytime you want to!"

"N-n-no I c-c-can't! You think I w-w-want to?"

"I know you do! It gives you a name!"

"I c-c-can't!"

"You can, and by God, you will! Now, listen to me, you whimpering little bastard! You're going to stop that silly damn stuttering right now this minute, or you can get the hell out of here? *Stop or go home right now!*"

He glared at the boy. There was terrible silence.

"I said, you understand?"

Real tears rolled down the boy's face. He writhed clear in his soul.

"Answer me!"

The boy's mouth opened, and the word came out after painful effort: "Yes."

"Yes what?"

The boy's lips shaped the sound, and he forced the word out with excruciating care: "Sir."

"Say it again and say it clear!"

The boy swallowed. Sweat poured down his face. Everybody sat in terrible tension. He took a breath and said, "Yes . . . sir."

The man glared relentlessly: *"Yes, sir, what?"*

The boy was trembling. His eyes were locked with the man's. He swallowed and said, "Yes . . . sir . . . I . . . can."

"Say it again. There's nothing hard about it. Say it fast."

"Yes . . . sir . . . I can."

"I said, say it fast, boy!"

"Yes, sir . . . I can!"

"Again!"

"Yes, sir, I can!"

"Again, God damn you! Say it till I tell you to stop!"

And the boy said, "Yes, sir, I can. Yes, sir, I can. Yes, sir, I can. Yes, sir, I *can!*"

A look of wonder and of joy came into his face. He seemed to want to throw his arms around someone and hold them, if he only dared.

"I can, I can, I can! Listen to me! I can!"

Wil Andersen hitched up his pants and walked off saying, "Hell, *I* knew you could all along."

Black Charlie's face was glistening wet. The silence stretched beyond endurance. Then Stuttering Bob took a deep breath and said the first, unfettered sentence of his life. It came out in a low, clear tone.

"Gol-ly, it looks like a man our age just can't do nothing right around here."

Nobody looked at him, because great tears were rolling down his face.

14

The earth rolled like a ball down the slope of time. Three whole weeks had whisked by before the calf roundup was done and Jesse said good-bye. June was just a notch away, and there was a world of things to teach the boys before the beef roundup and the drive in mid-July. Wil lived by an immense calendar printed on the sky and smoked his fingers yellow trying to make haste slowly.

Yet, in just weeks, the boys were tanner, leaner, quieter, harder to tire, and had learned to sleep at will and wake on the instant. Wil himself had not been sleeping well. It was the first time in his life that he'd found himself too tired to sleep. A surface doze was as close as he could get to rest. His eyes began to look out of caves.

The Old Woman said, "I don't know why that should be, Mr. Andersen. I think the boys is working out just fine."

"Sure, sure, but you got to watch 'em every minute. Got any coffee?"

The Old Woman said, "You know where it is."

Wil filled a tin cup. "Godamighty, Charlie, there's so damn many things that can happen on a roundup, even when you got seasoned men, and these are only boys, little boys, just boys!"

Charlie had gone to the drawers in the chuck box at the back of the wagon. He came back with a brown bottle in his hand.

"Not little, not just, maybe not even boys. I think you frets too much and don't sit back and really look at them. I think I know what you're thinking."

"What am I thinking?"

He poured alarming amounts of whiskey into their tin cups. "You keep thinking what Charlie Schwartz's mother said. You keep hearing her say that thing. *What make you think you can take care of ours when you did so bad with yours?* Hm?"

"Who told you that?"

"Why, young Charlie did himself. And he say he was so ashamed he wanted to run off and never come back."

"Did he, now?"

Black Charlie sipped, as for flavor, but Wil just swirled his around in the cup. He nodded. "Yes, a mother piping up like that would make a boy feel pretty bad. And, God, Charlie, I can't begin to tell you how it made *me* feel. If he'd started running, I'd of gone right with him, and nobody'd ever heard of either of us again." He looked away and asked casually, "He tell you what I said back to her?"

Black Charlie turned away to wave off flies and

lied casually, "Don't recall. What I think is, you think too much. You poor old brain, it like one of them parrot birds that keep saying the same thing on and on and over and over. Why you do that?"

"I don't know, Charlie. But you're right, I do. And I don't mean just things like the day Annie and I took the wagon and went out to bring our boys back home. No, like you say, it's things like what Mrs. Schwartz said. And like that last time I was talking to Smiley and the Boys out in front of the house. I keep remembering over and over the place where Smiley said, 'Mr. Andersen, we leave it up to you. Say the word and we'll forget the whole thing.' I was real relieved and pleased with them for backing down, but I couldn't say a word. There was my chance, and I just couldn't take it!"

Black Charlie kept his face averted. Its wrinkles were all arranged to look calm, but inside he was horrified at being confided in so nakedly.

"To tell the truth, Charlie, that came to my mind like a shot when that long-haired bastard in the bar said *a man too old to know when he's lucky.* I wanted to kill him because he was so right. All I had to say was *stay* to Smiley and the Boys, and I couldn't. Everything that's happened since has been because I didn't say that one little word. An old man died a bad death the other day because of me. And his son's crippled for life because I couldn't say *stay*. And then I turn around and take it all out on a boy that stutters!"

He emptied his cup suddenly and swallowed easily, as if he couldn't taste the liquor's ragged strength. Black Charlie said, "I got a feeling I'm wasting this on you, Mr. A., but let's just have one swaller more."

"No, Charlie, no. I got to keep my wits about me." He pulled his cup away and went for bitter coffee.

"Don't drink that stuff. That for waking, this for sleep. Go sleep. Least go lay you down a bit."

"What about you, Charlie? You don't sleep any more than I do. You're always up and around."

"Old men sleeps in different ways from young. They don't lie down and die like boys. They float. They ain't willing to let loose anymore. Me, I sit and sip and look back. And I got plenty to look back at."

Wil glanced at the white-headed black man in alarm, as if he sensed what was coming. Confidences are a peculiar responsibility. There's no way in the world to prove you've honored them.

"Same as you, I made me a mistake or two in my time. Mr. A., I'm gonna tell you something I never told a living soul before. When I was twenty-five, I was about the most pig-headed young stud in Mississippi, Arkansas, and parts of Louisiana. I got whip regular every Tuesday, Thursday, and some Satiddys if I didn't have nothing else to do. Well, sir, one day I up and decides my own brother's wife she the onliest gal in the world for me. I decides that Love's more important than folks, and I be better dead than alive without her. You'd of thought I could read your white man's books! Well, she ain't having none of me, but he up and almost kill her, then he start on me. Only I'm too big. To my dying day, I never forget how easy it was for me to break his neck. It snap like a flower on a crispy stem."

Wil stared at the other man as if he hoped it was all a joke.

"Oh, I run away, but I never run far enough in all these years to forget the look on his face. There been others, all right, but he was my own brother, and he die *surprise*. Now, you tell me if that ain't something to have to live with, Mr. A. You neen to be so proud to think you's the onliest jackass in the world. Why, man, why you think I got somebody else's name? I ain't Charlie Nightlinger. He was the best cook in the West. I's only Black Charlie making echoes."

Wil finally looked away and shook his head and smiled. The black man had never seen him smile before. He suddenly felt a bit afraid, a bit embarrassed. The feeling grew when he heard the other say,

"Funny, but you're one black son of a bitch that I never pictured making a bad mistake. Burn a biscuit, but hardly more." He rinsed his cup in the tepid tub and walked off unsteadily, saying, "Welcome to the human race, old man! I've lost a saint and gained a brother."

That night he slept.

The next morning Horny Jim remarked that the Old Man was almost human this morning. Weedy lowered his voice to answer: "He ought to be. He got last night's sleep out of a bottle. When I come in from my round, I seen him and the Old Woman passing a bottle back and forth and just simply *swilling* it down."

Horny Jim looked at him doubtfully. "You jobbing me? He said himself there'd be no coffin varnish in this outfit. You heard him."

"Well, some preachers don't listen to their own sermons. The Old Woman keeps a whole big bottle of tonsil paint back in one of them drawers in the chuck box."

The word got around, and everybody took a good look at Wil Andersen to see the traces of being dead drunk last night. Oddly enough, he looked better than he had in weeks.

Four Eyes said thoughtfully, "I knew he might be the number-one son of a bitch around these parts, but I never thought he was two-faced, too."

Supper was different that night. Nobody talked much. When it was over, little Fimps' crap game was quieter than usual. He didn't seem so set on winning everybody's last cent. Four Eyes was slower than usual learning his dozen notes from Charlie Schwartz, and everybody else just sat and sneaked little glances at the Old Woman. It was around that time of evening for him to go meditate among the brush. It was a ceremony neither casual nor to be rushed. If they were lucky, Mr. Andersen would go out to set the first guard around the same time.

They were lucky. The chuck wagon stood before

them wholly unprotected. Somebody hissed, "All
right, Weedy."

Weedy got up slowly, as if he were going to his
own crucifixion. He'd drawn the lot to do the job,
and it went against his every Christian principle. He
was a long and gangling young fellow who seemed
to have been put together by an amateur, then given
pimples by a pro. He became a part of the horse
when riding, but afoot he seemed to be coming apart.
As if his saddle were the anxious seat, Weedy talked
a lot about the Hereafter in that awe of those whose
religion is based upon a fear of hell. Now and again
he embarrassed everybody by reciting Scripture. His
quotations were seldom apt, and his memory never
letter perfect, yet he kept before everybody the image
of his dreary God and gave every day a passing
touch of gloomy Sunday.

It had been important to include him in the drawing of the lots. A bastard this pious had to be included in all shenanigans or he'd be sure to feel left
out and tell. Yet nobody had thought he'd pull the
short one. God just couldn't be that mysterious. And
Weedy, who'd been sure his deity would protect
him from active participation in such a sinful thing,
was secretly staggered that he himself had been
chosen as the Instrument of Sin. It must be punishment for exaggerating about that drink he saw the
Old Man and the Old Woman taking. It had been
sinful of him to describe it as "swilling."

Weedy rose to doom and moved over to the end
of the wagon. Then he just stood in front of the
chuck box in a cold sweat while several voices hissed
him on. He looked all around, then opened a drawer
gingerly, as if he expected a rattlesnake to jab out.
There was nothing in it but one-pound sacks of Arbuckle coffee. Another held beans, and the third one
was a jumble of linament, pills, salts, quinine, and
calomel. He turned around and shrugged at the boys.
Young Charlie Schwartz growled, "Gawdammit,
Preacher Man, don't dawdle!" Weedy opened another.

It rattled like caissons. Everybody jumped, then swore at the dang fool for not remembering the drawer with the tin plates, knives, forks, and spoons. The next drawer contained tobacco for chewing and smoking, lots of bibles, matches, and a brown bottle. Weedy pretended he saw nothing and closed the drawer again.

Four Eyes whispered, "Look in with the linament again! It's snake bite, ain't it?"

Weedy said, "I already did!" but opened it again and saw another big dark bottle stashed away in the back. There were sounds in the dark. Startled, he pulled the bottle out, slipped it in his shirt, and walked to his bedroll trembling. He was a Thief.

The Old Woman came back belching softly, almost melodiously. Horny Jim waited for a moment then quickly felt the bottle through Weedy's shirt. Weedy sat as if all the Eyes of Heaven were on him. Suddenly he pulled the terrible thing out and pushed it into Horny's hands. Horny quickly jammed it inside his own shirt.

The Old Woman noticed that something was going on but didn't deign to look. He muttered, "Boy secrets," several times and took an inventory of the kindling in the rawhide cradle underneath the wagon. A full coosie always made him feel secure.

Horny Jim got up, stretched with his back to the wagon, yawned, and said, "Well, I think I'll take me one, too, and turn in. Been quite a day." He strolled off into the darkness, and silence closed around his corner of the night.

The others found it hard to keep from staring out there. Night-blind as everyone always is from sitting around the fire, they couldn't have seen him even if they went out with burning shucks. Hardy Fimps whispered, "What's taking him so long?" and somebody muttered, "He'll drink it all himself!" and got up and followed. Cimarron laughed and said softly, "That was so *small* a bottle!" and slid into the darkness after the others. Four Eyes and Stuttering Bob

hurried after him. Charlie Schwartz muttered, "Dang
fools going in a bunch! They're gonna get us all in
trouble. Slim, get them back here before Mr. Andersen comes in." Slim frowned. "You come, too." When
they'd gone, the fat boy grabbed Weedy's arm and
whispered, "They can't leave us all alone! Come on,
Weedy, let's go hear the owl hoot!" and dragged him
bodily off into the darkness with the surprising
strength of the fat.

The fire was low. The Old Woman had been too
busy to notice the flat bedrolls. Wil came back woozy
with fatigue and lay on his bed with arms folded.
He didn't expect rest. He'd even gone beyond envy
of these boys lying all around so deathly still in
sleep. Then he heard Fats way off on guard crooning
softly to the cattle. The boy had a wonderful way
with them. Nobody else could night-sing the way he
did. Restlessness vanished at the first sound of him.

The boy didn't usually sing like this unless there
was a little something stirring. He'd said, "I save it
till it's needed." Wil wondered why it was needed
now. Maybe he'd better get up and go see. No, he
was dog-tired, and Singing Fats would take care of
it. It was good to hear him way off there in the
night. Wil closed his eyes.

Then he opened them suddenly. Fats wasn't on
the first guard. What the Goddamn hell was he doing, then? Singing in his sleep? Now there seemed
to be two voices. Hell, three. Good God, it sounded
like a whole chorus! He'd swear there was a saloon a
mile off down the trail. In moments, it began sound-
ing like it was only half a mile away.

Wil sat up. The Old Woman was standing there
with a big mixing spoon in his hand staring off into
the darkness. Wil stood up and looked at the bedroll nearest him. It was flat as a pancake. So was the
one beyond it. He said, "Charlie, what the hell's going on here?"

The two of them started in the direction of the
singing. They walked carefully and stayed together,
as men do facing strangeness on the prairie. There

were no words to the singing. It was just *la*-la-*la*-la to this tune Charlie Schwartz was teaching Four Eyes. The two men slowed. The darkness away from the fire was almost impenetrable. It was their feet that told them they'd come to a little hill. They began to skirt it. The singing got louder, but never loud. Even now there was a respect for the night rule on noise.

There was a warm stirring in the blackness ahead. A young voice said, "Weedy, you pious bastard, you keep taking long swigs like that and you're gonna miss your turn next time."

This was very interesting. The two men hunkered on the edge of the party and listened.

The song swayed on through the starlight, and Wil peered hard to see who all was here. He couldn't make out faces, but it seemed to be just about everybody but the two on guard.

Horny Jim's voice said, "I got to go water the garden. Hold on to the bug juice when it gets to you, Bob. I don't want to lose my turn."

Somebody called out softly after the stumbling figure, "Don't wake up Mr. Wil Crud-Face Andersen!"

Wil turned to the Old Woman. He couldn't make out the other's features, but the sight of all those glowing teeth meant great silent laughter.

A very familiar voice said, "That's right! Fill up his hat, but for gawsakes don't wake up old Iron Nuts!"

Another voice called out, "Hey, Shorty, if he asks after me, tell 'im I'm on the second guard, so there ain't no point in going to bed. I wonder *why* that old bastard always gives me the second guard!"

That sounded like Slim. It had more deep notes than high ones. Then, over the plucking of the guitar, came Four Eyes' voice: "Hey, Charlie Schwartz, you there?"

"I think so. More or less."

"You sure some Italian made up this here song? Don't sound like nothing but pure Montana to me. Who ever heard of a wop cowman?"

"That's what my uncle is."

"Honest?"

"I think so. More or less."

Stuttering Bob's voice came down from the other end of the group: "Weedy? I warned you once about taking such long swigs!" and Weedy's voice complained, "I ain't got the bottle! It's way down there somewheres!"

A hand pushed the bottle into Wil's middle. He took it and passed it on to the Old Woman, who automatically took a pull and coughed.

While several sang *la*-la-*la*-la softly, two talked: "You know, curing your stutter wasn't no great thing. Anybody as mean as Iron Nuts could of done the exact same thing."

"And I'll tell you something else. If I'da knew anybody wanted me to stop, I could of stopped all alone just anytime!"

"I bet."

"I could!"

"Don't job me, mister."

Singing Fats's voice rose over the argument: "Hey, you want to know something? I never been drunk before, and I think I kindly like it!"

"This your first time? Oh, man, you are a farmer!" That was Horny Jim.

"All right, Mister Smarty, how many times you been drunk before, huh?"

"Lordy, I'm too drunk to remember!"

Charlie Schwartz hissed, "Keep it down, you dang fools. You wanta start a stampede?"

There was a lull; then somebody answered, "*Yes.*"

Weedy was stumbling down the middle of the party. "Lord Amighty, I ain't used to this. I'm gonna bed."

Somebody said, "Ta-ta," and everybody else took it up in a storm of soft ta-tas.

Then Slim's low voice spoke, "You know something, girls? Sometimes I think if old Iron Nuts calls us 'honyocks' just once more, I'm gonna let him have it."

"Have what?"

"It."

"What's it?"

"I ain't decided."

It sounded funny coming from Slim. He was usually such a responsible citizen.

"Hey, what ever happened to the bottle? It should of come round a long time ago."

"It coming."

Somebody down at the other end laughed. "Hey, you know who that sounded like just then? The Old Woman!"

Horny Jim was apparently back. His cracking voice came through the music: "Now, there's one fine nigger! You know, he can sew on a button as good as my maw. And I wouldn't be surprised if he didn't cook a shade better!"

Hardy Fimps piped up: "Maybe so, but if he tells me to go out and hustle wood for his damn fire just once more, I think I'm gonna let him have it, too!"

Wil smiled at the Old Woman but got no glow in return.

Charlie Schwartz said, "Oh, I hope I'm around to see that. Got any messages for your folks?"

Charlie Schwartz stood up, then Slim. They swayed in outline against the stars. Slim said, "Well, I think we better get back. No point in giving the Old Man any *more* bags under his damn eyes."

They started picking their way through the party.

"All right, all right, only I want to know what ever happened to the bottle."

Then Horny Jim's voice came up happy with a great idea: "Hey, let's all have a circle jerk!"

And Hardy Fimps said to somebody beside him: "You ever notice how pink the Old Woman's palms is? It's kind of pretty."

"Horse apples."

"Well, it is!"

"Horse apples."

"That reminds me. I got to get back to my horses."

Two more wove by. Four Eyes stepped on Wil's foot and bumped the Old Woman in the head with his guitar. Then Horny Jim passed, telling the one ahead about the red-light districts in the Orient. The last one hadn't said a word through the whole thing. Now he bent over Wil and said with smiling scorn, "Adios, amigo."

The two men kept sitting there to give the boys time to get sandwiched in soogans before they returned.

Suddenly Wil burst out softly: "I tell you, boys ain't the same breed as humans! Remember what I told them about drinking? Wait till I find out which one brought that bottle!"

"Now, hold on."

"Why should I?"

"I brought it."

"You mean those little bastards stole your own whiskey out of the chuck wagon? Oh, Charlie, this is the end of the whole roundup right here and now!"

"Now, hold on, hold on. Take a draw on this."

"Don't waste good whiskey on a man that's mad."

"Then sniff it."

"Jesus, what is that? They make it themselfs?"

"I begs your pardon. That's my own special recipe of cough syrup and tonsil loosener and gargle."

"How the hell could they get drunk on *that*?"

"I'll thank you not to ask into my private personal recipes."

"I don't care what brand of horse it is, they broke in your chuck box and stole it."

"How you know I didn't say they could take a gargle anytime they needs it?"

"You know damn well you didn't."

"Yes, but do you? Me, I don't care. It's gone and done. Only thing that makes me mad is a person's *second* mistake. And believe me, Mr. A., ain't nobody *never* gonna take another draw of Black Charlie Nightlinger's cough syrup agin without leave."

Wil Andersen sighed deeply, clear in from his soul.

He said, "All right, all right. But, God, Charlie, how tired I am of you and boys and horses and cows and worrying!"

But the next morning he was up and roaring as loud as ever. And all the hungover young boys gritted their teeth and hated him in bitter silence.

15

There was a lot of talk about this red savage with a Christian name, Chief Joseph and his Nez Percé. They'd risen somewhere out in Idaho territory and started north away from their ancient home. When the Army came to take them back, there was a running fight and there were soldier dead. Then they vanished. Rumor had them only a hundred miles from Virginia City, with Bozeman next. But everybody with a level head on his shoulders knew that General Howard and his large force of well-trained cavalry would soon round up all seven hundred and herd them back to the reservation long before they ever reached Yellowstone. Yet front pages all over the country ran mile-by-mile accounts of the chase, and the nation's sympathy was stirred by this strangely undefeated band of homeless savages.

Wil was more interested in the early heat. The grass was already drying. He pictured what it would be like in late August in the badlands between here and Belle Fourche. There'd be next to nothing for the herd to eat, nothing but perfect tinder for a prairie fire. If an accident of lightning didn't turn it into a racing wall of flame, the Indians probably would.

Custer and his men were only dead a year, and still not properly buried. The rains and coyotes had un-

covered their bones. Sitting Bull was still unconvinced
that he should come down home from Canada and be
a good Indian. The main Sioux forces were contained,
but there were still small bands of warriors that
roamed the territory stealing horses and cattle, attack-
ing stage lines and lone ranches, and killing outnumbered whites with the desperation of a dying people.

They'd be roaming all through the crackling-dry
plains that the herd would cross. Wil knew that the
red man didn't like the heat any more than anyone
else. Normally the chances of a raid in July or August
were less likely than September, when the first cold
winds swept down and stirred the blood. But these
people were hungry and doing things they'd never
done in memory. Little you'd learned about them
meant much anymore.

He began to push the boys, and push them hard.
They rounded up the herd a second time and cut out
for market the castrated males that went by the European name of "steer." When there were fifteen hundred head, Wil plucked a blade of half-dry grass,
nibbled it thoughtfully, and said, "Get the boys
together."

He looked at them coming in. Their clothes fit better.
Every hat had character and bent to its owner's style.
You could see it and know who it belonged to. They
didn't complain about the weather now, or hunger, or
the idiot that calls itself a cow. Instead they bitched
like full-grown men. And around the fire, they liked
to listen to one another's stories and to tell their own,
but they didn't chatter like Miss Fanny's boys. As their
mutual respect grew, they interrupted less and gave
the other man a chance to have his say. Or lay and
looked into the fire and listened to Four Eyes think
out loud on his guitar.

Best of all, Wil could see that the job came first.
They did what they were paid to do with all the skill
that they could muster. And when they needed help,
they asked for it. Yes, they were as ready as time

would allow. Only years and happenings could make them better.

Not all of the boys got down. This was under the theory that if it can't be done in the saddle, it isn't cowman's work. Wil hunkered and drew in the dirt with a twig. The oval was the herd. The dots were riders.

"I'll ride pilot, of course. Slim and Cimarron will be the point men. They'll ride up here not quite at the head. The swing men on the near side'll be Charlie Schwartz and Stuttering Bob. On the far side, Shorty and Singing Fats. Down here on the flanks, Four Eyes and Horny Jim, and Weedy and Sweet Nose. You'll all take turns riding drag, except the point men. They stay put. You, Mr. Fimps—I decided to make you the wrangler and the Old Woman's right hand. But you'll still take your turn at night hawk, so get used to sleeping in the sun, boy. You been chose."

It's not often that an undersized eleven-year-old can manage to look distinguished. Hardy Fimps folded his arms and looked out over the prairie as if he'd just received an honor long overdue.

Wil stood up and unkinked his knees. Stiff, stiff. "Now, remember this one thing, and we'll do all right. Nobody leads a cow nowhere. The feather-headed thing's got to think it's going its own way. All you do is nudge, and more often than not, a nudge is all you need. That big hunk of beef you call Bull Durham's gonna be the leader. As soon as the drive begins, he'll push himself right up front, and he'll stay there. And the time will come you'll love that bull. You watch and see."

The boys lounged on their saddles, knees hooked over the horn in a variety of ways and some leaning on the rump. All sat with a certain cocky ease in the way most comfortable to himself. Only a greener thinks there's just one way to sit in a saddle.

"'Course, nobody knows better'n me that there's times when nothing'll move a critter. Build a fire under him, and he'll just stand there glaring at you.

Sometimes you think the damned thing can read your mind, the way it goes contrary to what you're gonna do before you do it. A cow can cover the shortest distance in the longest time of any living thing that don't have roots. But you can keep 'em moving as long as you're not too anxious. They know when you ain't thinking peaceful thoughts. But when you are, we'll make maybe eight or ten miles a day. Depending."

The boys stirred and stifled yawns. Wil saw this in a certain desperation and yet went on. He knew that a team looks on its coach with alternate boredom and loathing. Only after victory do they love him. And all he can do is lecture them over and over on the same old things day after day, as if everyone were deaf or a moron or bored and shutting him out. He doesn't aim at the stupidest. When they catch on, it's theirs for good. It's the brightest that bore easily and make the worst mistakes. They're the ones he tries for, and Wil tried desperately.

"Take care of your horses. No outfit's better than its cavvy. The whole drive depends on what condition the horses are in. Keep your saddle blankets clean and dry. Change mounts at least a couple times a day, and check their hooves. And when you've done all that, help keep the Old Woman supplied with firewood. And take *care* of yourself. The only way you can be useful to the outfit is to take care of yourself so good you have a little time to spare for the job. You're on your own."

That part was all right, and they almost liked the man-to-man way he was talking. Then he had to pour cold water on the whole thing with some of the most shocking advice they'd ever heard in all their lives. He looked away at the hills and seemed to repeat to himself something he'd read somewhere.

"*Look on no man as your father, no woman your mother, nobody your brother. And if you're asked is that your son, say I do not know him.*"

He cleared his throat and said, "That's all. School's

out. Say your good-byes. Now the work begins. You'll
never forget this summer. Let's get it over with."

All the families but one came to see the boys off
at dawn and stare after their vanished boyhood. The
mothers fretted to see them no longer between hay and
grass and acting that way. The fathers sighed with
proud relief. The Schwartz children came, but Mrs.
Schwartz was having innard trouble again and didn't
feel up to it, and Aaron had gone down to Virginia
City to find out about this Nez Percé thing. Apparently
everybody there and in Bozeman was running around
like chickens with their heads cut off and getting ready
for a great big red Injun siege.

Young Charlie seemed unconcerned that his were
the only parents missing. In fact, he remarked that
they were the only ones that thought their son man
enough to go off on a big drive without coming all this
way to yell things like, "Keep your feet dry!" He
asked one of his sisters if Mother had mentioned what
she'd like him to bring her from Belle Fourche. The
girl shrugged and said no. Charlie mounted, and without even nodding good-bye, walked his horse a ways
out toward the herd, then waited.

Wil was saying his good-byes to Annie, him on
Sad Sarah and her on the top step of the porch.

"What you want from Belle Fourche?"

"Oh, lands, I want a great deal!"

"Got it wrote out?"

"No, you'll remember."

"What?"

"All I want is everybody to come back in one piece."

"Godamighty, Annie, you know somebody always
breaks a arm or leg or neck. Don't you want us back if
we're not all in one piece?"

Her voice lowered and became intense: "Wil, those
boys are dears, every one of them. But if you have to
leave 'em all beside the trail, I want *you* back here
before the first snow falls, hear?"

To a little, moral man it would have been no less than tiger talk, and terrifying. But the corners of Wil's mouth turned up. "You giving me orders, woman?"

"Yes, I am."

"I'll see what I can do." He looked around and sighed through his nose. "Well, Annie, old girl, here goes."

And he rode off with young Charlie Schwartz. Their hooves made only the smallest sound in the meadow grass. The others hurried after.

16

The drive was beginning. Wil described the bed-ground he'd chosen ten miles up ahead and sent Black Charlie and the chuck wagon on alone. As they parted, Wil half-smiled and said a little wryly, "Well, Charlie, here we go."

Charlie returned the smile and shrugged. "That's right. Here we go." Then he cracked his whip over the kitchen string, and the wagon rocked off straight across country behind its team of four.

The valley was an ocean of brown hide and staring eyes. There were endless snorts and a vast clacking of horns as they stirred restlessly in the waiting pack. Something was going to happen, and every critter in the herd was eager to be alarmed.

Wil placed his men. He was everywhere. Exploding with furious energy and cursing like a master, he shaped his forces around the herd.

The boys sat in place, watching him. He walked Sad Sarah restlessly back and forth, finally took a deep breath, and raised his arm. His shout made the whole valley vibrate. "*All right, boys, let's go!*"

The boys' high voices passed the call up and down the line. They began yipping and nudging. The great herd came to life. Slim moved against the tremendous bulk they called Bull Durham. The great animal stirred, moved, and pressed on ahead of the others. They followed. The herd began to flow. The drive was on.

Wil had given the order to press hard the first few days so every last critter would be too tired to do anything but graze and drink and sleep when they got to bedground each night. The boys really worked. They got clear down to the Bozeman Trail in just three days. By then, man and breast were beginning to get the feel of the drive and to move as a part of something bigger than themselves. Those with push pushed ahead, and those with less let them; each critter found a place for itself that it would keep to all through the drive.

The boys had a few things to iron out, too. Early in the drive they began to split the blankets. After a hard rain, they found that if they doubled up they could sleep on a tarp as well as under one. Unexpected pairs tried each other out and became bunkies. Only Slim and Weedy slept alone. Nobody would have Weedy, and Slim would have nobody.

The Bozeman Trail crosses the Shields River a couple miles before it empties into the Yellowstone. Then it crosses the Yellowstone itself hardly twenty miles farther to the east. Wil had fretted about this right from the first. It meant pushing the herd twice through big water in as many days. Deep river crossing is a danger at best, and he had green men who'd never crossed a stream deep enough for a horse to swim. And, of course, at the beginning of a drive a herd is techy as a bunch of scared old women. He couldn't roll cigarettes fast enough, thinking it over.

At the fire the second night he cut into the craps and poker and music lesson: "Hold up on that a

minute. I been thinking about this river-crossing thing.
It ain't going to be no great big thrilling adventure.
Old hands hate it."

He squatted down and drew the Shields and the
Yellowstone in the dirt. "So I decided to take a chance
and leave the trail for a spell and cross the Yellowstone
in the morning. It's a little swifter here, and deeper,
but it'll save us another crossing two days from now.
I never did figure out why John Bozeman laid out his
damn trail like that."

He stood up and hitched his belt. "We'll have to
move fast. We got to get the herd across before the
sun's up over the mountain. You can't swim a critter
into the sun. The light on the water upsets their
feather-brains all to hell, and sure as you're living,
they'll turn right around and try to go back. *And don't
you let 'em.* If they start milling in the water, we're
in bad trouble. Try breaking up a cow-panic in water
over your head. That's when you'll see how much of
a big adventure it is. Pick a real good swimming horse.
That water's fast and cold. And be sure to loosen your
cinches, hear me? Loosen your cinches. All right, go
back to your little games. Some of you may not be
around to play 'em tomorrow."

Eyes glared at his broad shoulders as he strode off
into the darkness. Weedy mulled the man awhile,
then said, "Wouldn't it be nice to be that smart and
know just about everything? You could spend your
time doing nothing but yelling at everybody." Then he
looked up at Wil Andersen standing over him button-
ing his pants. A great stillness settled around the fire.

"Oh, I ain't all that smart, Weedy. For instance,
when I made up my mind about this crossing tonight,
I plumb forgot one thing. And it looks to me like just
about everybody else has, too. Except maybe Black
Charlie. What about eating tomorrow after we get
across?"

Eyes began to turn to the chuck wagon. The Old
Woman busied himself, and began whistling with
great unconcern.

Wil said, "No, it won't float across. Not in water that fast. What we got to do, boys, is put down our cards and our guitar and our dice for a little while and go out and build us a raft. Right now, tonight."

They looked at him with blank faces.

"And what's more, we're gonna have to go a long ways to get us the wood, because the herd's a little restless. When they're like this, you have to go a mile to spit. So we'll be chopping and dragging logs most of the night. How'd you like them apples, hm?"

He stood a moment, then snarled, "*Get off your asses!*"

It was a busy night. They had to choose between a few big logs and a lot of little ones, chop them down, and drag the dang things a quarter of a mile back to the river. Then they lashed them together, rolled the wagon on, and tied it down tight. By then the boys were glad to go on guard and get some rest just riding. The Old Woman divided his time between imperial supervision and keeping the coffeepot filled. On top of that, he turned out an almost endless batch of bear signs that filled the night with warmth and reassurance.

Hardy Fimps spoke through crammed cheeks: "Mr. Nightlinger, how come they call doughnuts bear signs?"

"Put one on the ground, and you see soon enough."

Wil divided his time between keeping an eye on the guard and holding the noise down. When it was done, he said, "Boys, you did a good job. It won't be light for another half-hour, so I want you to eat and have yourselves a nice little rest. We all want to be full of piss and vinegar when we start that herd across."

There was nothing much inviting about crawling under their soogans in sweat-soaked long johns. They spent the next half-hour shuddering around the fire and letting the Old Woman dab something on their blisters in between fixing a big breakfast.

Hardy Fimps now spent most of his waking hours

with the big black man, and most of that was spent in asking questions.

"Mr. Nightlinger, I never thought cowboys was supposed to do things like chop wood. Ain't that kind of thing for farmers?"

The Old Woman poked at the pancakes in the Dutch oven. "Not if you wants to eat, sonny."

The boy looked at the cradle underneath the wagon. Only a couple hours ago he'd had it so full it sagged down to the ground. Now it was almost empty. He decided to dig the next firehole a little smaller. As if reading his mind, Black Charlie said, "The less fire, the less food."

The boy sighed. The distinction of being night hawk and wrangler had its drawbacks. Swapping his bed for a lantern, he slept part of the day in the noisy camp and herded his horses part of the night. It was true that the Old Woman kept him chomping on tidbits the other boys never got. But this was in trade for keeping that hungry sling under the wagon loaded with firewood, and a hundred other chores around the camp. And if he didn't keep a sharp eye on the saddle band, he'd lose a few horses in the night. Then he'd have to scour the range for them so he wouldn't be late bringing up the remuda when it got light. He really caught it from Mr. Andersen when he was late with the horses. The man snorted, "You got the easiest job in the outfit, and you're late most of the time! I want that saddle band right here in camp before anybody's finished eating, you hear?"

This morning Hardy brought in the band even before they'd started to eat. Wil said, "Why so early, boy? You ain't sleeping today. Today *every*body works to get that herd across."

Wil ended breakfast with an order to strip so they'd have dry clothes waiting for them on the other side of the river. Growed men might ride wet, but children shouldn't get a chill. The boys muttered as they peeled down and put their duds in the wagon with the bedrolls. Bare Fimps looked inquiringly at the Old

Woman, who shook his head. "I ain't dying nekkid.
Not in water that cold." He got up in the driver's seat
and sat with a certain swaying majesty as they dragged
the raft into the water.

The first splash brought paralysis. Wil and his lean,
hard body seemed too busy to notice. The ropes drew
taut. The raft floated. They dug heels in their horses'
sides and pulled into deeper and deeper water. It
wasn't until they were swimming that the raft began
to turn around. Wil shouted a warning. The swimming
horses snorted and coughed in the water. The boys
strained at the ropes. The raft righted itself and drifted
toward the godown on the other side that Wil had
picked for landing.

When the wagon was safe on shore and the Old
Woman whipping his mules up the bank, a certain
exhilaration took the boys. It was cold. The water was
ice, and the wind brutal. The whole thing was so
awful it was good. This was real adventure, no matter
what the Old Man said. When the chuck wagon was
safely up the slope, the boys shouted and raced back
across the river for the herd.

Slim got down to check his saddle. In the excitement, he automatically tightened his cinch. Then he
and Cimarron singled out Old Bull Durham. They
explained the situation to him, and the huge beast
allowed himself to be coaxed down into the water. The
rest followed solemnly.

Wil had picked a smooth place to cross, although
the current was strong. Figuring the drift, he set the
herd in a hundred yards up from where he wanted
them to come out. The boys narrowed the file down to
a dozen head and coaxed them easy out to the unseen
shelf. There they stepped off into nothing with a grunt
and wide eyes, and started swimming in dull outrage.
Reaching the other side, some showed their gratitude
by trying to hook the riders, then went on up to graze
as if nothing had happened.

Each time a pair of boys reached the far shore, they
turned around and swam back to guide another piece

of the herd. Wil sat his horse on the near shore and
watched, lunged in when he was needed, and kept
reminding everybody every two minutes about the sun
going to come up anytime now. The boys kept squinting at the brightening point where it would appear
and enjoyed a delicious panic. They worked together
like demons, and separately as proud rivals of all the
rest.

The sun was just coming up over the mountain when
the last of the herd entered the water. Sudden light on
the surface flashed in their eyes. They drew up. Those
swimming started to turn. Wil and the boys shouted
and beat at them to keep going. Those in midstream
fought to return. Some got by the boys and started to
mill. Panic set in.

That was when Slim vanished. His horse simply
sank. Wil blinked, unbelieving. The boys needed him
desperately, but he said, "Damn the critters! Let 'em
drown!" and lunged in where he'd last seen Slim.

In the packed mill, Slim's hand, then head, appeared.
Wil shouted, "Grab a tail! I'll get to you!"

Black Charlie was on the far shore waving something. A gun. Wil went for it fast. He circled back
around and started shooting right up close to the panicked cattle. The gun roar gave them something new
to be afraid of. They hesitated, and in the hesitation
forgot to mill. Suddenly they were swimming hard
for the far shore. The boys screamed them on furiously,
beat at them, and swore in high voices.

Slim was dragged along. When they got up on shore,
he was still in the middle of the bunch. Let go, and
he'd be trampled. To get to him, Wil shot the nearest
cow in the head. It fell and made way for him. He
grabbed the boy by the hair and hauled him up,
wincing, across the saddle. The horn rammed into his
gut with each step. Away from the bawling critters,
Wil pushed the boy off and rode away.

But it wasn't Wil Andersen who impressed the boys
that day. It was Shorty. The quiet little fellow with
the broad shoulders and man's body revealed a talent

that awed them all. In the confusion of the midstream
mill, a steer had hooked Wil's Sad Sarah. She keeled
over on her side. Swept off her for a moment, Wil
dropped his Colt. On shore, he considered it lost. But
not Shorty. When the last of the herd was out of the
water, he dived and dived for half an hour and finally
came up shivering with the gun.

Swimming was unusual for a prairie boy, but to be
able to swim underwater was akin to genius. The other
boys were frankly awed. The Old Woman was wide-
eyed with wonder, and Wil Andersen impressed. He
said, "Remind me of this when we get to Belle
Fourche, boy."

The boy strode off with more of a roll than ever in
his walk.

It is good for a man to have his own specialty.

17

Wil posted two riders to shape the herd and let the
rest dry off, dress, and change mounts.

It was the first time the boys had been naked together. They stood on the river bank and peeked at
one another with secret interest. The Hebrew prohibi-
tions reached down two thousand years, even to Montana. Inevitably comparing their bodies, they were
envious of some and proud before others. But they
found that maturity is a little hard to pin down. While
Shorty had the body of a man, his voice was just beginning to change. Slim, who had the deepest voice of
all, had only a faint fuzz of pubic hair, and Charlie
Schwartz, who had the most grown-up mind, had the
body of a very little boy.

They looked at Shorty most. He had a great build. But it was Horny Jim who received the most comment. He was almost ludicrously lucky. They laughed and kidded him, and he was delighted. "My father says you don't get your full growth until you're eighteen or so. Think how big I'll be in four *more* years!"

They laughed, and for the first time, each boy was profoundly proud of being male.

Everybody was about dressed when Wil rode up with Slim's horse. It walked funny. The poor damn thing was filled solid with water, and looking mighty crestfallen. Wil was fit to be tied. He flung down the reins and planted himself in front of Slim.

"I told you to loosen your cinch! I told you a dozen times to loosen your gawdamn cinch, and what did you do? My God, boy, you pulled it so tight you cut his wind clear off! No wonder the poor damn thing sank like a rock. I ought to have my head examined, picking you for top man. You're just another yack sodbuster like all the rest!"

He rode off, leaving indignation in his wake. Instead of being glad Slim was alive, this crazy old man was in a stew because one of his horses got more water than it needed. Slim said nothing, but you could see he was angry and ashamed—especially since old Iron Nuts had saved his life today. At best, gratitude is a dilemma and not to lived with long.

The slaughtered steer added the first fresh meat to the menu in days. Wil watched the Old Woman pounding steak with the butt-end of his .45 and grunted: "You know, Charlie, someday you're gonna make yourself another navel doing that."

The Old Woman shook his head. "Oh, I never loads it." He demonstrated by pointing the gun to the sky and pulling the trigger. The roar made them both jump. He sniffed at the cylinder and added, "Very often," and went on pounding.

Everybody avoided Wil's eyes at the evening meal. He didn't mind. He seemed to relish their resentment. When they were all hunkered around on the ground eating, he said, "Did I pull out much of your hair this morning, Slim?"

Slim looked up startled. "No, sir."

Wil looked right at him. "And I don't guess my saddle horn felt very good either, digging in your gut."

Slim was at a loss. He shrugged and said, "No, sir." He poked at his food, then seemed to have an idea. He looked at Wil and said, "Uh, thanks for pulling me out, Mr. Andersen."

Wil grunted: "No need for that, boy. Nothing personal about it. I'd do the same for anybody. I'm still the mean old son of a bitch I always was. I can't understand how you poor boys put up with me."

Black Charlie was standing over there smiling to himself. Wil barked, "What the hell's so funny?"

"Nothing."

"Nothing, my fat fanny!"

"Nothing you'd want to hear."

"I'll be the judge of that."

The black man bent close. "It just kindly seemed to me that you's beginning to break your promise to Mrs. Schwartz."

Then he straightened and smiled big and wide right at Wil Andersen, and Wil glared back.

"Charlie Nightlinger, one of these days I'm gonna kick the daylights outta you."

"Anytime, Mr. A., just anytime you wants to try."

Sweet Nose was the one who drew pictures. He got the name from his habit of nausea at the smell every time he had to hold down a calf that they were branding. He worked very hard at being a regular fellow, but when everything was said and done, he did like to draw pictures.

The day after the river crossing, he rode up to Wil all breathless.

"Mr. Andersen, there's a big cat over on the far side stalking the herd!"

"Cougar?"

"Yes, sir, and big as all get-out! I thought maybe

somebody ought to get his rifle and settle the varmint's hash before he causes any trouble."

Wil didn't take the hint. He rode with the boy, his Sharps in a holster on his saddle. They tracked the cat for over a mile before they caught sight of it. It was a beauty. Big and well fed, it gave the impression that it was stalking more for excitement than hunger. The tail flicked rapidly as it watched the nearest steers. Wil murmured, "There's one good reason for not coming over here on the wild side of the river. Maybe Bozeman knew what he was doing, after all."

When he lifted the rifle, Sweet Nose whispered, "Mr. Andersen, sir, can I drop him, please? I never had a chance at a varmint this big before." He moistened his lips and added, "Everybody knows I'm as good a shot as Charlie Schwartz is."

The boy's eagerness was too much for Wil. He handed over the Sharps. The boy licked his lips again, raised the rifle, and fired immediately. He didn't miss by far, but he missed. The big cat vanished in a graceful blur. The boy sighed and waited a long moment before looking up at the silent man. Wil, of course, was glaring at him.

"Hasn't nobody ever told you about *squeezing* the trigger? Do you always just raise your gun and go bang-bang-bang like some damn nester? Dammit, man, press it *easy*! They ain't no rush. Try it again. Aim at that white rock way over there in front of that bush. Now squeeeeeeze it eeeeeeasy."

The boy obeyed and hit the rock exact center. Wil got up and took the rifle with no comment. The boy scrambled after him. "Maybe we better go on guard with our rifles tonight, hm, Mr. Andersen?"

Wil almost shouted, "I wouldn't trust any of you with a peashooter in a high wind."

Sweet Nose hoped desperately that Mr. Andersen wouldn't mention which of them had missed the cougar. Of course, the old prick did. He let it out when he was warning everybody to keep a sharp eye out tonight: "With the herd this jumpy, just a whiff of cat will be enough to set them off. And don't get no far-fetched ideas about me arming the guard. All we need's a lot of wild shooting like Sweet Nose did today and we'll have us the biggest stampede anybody ever heard of."

Sweet Nose was humiliated. But he listened when the Old Woman began tell about this gunfighter that kept his trigger finger rubbed raw to the point of bleeding to keep it light as breath on the trigger. He began rubbing his as he listened. Old Iron Nuts wouldn't see him miss again.

The cattle were restless all night. There was something in the air. Two nights later, when they got back on the Bozeman, it was still there. A feeling of suspense.

The stampede came the third night.

18

The day had been miserable since early morning. They came to a vast swath of rocky ground, the debris of an ancient glacier. It took hours to cross, because the cows decided that consternation was the only way to react to a rock. They began scattering in all directions. The boys rode back and forth trying to keep the herd in some sort of shape. In all this time there was no grass and no water. The herd began to get testy.

Wil rode on ahead to find suitable bed-ground, but there wasn't any within a reasonable distance. He had a choice between stopping for the night with a hungry, thirsty herd and going on till long after dark to a place where there was enough grass and water. He chose the second, and both cows and cowboys complained like beaten wives.

Even the Old Woman complained. He'd tried his damnedest the whole blessed day to disprove that dumb old joke about "a cook'll go out of his way to run over a rock"—and hadn't. Now he was getting a chance to prove it in the dark. But his main complaint was not about himself: "A man can put up with anything on a full stomach, and them poor li'l boys is empty as drums."

Wil gave in and gave the order to bed down right where they were. It's better to stop when you're nowhere than push through the dark to somewhere worse.

The night was pitch. The Old Woman sniffed at the sky and said, "It so dark you can't find your nose with both hands." Everybody looked and looked for firewood, and they sweated. The cold winds hadn't come tonight. The air was strangely humid. Man and beast were too tired to rest, and this feeling of suspense made for testy remarks and snappish answers. Even the coffee showed the state of things. It was weak, but nobody dared say anything to the Old Woman. That was a mistake. Later on, when he had time to sip it himself, he raged at the whole outfit for being so girlish they didn't dare speak up when he served them something straight out of the horse.

At midnight Slim and Cimarron came from their stint. They woke their reliefs and munched from a plate of biscuits the Old Woman had left out for them. Wil was awake. He snapped at Cimarron for not thoroughly waking his relief: "Look at the bastard! He's gone back to sleep! Don't you know by now a cowhand'll say 'Yes, I'm coming' when he's dead to the world? Shake him, and don't consider yourself relieved until he's on his feet." Cimarron shook Four Eyes hard. Singing Fats was already up.

Wil asked how the herd was. Slim shook his head. "Kind of funny. It's like they're waiting, just standing there waiting. I never seen them so quiet."

Wil's jaw muscles rippled; he sighed through his nose. "Fats, you hear that? Now, you're going out there and croon nicer than you ever crooned before. Them critters is tired and hungry and thirsty. On top of hiking over all them rocks today, they got a real beef. So both of you croon soft, and don't so much as sniff. All it would take is moonrise or a falling star to mustard the whole herd."

Just as Charlie Schwartz was no longer skinny and pale, and Stuttering Bob no longer stuttered, Fats was no longer fat. Of course, no one noticed. Even after the Old Woman took in his pants four inches, they were still a little loose, yet he was still Singing Fats to everybody—and a young man of special reputation.

He was the only one who never minded getting up in the middle of the night to do a two-hour circuit of the herd. It gave him a chance to do what he could do best: ride and sing. Out there alone, he went from one soft song to another without stopping. He usually used that tune Charlie Schwartz was teaching Four Eyes, but the words were his own. They dealt with everything that happened during the day, and people and horses. Like the others, he'd given names not only to all the horses, but to a good many cows as well. They were included in his songs, and he swore they noticed. His opinions of everyone but Mr. Andersen varied from night to night. "Four-eyed Joe/and his spik banjo/give him a tune/and away he go!" might change on some other peevish night to "Stupid Joe/all he know/is one damn song/and it's too long." But his lyric diary was generally tolerant of the boys and the Old Woman. They might make mistakes, but they were his outfit.

His songs about Mr. Andersen were equally consistent. They never failed to mention that he was a mean, harping, hardhearted old son of a bitch. "When he looks at you/with them eyes of blue/you wonder what'd I do?/I guess I'm through." When Fats sang about his boss, the lyrics had more feeling, ingenuity, and quality than any of his others. He reached his creative peak by way of resentment, and the drive was the better for it.

He also sang about Mrs. Andersen. He'd only liked her a lot until the night it struck him that there must be times when that fine, nice lady must submit herself to this terrible man. He was horrified at the thought, and from then on loved her passionately. He lowered his voice even lower than usual when he sang his promise to one day rescue her from this awful brute.

Tonight he'd been wakened from a dream of fair women—all named Annie and all wildly in love with him. When he started his circuit, he went at once into his secret song for her. He was so wrought up by the dream that he made the most extravagant promises ever, and sang them in his softest tone. It was so soft, in fact, that it could hardly be heard. Like people, the animals strained to hear the indefinite. Instead of lulling them, his song made them more restive than ever. After he passed, they stood dead still in breathless silence.

At the far end of the herd, he stopped singing when he met Four Eyes going the other way. He set the Ingersoll ahead and murmured, "I never seen it so dark." Four Eyes whispered, "And it's sticky. My glasses keep getting fogged up." He took them off to squint at them against the faint starlight.

One of the ear hooks caught on his hat string. The glasses flew through the air in a high arc. Then, as from an infinite distance, came the faint tinkle of broken glass.

It was a delicate sound, yet in an instant the entire herd was running as fast as it could go.

The panic didn't spread from this spot outward. It was as if all fifteen hundred head had been waiting for the signal and were simultaneously off and running. The sudden thunder of their hooves was like the breaking of a terrible storm. The clacking of their horns punctuated the thunder with terror.

The two boys were swept along like twigs on a flood.

Wil heard, and rose in the same instant. He roared, "*All hands and the cook!*" Moments later the Old Woman was dumping all the kindling he had on the fire.

The boys flung off their soogans and flung themselves onto their waiting night-horses. Few realized they'd used a flying mount. The Old Woman didn't share the cowman's panic at being caught afoot. Never fond of riding, he felt safest between wagon and fire. By now the flames were rising high in the air.

Cimarron and the others rode off after Wil Andersen. Charlie Schwartz yelled at Slim, "There's got to be somebody on the other side!" The two rode against the wild, horn-clattering current, across the bottom of the herd, and up the far side. Then they galloped wildly to keep pace with the violent rush. It was too soon to do anything with them. All they could hope for was to keep the herd generally together.

Wil, on the other side, was shouting, "Don't let 'em split up! Keep 'em together! We'll point 'em when they start to tire out!"

The herd did stay together for a while, and Fats and Four Eyes rode its crest like they'd never ridden in their lives. Four Eyes kept praying, "Oh, Lord, no gopher holes, no gopher holes, please, no gopher holes!"

Running isn't a cow's favorite pace. After several miles the movement began to slow. Now Wil began to press them from his side. He wanted to begin to turn them and start a mill. Once started in an endless circle, they'd have to slow down by the very compactness of the mass. He didn't know that Charlie and Slim were on the other side doing the same thing in the opposite direction.

Wil and his boys began to whip at the edge of the herd hard with their quirts. The herd began to turn.

On the other side, Charlie and Slim were startled to see the herd begin to press out at them. They veered away, and the herd came with them.

Suddenly the leaders of the herd smelled the rushing river and turned more sharply. Slim and Charlie found themselves being sucked into the center of a milling mass of cows.

Charlie yelled and pointed. Huge old Bull Durham was just yards from them struggling against the current. The two boys fought their way to him and began beating his rump. He tossed his head, bellowed, and began to make headway. Now they unrolled their slickers and began waving them and slapping the nearest critters. An eddy formed in the main current.

As the herd turned, Fats and Four Eyes found themselves riding all alone across the prairie. They never did smell the river, but they began to hear it as the sound of the hooves behind them faded. It was loud. Must be rapids. They swung sharply and started back —straight into a second section of the stampede that hadn't turned.

The two boys split and rode like hell. The herd passed between them and tumbled, with black surprise, into the river. Fats and Four Eyes followed to see what they could salvage.

Wil howled with anger when he saw the herd break in two. It was the worst thing that could happen. Once a herd began splitting up, you had no choice but to spend the next week combing the entire territory. Then he heard shouting from the center of the mill. He stared into the dusty darkness. *My God, did I catch somebody in that mill?* Damning himself, he dug in his spurs and lunged into the confused mass.

Bull Durham was coming at him. He swung sharply and watched in astonishment as the huge beast loped by with a large and orderly following. Charlie and Slim were on the other side nudging them back toward the bed ground. He guessed that they had maybe half the herd here and under control.

He swung again and headed for the bunch that had gone on toward the river. Less than a mile later he met them coming this way. The leaders were dripping, but both Fats and Four Eyes insisted that none had been lost in the rapids.

He said, "Whatever you think, we're taking a head count first thing in the morning," and rode on.

It wasn't until the dark hour before dawn that they got back to camp. Fimps and his precious saddle band were there before them, intact, untouched, coffee and hot cinnamon rolls waiting. He knew the tremendous fatigue that a well-fed man can endure, and he was there working between wagon and fire, and bitching about the lack of wood.

Wil sipped his scalding coffee and kept looking from Slim to Charlie Schwartz. Everybody else was pretty tired, but these two had come within speaking distance of death, and looked at everything now with brighter eyes.

Wil said almost to himself, "What I don't understand is how the two of you got in the middle of that mill."

Neither of the boys looked up from his plate. Eyes began darting between them and Wil. The Old Woman began to listen with a frown on his face. The inquiry had begun.

"Come to think of it, the only way it could happen would be if you were on the far side."

Slim swallowed a mouthful, looked up, and said, "Yes, sir, that's where we were."

Cold sparks came into Wil's eyes. "And what the hell were you doing there? I yelled for everybody to follow me."

Slim shrugged. "I guess we didn't hear you."

"I must have yelled a dozen times to follow me."

Little Charlie Schwartz wiped a hand on his shirt front and stopped eating. He spoke with a faint touch of patience: "Mr. Andersen, you told us over and over the worst part of a stampede is the critters scattering all over creation. So Slim and I went around to the far side to try and keep them in shape."

Wil's cold gaze became a glare. The boy's attitude of let's-be-reasonable-old-fellow caught him off balance. His voice trembled: "And I've told you over and over the best way to stop a stampede is to get 'em to mill, haven't I?"

Slim said, "Yes, sir. That's what we tried to do."

Wil's anger turned on the tall boy: "You tried to

bend 'em *our* way? Good God, you might of caught us all in a mill!"

Both boys stared.

"You knew we were on the other side, and you *still* tried to bend them our way? Judas Priest, you got a grudge against all your little friends? I thought it was only me!"

Young Charlie shook off dismay long enough to snap back, "We was just trying to use our heads!"

Wil lunged forward, swept the boy up by two handfuls of shirt front, and held him face to face.

"But you didn't try hard enough! You're the smartest little bugger here, and you came within an ace of killing every one of us tonight! And it's only pure damn luck that you and your friend here aren't jelly somewhere out there on the plain! I wrapped that mill right around you two! *You almost let me kill you!*"

The big man sounded near tears. The Old Woman dropped a pan with a loud clatter. The moment broke. Wil put the boy down as if shoving him into the ground.

Wil walked in a small circle, then turned on them. "There's *got* to be a boss, and he's got two uses. One is, he makes everybody work together, and the other is, he's the perfect man to hate. You can go on hating him for everything, even blame him for the weather. And laugh when he makes mistakes; and when he don't, you can complain he's got too rich. It's the price he has to pay for making something of himself."

His voice gave out. He ended in an almost helpless tone: "So hate ahead, but take my orders or we'll all end up right where we fall."

He threw his coffee dregs out in a brown arc and went to get some fresh. There was a thud-thud of hooves, and a new boy rode up. Everybody stared at him until he fished bent glasses rims out of his pocket and put them on. He smiled and said, "Keno! I found 'em!" and got down.

Wil looked down at him through the steam of his

coffee. Under that gaze, the boy felt he had to say
something. He had to perform to keep that special
attention.

"They was right where I lost 'em!"

He took the rims off, straightened a kink, and held
them up beamingly.

"Yep, that's what started the whole jamboree!"

Wil's eyes took on a new look. Everyone else grew
still. But the damn fool kept yapping on.

"Me and Fats met at the far side and stopped to
pass the time of day. My glasses was all steamed up.
I took them off to wipe and dropped them on a rock.
And BOOM, the whole dang herd was off in a cloud
of dust!"

Then he grinned.

Perhaps if he hadn't been so cheerfully frank, perhaps if he'd lied or said nothing and let it stay a
mystery.

Or simply not have grinned. That was it. The idiotic
conviction of the young that *Nothing can hurt me!*

Something in him snapped. Wil swung out and
knocked the boy flat with the back of his hand. Dust
rose up around him.

The Old Woman said, "They's fresh coffee, Mr.
Andersen."

Wil stared at him as if he couldn't place the face,
and stalked off into the darkness.

Four Eyes sat up, glared after the Old Man, and
said softly, "He's gonna be sorry he done that. You
don't have to be growed to get back at somebody."

19

Wil knew there had to be missing cattle, but nothing like what the count showed next morning. They were over three hundred shy. He pushed his hat back with a forefinger and squinted at the endless scenery, too tired to give the order to go. Even if he got the whole three hundred back, there'd still be the herd's loss of all that weight last night. He winced at the pounds converted into dollars.

The night of the stampede, they'd bedded down about five miles from where the Bozeman forks. The Yellowstone was at their left and the Stillwater maybe ten miles ahead. The stampede had taken the herd clear on across the shallows of the Stillwater and into the great plain at the foot of the northern Absarokas. There it was every critter for itself. They spread out over an area of thirty square miles and began grazing as if nothing had happened except a little change of scenery.

Wil divided the boys up. Part pushed down from the Yellowstone, part pressed forward along the Bozeman, and the others swept south among the foothills to see what they could find. He sent the Old Woman and Four Eyes with the saddle band on ahead to where the trail crosses the Clark Fork. There they'd meet the gather and stay until the count was right. The wagon rocked on over the rough ground with Night-Hawk Fimps sleeping by daylight in the rear.

Wil himself took the hard part with Slim and Cimarron. They would comb the foothills of the Absarokas. It was a tail-breaking job, but three hundred is a lot of cattle to be missing. He'd intended to go first and have the boys work behind him, but as each took a valley to work, the order kept changing. Very shortly he found himself with a big gather, and way behind. He fumed but was too tired to reorganize the search. All right, let them do the hard work. He'd start hazing these back and let them catch up alone.

The two boys had picked their best, a pair of rim-rockers that could take the hard riding all day long without rest. Right after they left Mr. Andersen they came to a wide valley. Slim wanted both of them to work it, but Cimarron ignored him and went on ahead.

The dark boy liked to work alone. Being with other people always made him do a lot of dang-fool heifer things so that they'd be taken with him. But while that might be nice for a while, he liked better being alone out in the middle of nowhere with only his shadow moving along beside him for company. It was a very handsome shadow, and all he needed.

There was nothing lazy about Cimarron. He worked hard and fast, wove in and out of the gullies, and flushed out a surprising number of fugitives. He pushed them up to join Slim's gather, then turned around and went farther south.

By the middle of the afternoon he hit the Clark Fork about ten miles from where it comes out of the Ab-sarokas. This was the first week of September, 1877, and neither a good time nor a good place to be. If he'd been on the other side of the river and seen the story written in the dirt, he might have guessed that something was up. As it was, all he knew was that the air seemed colder and that there just might be one last critter around the next bend up ahead. He could just hear what Mr. Andersen would say if he came all this way and then left behind a couple head.

He'd just decided to call it quits. Even the fastest damn critter couldn't have come this far since last night. Then he noticed the tracks. It looked like two or three head, with two horses pushing from behind. The tracks were fresh. He followed fast, frequently glancing ahead.

In no time he saw the dust up ahead and dug in his

spurs. When they heard him coming, the two riders left their steal and took off up the river fast.

There were three head, and all of them Double-O. Cimarron swung them around and started back, wishing to God he had his gun. Mr. Andersen had no right.

He hadn't gone a mile when he heard them behind him. It was the same two riders, and they weren't scared now. Well, neither was he. He turned around and waited for them.

The boy's eyes went wide when he saw that they were U.S. cavalrymen, and one a sergeant. All the same, he kept his right side away from them so they couldn't see he had no gun.

They pulled up wide apart, with their rifles leveled from the saddle. If he were armed and a good shot, he couldn't have gotten more than one of them before the other got him. They were seasoned horse soldiers and looked like they'd been through hell and back. They were in no mood to be messed with.

Seeing Cimarron's age, their faces relaxed a little, yet they kept looking him up and down as if speculating on just how grown-up he might be.

"Drop your gun, boy."

"Not before you drop yours, soldier boy. Just slide them back in their holsters, *amigo*, and I'll be satisfied."

"And you just keep both your hands in sight."

"I've heard a lot of sneaking things about the Army, but I always thought you was slicker than to come right out and rustle off the range."

"We ain't rustling a damn thing, sonny. We'd of looked up your outfit from the brand and paid every cent that's coming to you top price. The Army don't bargain about supplies. Our outfit's tired and hungry and days ahead of our train. And we're *taking* this beef."

"Soldier, you will nothing until you get Mr. Andersen's okay. This is Double-O stock. It ain't mine to give away."

"Sonny, that works both ways. You ain't moving nowhere with them cows without Colonel Sturgis' okay. So how do you like them beans, little Mr. Pepper Gut?"

"Fine by me. One of the two of you'll be the first soldier I ever dropped."

"And the last."

"Soldier, that don't bother me one bit. Go right ahead. Reach for your rifle."

The older soldier with the red-gray moustache sighed. "First this bunch of redskins makes jackasses out of us, and now we get stopped by a schoolboy cow nurse. You know, Stew, some operations is all of a piece. You can be surrounded by wild Injuns ten to one, and the only chicken hawk in the whole territory will fly over and crap in your eye."

The other soldier squinted at Cimarron. "Which side of the river was them Injuns on?"

"What Injuns?"

"What Injuns! A whole tribe going the exact same way you just came from!"

"I been looking for strays in the hills and tending my own business. If we passed any Injuns, it was at night. Did you say a whole tribe?"

"Something like a hundred bucks and at least three hundred women and children and old folks."

The other soldier said, "Maybe more."

The boy looked from one to the other. "Where they from? Wyoming?"

"No, no, these is Nez Percés."

The boy smiled, all radiance and scorn. "You mean to say these is the ones from clear way over in Idaho? Chief Joseph's bunch? No wonder you look so wore out! Them red savages must have run you boys four–five hundred miles!"

The older soldier turned to his companion. "I'd like to know what the hell's so funny about the Army getting its tail run off by a little bunch of redskins! I sometimes think the whole damn Union's laughing at us."

Cimarron was so amused he didn't notice the sergeant edging farther around his right side as he spoke to his companion. Suddenly the soldier made an exclamation of disgust. "She-it, this kid ain't got no gun! Stew, we been buffaloed by a baby! What'd I tell you about some operations being all of a piece?"

The rifle came up with a big, gritty finger curved around the trigger. "Come on, sonny, we're gonna see Colonel Sturgis."

It was an order to be obeyed.

The camp was only a few miles up on the slopes of the Absarokas. It was the disheveled camp of men whose commander was weary and frustrated. The little tents were not in line, and you couldn't tell the guards from anybody else. In fact, it was odd to see a camp at all, and horses grazing, when they were supposed to be out chasing redskins for all they were worth.

The gray-haired colonel looked wearier than a commander in the field should. But he was cordial. Perhaps it was the sight of fresh beef that made him smile for the first time since last June, when this whole idiotic mess began. He immediately wrote out a military voucher for the three head and signed it with a flourish.

He said, "Son, have no doubts about what you have done. These may be your employer's property, but I'm sure he'd have given them freely to his country in this crisis."

Cimarron looked at him with cool eyes. The old soldier sounded as if he were reading out of a book.

"You may not know it, but our forces under General Howard have had a run of bad luck that's almost too much to believe. Everything's happened to us, from bad weather to unreliable scouts and a terrible lack of public sympathy. And on top of that, this Chief Joseph may claim he's no warrior, but he's turned out to be the best damned military man and tactician I ever heard of."

The boy and the men saw the terrible need in the old soldier to explain. They listened in restive embarrassment.

"That wild savage's fighting us on our own terms, and, by God, he's winning! I never thought I'd call a naked Injun brilliant, but that's exactly what he is. And he's lucky, yes, he's had the benefit of some very lucky accidents."

His eyes fell on the boy's hands. They were folding and refolding the voucher. He straightened up and concluded his address briskly.

"But, by God, I'm going to run him down and bring him and his people back where they belong if it takes the rest of my life! Tell your people that, son, tell everybody you meet that Colonel Sturgis and the Seventh Cavalry may be set back a mite, but we ain't licked!"

The boy glanced at the men standing around. They were all looking away somewhere. The colonel said, "That will be all," and they saluted and left. Assuming it was required, Cimarron saluted, too, and followed.

While he was saddling up, the sergeant with the red-gray moustache said, "Pass the word along about these wild savages, sonny. They been hitting ranches and hunters and travelers all along the line. They think all white men's their enemy, and they're raising hell and putting a prop under it. But you needn't tell nobody about Colonel Sturgis not being licked. He is, or he wouldn't of said he wasn't. He lost a boy with Custer last year, and he hates redskins so bad he don't think straight. He's been making so many bad mistakes the men's near tears most of the time. Including me. But from the way Chief Joseph's already outsmarted two generals, the U.S. Army, and all of Washington, D.C., I don't guess a tired little old colonel ought to feel so bad."

The boy looked down at the man from his saddle. "No red savage will take cows from the Double-O like you did. This little piece of paper is maybe no good, but Chief Joseph won't even give us that. I know the savage. My people know them. We also say the good Injun is a dead one."

The handsome boy spoke with a startling hate for

one so young. His burning eyes seemed to be remembering awful things.

Suddenly he kicked his spurs in deep and set off at a full gallop. He was going to save his outfit from massacre! Yet he still glanced down now and then at his swift shadow on the ground.

20

Wil Andersen and Slim came back with nearly two hundred of the missing cattle. The boys bringing up the main body of the herd swore they'd flushed out at least that many, too. Wil grunted: "And I guess Cimarron will almost have to bring in another two hundred himself—just to keep everything on a real high level of cowmanship. I don't suppose nobody's been noticing whose brand is on all this new beef." There was silence, and he said, "All right, let's take another damn count."

The boys sighed audibly. It looked like they took more counts than they did anything else, especially eating and sleeping. They strung out the herd and squeezed it four or five abreast between young Charlie Schwartz and Hardy Fimps, who'd turned out to be the most reliable counters.

Charlie used knots in a string to keep track of hundreds; Hardy leaned toward beans, which he transferred from one vest pocket to the other without running afoul of his dice.

Fimps had turned out to be not only a good counter and wrangler but also the best sleeper in the outfit. He could sleep soundly in the chuck wagon all day

in the middle of wildest confusion, yet never seemed
to mind being roused to take another count. He was
like some great concert star getting off the train in the
middle of the night at a hamlet where he'd be perform-
ing brilliantly; the inconvenience was the burden of
his talent. Full of strong coffee and on his gelding
named Minnie Q, he was wide-awake and ready to do
the count all alone.

Wil began to fret when Cimarron didn't show up. It
just about had to mean the beautiful little bastard had
got himself into some sort of trouble down to the
south. The Old Woman said, "No, maybe he just got
loose in the foots and free in the fancy. Cimarron ain't
no fireside boy, you know. He don't belong to nothing
and nobody except himself. Could be he just cut his
picket pin and drifted."

Everybody was looking at him. Wil felt tired and
mean. He turned to young Charlie Schwartz and
asked, "You're his bunkie. You think that's what he
did?"

Young Charlie looked at the ground in what would
have been blushing confusion if he hadn't been so
tanned. Then he looked up and set Wil Andersen back
on his heels. "It takes more than sleeping with a man
to know what's on his mind."

Wil looked at the ground. The Old Woman was
smiling, but it was a good point. Wil almost liked the
boy for a moment there, because you could see he was
worried about Cimarron, too.

There were maybe three hours of sunlight left. He
decided to go look for the boy himself.

Of course he wasn't really worried. Of all the boys
in the outfit, Cimarron could take care of himself best.
Young as he was, he must of covered one hell of a lot
of territory all alone, and completely on his own.

What really set Wil looking for the boy was the
rankling possibility that the Old Woman might be
right. Maybe he'd finally had enough. Maybe he'd got
so mad at Wil that he'd given up the Double-O in disgust and left without even asking for his pay. The

possibility hurt. He couldn't stand the idea of this particular boy giving him up as hopeless. It would be like his own two boys saying all over again *We'd rather be dead wrong than right and agree with you.*

Wil rode close to the foothills. He had a hunch and a hope he'd find the boy way up some one of these twisting little gulches. He'd be trying to get some big old critter out of the brush, and the critter would be trying to get back in. Wil remembered saying over and over, "When I send you out for some stupid cow and it takes you all summer to get her to move six inches, try for seven, and don't come back without her." And that's just what Cimarron would do. All alone and too proud to call for help. He half-smiled at the cussing out he'd give the boy, and then, by grab, he'd give the boy a little wink, and they'd go on about their business.

He looked up a boulder-filled gulch. His hunch grew stronger. When he saw the right hoof prints, he knew he'd found the boy. He spurred Sad Sarah. The horse didn't share his eagerness, but picked its way with care. He spurred again. Sarah stumbled and went lame.

Wil got down, stood with his fists on his hips, and said, "So much for hunches." It was a good hour back to camp by ankle express; with a limping horse, three. He threw back his head and groaned, "Jesus Christ, I did it again!" But he set out at once. No point burning daylight.

He wondered how long it would take the boys to miss him and start looking. He should have told somebody where he was going. Still, they'd know if they used even a shred of horse sense. Who'd come after him? Slim, probably.

Then, about a half-mile off he saw a rider really making dust. He was coming from the south and headed for the herd. It had to be Cimarron. He drew and fired into the air. The rider didn't slow for a moment. Long after he disappeared, Wil watched to see if the boy had been followed.

When Cimarron got to camp, they were wondering where Mr. Andersen was. The Old Woman said coldly, "He's got to be gone off looking for you, Mr. Pretty Face." But Cimarron was sure it was Indians that fired the shot. The Old Man's whereabouts was secondary to the news of the uprising. He was deeply excited and got everybody else excited, too, except for the Old Woman and Charlie Schwartz. Neither was swept up with the heroic possibility of having to fight off hundreds of wild savages.

Young Charlie said, "Oh, come on, Cimarron! If it was a bloody uprising, why are they running away? They don't sound like wild savages to me. I bet they're just fed up and moving somewhere else."

Cimarron glared at him. "All right. When they start driving off the herd and lifting all our topknots, you can try to reason with them if you want to. You talk like a real plow chaser, Charlie Schwartz. I've seen what redskins do when they're riled, and I know the only thing that'll stop them."

"You've only seen Apaches, and they're nothing like the Nez Percé. Chief Joseph's people have always been friendly and sensible."

"They are all friendly and sensible until they want something, amigo."

The Old Woman broke in: "But not you and me, hm? Lookyere, boy, why they shoot at you from clear a quarter of a mile away? What that do 'cept warn everybody all around?"

"When they're on the warpath, they're just plumb crazy."

"Well, the way they outfox all them generals, look to me like it's a good way to be crazy. Wasn't no Injun shot at you."

"Why would a white man? Ain't no rustlers around here."

Young Charlie squinted over at the mountains, then said to the Old Woman, "I got the feeling it was Mr. Andersen, and he wanted help. Nothing else that it could be."

Cimarron's eyes went wide. "And you want us to go out there without no guns and find out?"

"I don't want to, but we got to. Mr. Andersen's out there all alone."

"Well, I ain't. I'm gonna get our guns from the wagon and get ready to make a stand. What do you say, boys?"

They all agreed. The Old Woman spit in the fire and said, "She-it." They looked at him, and he added, "You got to get by me first. I'd say your first job is to go out there and find Mr. Andersen. That's what a cow-*man* would do."

"What's so damn manly about going out there and getting ourselfs killed?"

"He need help. 'Sides, there ain't no Injuns out there."

"How do you know?"

"Because I ain't scared."

Young Charlie went to his horse. The Old Woman said, "You know, Pretty Face, you ought to be the one to go. He went out looking for you."

"Give me my guns and I'll go all alone!"

The Old Woman spit in the fire and leaned against the wagon with folded arms. The boy dug his hands in his pockets and muttered to the ground, "Way things are, we ought to just *take 'em!*"

Nobody dared look at the Old Woman, but they all agreed, and the Old Woman knew it. He got a faintly amused look on his face and began smoothing the splinters off a wagon slat. Without looking up, he said, "If you was growed men, I whittle me a club. Being what you is, I whittle me a paddle."

Slim said, "All right, girls, let's get out there and ride herd," and sent them to their positions. The boys rode off, setting up a system of signals in case of attack.

Young Charlie rode alongside Sad Sarah's tracks. They were new and clear. He lost them at a place where the wind came down from the hills and dusted them over. Without wasting time, he rode up to the top of a steep hill and took a look. The first glance showed him a man walking ahead of a horse maybe a mile off. Young Charlie was there in no time.

The man kept looking at the boy as if he didn't recognize him. Charlie told him about Cimarron and the Indian news, but nothing of the mild mutiny. What had to be done next occurred to both of them at the same time.

While the man hesitated, the boy spoke: "Mr. Andersen, I think you ought to take my horse and go on ahead. Cimarron's no coward, but he's sure making everybody spooky as heifers. I'll come along with Sad Sarah."

"Boy, it'll be way after dark before you get in."

"I've rode night guard slower'n this, sir."

"But this time you're alone in Injun-country with an uprising going on somewhere. For all we know, we're right smack between the techy redskins and a bunch of chuckleheaded cavalrymen."

"We never been *out* of Injun country, sir. I ain't scared, if that's what you mean."

"You're a damn fool if you're not."

He began unbuckling his gunbelt. "You probably won't need this, but it'll make us both feel better."

It could have gone around young Charlie's waist twice, with some left over. The boy slung it over his shoulder and across his chest, with the gun on his right hip. There was a wonderful glow on his face.

Wil took one look at him before riding off. The boy looked very small but completely undismayed.

The man set out wondering if he was making another one of his damned mistakes.

21

It was sunset. The herd spread like a vast brown sea beneath the molten sky. The boys sat in their positions around it, waiting.

Over against the darkening east were the Indians. In the rear were several hundred women and children and old people. In front, the eighty naked warriors in just flaps and war paint.

In between, two small parties were coming together to parley. On the night side were three fierce-faced, lean-bodied men with painted hair and faces, and little slivers of bone piercing their noses. Their naked legs guided splendid Appaloosas with bright feathers in their manes.

Facing them were Slim and Cimarron, whose backs looked surprisingly purposeful to Wil. Black Charlie was beside them on a mule. The canny old warlock knew that black was fascinating to the red men.

Wil walked his horse out to join the boys as if he were in no particular hurry. Getting nearer, he saw that Cimarron was wearing a red sash around his waist. Wil was surprised that the boy honored the old tradition of the desperado flag. It looked like his sign language was pretty good, too.

Cimarron was going through a fairly elaborate greeting. It ended with a sudden, blunt question. *Who are you?*

Nez Percé.

Where do you go?

The warriors moved restively. The questions irri-

tated them. Their speaker looked at Wil and dismissed
the last question.

Boy talk.

It was Cimarron's turn to move restively and be irritated. Without taking his eyes from the warriors, he
said, "Mr. Andersen, this red savage, he says I ask a
foolish question."

"Maybe it was."

"I only ask where they were going."

"Then it was foolish. You don't ask a white man that.
Why ask a red man on the warpath? Find out what
they want that they can't take anyway. But go easy."

With no ceremony at all, the boy asked bluntly,
What do you want?

Wil started to interrupt. The Indian answered, *Cow.*

The boy snapped at him: *What for?*

The red man looked very impatient: *Not for wife
like cowboy.*

Wil smiled at the sarcasm. The boy was very upset.
He couldn't stand being treated like a boy by savages.
He started to answer in anger. Wil interrupted: "Ask
him how many."

The answer was precise: *Ten*

The boy's next question carried fatal logic: *What
have you to trade for them?*

The answer flashed like knives in the air: *Your lives.*

The boy sat up taller in his saddle and stunned
everyone in reading distance with his reply. *Among
my people, the seller sets the price. One of our cows
will cost you all of your lives.*

It was out before Wil could stop him. The three
Indians were enraged. Wil stepped his horse forward
and signed expertly: *If you have finished talking with
a boy, go ask your chief to come parley with a man.*

The warriors swung their horses around brutally and
raced away.

"Boy, when you decide to get people killed, ask
them first, huh?"

"But you can't talk soft to them! They're savages!
They don't understand. They'll just take advantage of
you. You got to stand up to them."

"My God, you think the way you stood up to them saved us?"

"It got us a parley in the first place. When we saw they were going to attack, we rode out to make talk."

Wil blinked. He'd wondered why the Indians hadn't just stolen what they needed without all this fuss. It slowed them down.

"You only stalled them. There's hardly a dozen of us against maybe a hundred real mad Injuns. And if you say one more thing to rile them, I'll warm the seat of your pants, you hear?"

"Well, all the same, I still think we'll parley a lot better wearing our guns where they can see them."

"I'm not giving you no gun, and that's final. If you shoot *it* off the way you do your mouth, we'd all be roaming around hell before morning."

The boy wheeled his horse.

"Hold on, you're not going no place. Stay right where you are."

"You can do your own sign language—sir."

The man looked at him with cold eyes. "I got other uses for you. *You stay put.*"

The sunset was at its brightest. Soon the prairie would go abruptly dark like a lamp blown out. A small procession was coming this way. At its head rode a big man in his late thirties. He had been called handsome and even noble by white men. His name—Thunder Traveling to Loftier Mountain Heights—fitted him perfectly. He was neither warrior nor of the Dreamer sect, yet he wore the bone splinter in his nose and the upswept curl of the Dreamers. His face had the flowing, anxiety-free expression of a man who knows where and when he will die, and is content.

He stopped his dappled horse and raised his hand. Wil Andersen raised his. He said, *I am the chief of this drive. These are my cattle, and these boys are my borrowed sons. They do not always do as I wish, but they are not bad.*

The Indian seemed to want to smile, but he did not. *I am the man you call Chief Joseph. I, too, have unruly sons. Yet there is a difference. My unruly sons have no home.*

But your sons will be forgiven. Mine will not.

Who will forgive them?

My people. Even now there are multitudes that cheer you on your way.

I do not hear this cheering. Only the sound of your army behind us.

Cimarron could not remain silent: *And it is close! The army chief has vowed to follow you to the end of his days.*

Wil slapped the boy's arm. "Idiot!"

"But it's true! I talked to him, and he gave me this paper for three of our stock."

He held out the voucher. The Indians looked at the paper fluttering between the boy's fingers. *Paper, white man, death.* Feeling the anger of their riders, the Appaloosas moved restlessly. One of the warriors spoke sharply to Chief Joseph, and the others grunted assent. The chief did not answer. He sat watching Wil Andersen.

Wil took the paper, read it, and tore it into small bits. The wind carried them away into the evening.

He faced the chief. *You are hungry. Take what you need.*

The boy was outraged. He almost yelled, "You're a damn Indian lover!"

The Indians had heard that term before. They brought up their rifles.

Wil clenched his teeth and said, "I was hoping I wouldn't have to do this." He swung down, pulled Cimarron out of the saddle, and sat on a rock. Then he spanked the boy hard. Cimarron fought savagely, but Wil went on and on until his hand was numb.

The Indians spoke excitedly. It was shocking. They never laid a hand on their children. The sight was revealing—and satisfying. They'd known all along that the white man was a savage.

Released, the boy jumped on his horse and thundered back to camp crying tears of anger and humiliation.

Wil knew what the consequences of the spanking would be. For that reason he sent Slim back to camp, too, so the boys could all work it out together. The Old Woman followed, frowning. Alone, Wil went to cut out the beef that the Indians needed.

Chief Joseph took no more than ten. As his men herded them away, he turned and looked at Wil Andersen.

You are a wise man. But we are caught in a time when wisdom is a thorn in the foot of a runner. You weaken my purpose. You weaken my anger. You destroy me more than the guns.

Then the sun dropped behind the horizon, and they faced one another in darkness.

22

Cimarron packed his things furiously and shouted and cried hot tears and didn't give a damn who saw them. He was leaving this damn outfit. And when he got his guns back, he was going to blast that old son of a bitch in his tracks.

Four Eyes adjusted his glassless rims and said, "So will I!" He meant well, but he made Cimarron's threat sound kind of silly. The *two* of them couldn't blast Andersen in his tracks. Then Shorty said, "Me, too," and the whole thing went up in smoke. It's good to have your friends walk out with you, but everybody taking a shot at the boss is more like an ambush than a thrilling shoot-out between Right and Wrong. Cimarron cursed them silently. Damn it, he'd wanted to do this thing alone.

In no time everybody was packing. They'd all had

enough. Wil Andersen was beyond endurance. Even Slim and Charlie went for their bedrolls.

The Old Woman leaned against the chuck wagon with folded arms and sucked a tooth. When there was a lull, he said quietly, "Supper ready."

They hesitated, and he went on: "Cain't travel on a empty stomach. Grab your plates." As if ashamed of having stomachs, they lined up in silence and stood eating in silence.

The Old Woman said, "If you boys don't mind me asking, where you going? Home? I mean, you gonna go walking in and say 'Hi there' and that's all there's to it, hm? Surely somebody gonna say 'My, you's home fast! Drive over already?' Then what you gonna say? Well, let's see, what can you say? I guess nothing but God's truth. And how would it go? 'That terrible old Mister Andersen done hurt everybody's feelings, and we got so mad we up and left him and his danged old cows way out in the middle of the badlands 'bout halfway 'tween here and Belle Fourche.' Hmmmm. I wonder what they gonna say to that."

The boys ate hungrily only half-listening.

"Well, that don't matter, just as long's you get away from this mean old man. Next time you tries to get a job on a drive, they just might say 'Ain't you one a them boys that run off in the middle of Mr. Andersen's drive?' But that no never mind. They's always a chance you run into somebody that ain't heard about all this. So just you eat a good meal, 'cause you's got a long way to go before the next one. Long's you take off outta here before he gits back, everything'll work itself out on the long ride home. Home! Just think of it! Home, and your mammy saying 'Oh, my little boy's come back to me!' Won't that be nice?"

The boys knew what he was trying to do, but they ate on in silence, and the food somehow tasted good. They began sitting down.

"Yes, best thing to do is just simply tell them the God's honest truth. If you get fancy, they'll begin comparing all your stories, so better stick to the facts.

Sure, maybe you did all bust your asses getting him to take you on in the first place and pulling all them coy little boy tricks that makes a man go ginst his better judgment. But it ain't your fault he turn out to be so mean and stupid and hardhearted. Fact is, Wil Andersen don't know the first thing about cows or horses or men or boys. Specially boys."

He was building up the fire under the Dutch oven; something sweet inside smelled very good.

"Oh, he may sleep just a hour here and a hour there, and run around all the rest of the time seeing everything's did right. But he only *look* like he doing all the work. He showing off. We's really the ones that's keeping everything going. Us is the ones that does the work! We don't start stampedes or try to get ourselfs drownded or have shoot-outs or get drunk behind a hill or almost burn down a barn learning how to smoke. Not us. We's beyond all that. We's men that don't have to be told what to do."

He was going around serving them seconds for the first time on the drive, but whacking the edge of the plates hard with his spoon.

"No, the honest fact is, Wil Andersen don't really know nothing. It may be his herd, but we got better ideas how to get it to market. And if he won't listen, then we just going off home. Ain't got nothing to do with how many years it took him to raise a herd this big or what little things he may have pick up in all that time. Main thing is, smart or dumb, we's *his* boss, just simply because they's *more* of us, and that's all there's to it. We votes just the same way. Right or wrong, it's what the *most* want, hm? 'Course, a growed-up cowman'd die 'fore he left his outfit in the middle of a drive, but we's just little boys, and the rules doesn't apply to childrens."

The eating began to stop. Nothing tasted very good anymore. Cimarron spit the last mouthful out. He hated that damn nigger.

"And in case you wants to know, that herd of critters out there don't just mean a lot to Mr. Andersen. It

mean everything. It all he got in the world, and if
something happen now, that man got to start all over
from the beginning. Ain't easy at fifty-five. That's when
a man's lived three times longer than any of you has.

"But they's something even more important to him
than that bawling herd. I jes give you a little hint what
it is. Once he had a couple boys, and he was mighty,
mighty fond of them. The sun rose and set on them.
He spoil them boys, still, they always held he was too
hard. So they sneaks off and has theirselfs a little
sip of bug juice now and again. And when they
gets behind paying for their drinks, they plays a little
cards to win some money to pay up what they owes.
In no time they wakes up and finds they owes money
to the wrong people, and 'fore they knows it, here they
is packing shooting irons just exactly like the ones I
got locked up in the wagon here. And here they is
sticking them guns way deep in the bellies of people
they don't know and asking for money that's not theirs.
Now, nobody likes that, and it don't last long. And all
of a sudden one day here they is full of holes and falling down to the ground and making dust. And everything mighty still. So who's to blame? That mean,
nasty, hardhearted old daddy, or the poor dead boys?"

There was silence on the prairie. The fire flicked in
their staring eyes.

"I don't know. You don't know. All anybody know
is Wil Andersen loved them boys, but they stuck guns
in people's bellies and asked for gold. And whoever to
blame, Mr. Andersen, he the one that has to go and
lay them boys into the wagon and spread a tarp over
them. And then drive all the way home and watch
while Miz Andersen wash them clean and help dress
'em in their best and lift 'em in a new pine box. Then
he digs a hole and puts the box in and covers it all
over and beats the earth down firm. He cover over all
them years and all that love and hope and faith that
his boys was good. Bury it deep and cover it over and
have nothing to show for all them years.

"Nothing except just one little old question that'll

nibble at his heart till the day he die. Every single day
Wil Andersen looks back and asks himself, *Was it my
fault?* Because if he's to remember even one good little
thing about them boys, then he knows he was wrong.
They was bad all the way, or he was wrong all the
way. They's no give and take with remembering. It's
all *re*joice or all *re*gret, and Wil Andersen ain't the
laughing kind. Was it his fault? Not a night goes by
that question don't set down on his chest and stare in
his face till dawn."

By now nobody saw the fire they looked at. Each
boy was older by as many years as his mind allowed.

"My God, ain't none of you wondered what he
meant when he answer Mrs. Schwartz that way? He
says, *I promise not to love them.* He was promising
not to be easy this time. He was promising nobody'd get around him so they could go off and get
theirself killed. He was promising not to care if you
hated his guts and cursed his name all day long and
all night, too. He'd not give in and let you hurt yourselfs. It was a promise to get you back alive and in
one piece, even if he didn't himself. That's the kind of
mean, hardhearted old son of a bitch *he* is, this Mr.
Wil Andersen of the Double-O!"

Charlie's voice had sunk lower and lower. When he
stopped, there was only the crackling of the fire.

There was the sound of a horse walking this way,
and then a man. Suddenly Black Charlie Nightlinger
straightened up and said harshly and loudly, "I puts
this tub of hot water here so's you can wrench off your
plates in it. It ain't for dumping in everything you can't
get down. The leavings go out there. The scrape plates
here. And the next time I catch one of you stink-pants
little baby boylets just dropping in his plate and an-
kling off, I'm gonna tear his arm off and beat his head
in with it, stomp his ribs, and piss on what's left, you
hear? Now get your jizz-stiff bedrolls outta my wagon
and let me think what we's having for breakfast *if* we's
having breakfast."

The rush in all directions was almost beautiful. Wil

watched them scurry about their separate businesses for all the world as if school were out. Nobody looked at him.

He knew, of course, that each boy was saying to himself, "Well, all right, I'll give the old son of a bitch just one more chance. Just one."

23

The Clark Fork River was a hair over a hundred miles on their way. It was deep and swift at the point they crossed. Wil Andersen sent the boys up and down stream looking for godowns for crossing. When they came up with two choices, he took the hard one, of course. Instead of the shallow ford just a mile downstream, he decided to take the whole herd south several miles out of their way.

Cimarron got mad all over again. "Can't you see what this crazy old fool does? He covers up them Injun tracks!"

Once across, they picked up the Bozeman Trail again and continued due east toward Fort Smith on the Big Horn River. The cattle moved better than ten miles a day, grazing as they went and getting plenty of water. Days, each critter took its established place on the trail, and nights they all bedded down nice as anything. The drive had become a way of life. Wil wouldn't admit it, but they were beginning to put back on the weight they'd lost in the stampede. Life flowed in a highly desirable monotony.

Yet Wil Andersen was restless. The fort was only a few miles from the battlefield on the Little Big Horn. It still meant trouble to everybody that heard the name. He decided to ride on ahead to the fort and find out how things stood in these parts. He told Black Charlie where to make camp, put Slim in command, and left before dawn. On the way he passed a pair of bivouacked wagons and a couple teams of pretty good horses. Nobody was up yet, so he went on by. It wasn't until late the next afternoon that he found out about those wagons. He saddled up immediately and made dust back to camp, but by then it was too late.

Four Eyes, in his glassless rims, brought the horses up while the boys were eating breakfast. Shorty helped him put up the remuda line around them. Before the boys went to pick their first horse of the day, Charlie Schwartz said the ones on the near side ought to hop to it, keeping the critters out of all the little gulches they'd been seeing along the base of the Pryor range. Fetching strays was slowing things down considerably and you could see for yourself how dry the grass was getting. When he finally said they couldn't afford to burn daylight, nobody was much surprised. They just went on eating while he took up a lot of other things.

In fact, young Charlie Schwartz covered just about everything except what to do if they ran across two big wagons full of young women.

Slim and Cimarron were walking their horses at their regular point positions when they first saw the wagons coming west along the Bozeman. Each was driven by a female, and beside her sat another. The oldest one looked thirty-five if she looked a day, and the rest might be as old as twenty. But in spite of their age, all of them were lookers. The boys stared hard, and the women waved. They lifted their hats with a certain reserve.

It was a minute before they realized the women wanted something. They rode cautiously over to where the wagons had stopped. They took off their hats, and Slim said, "Good morning, ma'am," to the older one. She'd been looking both boys over and picked Slim as the one to talk to. All three of her girls were fasci-

nated with Cimarron. The way he didn't take any
notice made him look even better.

"Son, where's your dad?"

"In Bozeman."

"No, I mean, who's running this drive?"

"I am."

"Huh?"

"Least till Mr. Andersen gets back from Fort Smith.
But we don't expect him till tomorrow sometime."

"Oh, he must have been that *good*-looking man that
woke us up this morning riding by. Gawd, that was
a lot of man."

Slim had never heard a woman talk like that before.
He looked at the ground. Cimarron tucked his shirt
deep in his pants and inspected the girls in the back
wagon with cool eyes.

"Well, hm, what's your name, young man?"

"Slim."

"Oh, how nice! Ain't that a nice name, girls? And
what's *yours*, honey?"

Cimarron ran cool eyes down to her full bosom and
addressed his answer to her cleavage. A shudder ran
through her. She felt for her shawl to cover up. *First
time I been looked at like that in Gawd knows how
long.*

She cleared her throat and turned back to Slim.
"Well, tell me, Slim, dear, how many men in your
outfit?"

"Uh, two. Mr. Andersen and Charlie Nightlinger.
The rest is just boys, I guess."

"By, hm, boys, just what do you mean, dear?"

That was the first time he'd ever been called "dear"
by a strange woman. He blushed and said, "Cowboys."

"Yes, I *know*, dear, but I mean about how old would
a cowboy be?"

"Oh, anywhere from eight to eighty, I guess, ma'am."

She turned quietly to the girl beside her. "Eight to
eighty! Half of them's lost their teeth, and the rest
probly ain't got their first ones yet. We'd do better if
we were dentists."

Slim said, "Most of us is going on fifteen, don't you guess, Cimarron?"

"I donno." He was looking at the far hills so the girls would keep looking at him.

"Only *fifteen*?"

"Ma'am, we're old enough to push a herd from Shields Valley nigh onto two hundred miles back, and we're going on again that far to Belle Fourche in the Dakotas."

"Now, no offense. In this kind of country a flock of helpless girls likes to know they got real men around. I mean, men to take care of us a little along the way." Her eyes slid down him. "Think you could?"

He said, "I guess so. What's the trouble, ma'am?"

She looked at her companion, who shrugged. Laughter came from the rear wagon. They looked back. Cimarron had walked his horse beside the buckboard and was just opening the driver's bodice. Two milk-white breats flowed out into the light of day.

Slim was aghast. The girls were mesmerized, and the woman outraged.

"You, Patsy Fenn, cover yourself up this instant! That's valuable merchandise you're putting on display! This ain't no vacation! It's a business trip, and we *talk* business before we allow favors! Get them things back in. And you, sonny, if you got any more handling you want to do, you'll kindly deposit one silver dollar with me right now. And then you'll conduct yourself *inside* the wagon with the young lady of your choice, and do no more shameless things right out here in front of God and all them staring cows!"

Slim was staring, too. It irritated her.

"What's the matter with *you*, boy? Ain't you never seen a real, genuine lady of pleasure before?"

In some confusion he hung his hat on what passed for his saddle horn and swallowed twice. "I don't know, ma'am. Everybody talked about Nettie Calhoun in Bozeman, but my dad says they always talk about ladies that make hats. Anyway, she didn't look nothing like you."

"And just exactly what do you mean by that?"

The boy writhed.

"Will you kindly answer my question?"

He was blushing furiously. He swallowed and said to the far horizon: "She was kind of flat-chested." For the second time that morning, Mary Derrydimple plucked at the neck of her dress. She smiled.

"Well, now, if you noticed *that*, you ain't so much a boy. I guess they grow up faster out here on the range, Phoebe. Come on in, Slim, and let's have ourselves a little talk. You're going to be surprised the way we fixed this wagon up."

Cimarron was tethering his horse to the back wagon wheel. He dug into his pants for money, tossed a coin to Mary Derrydimple, and started for the back wagon.

She shouted so loud all the cows looked up. "Just hold on there a minute, young man! I said a dollar. Ain't no less for juniors!"

He walked back, plucked the coin from her hand, and started untying his horse. The two girls in the rear wagon wailed "Awwwwww!" Mary was visibly upset.

"Young man, you got any idea how far we come and what terrible dangers and unbearable discomforts we've put up with just to bring a little sunshine into your sad and lonely lifes? Why, just looking at a pair of girls as pretty as Patsy and What's-her-name back there ought to be worth a dollar to you! What's more, we got the insides of these here wagons fixed up like the prettiest parlor you ever seen in all your born days! You won't believe you're out in the middle of nowhere. And when you lean back in the tub and let the girls scrub you down and then lay down on your first *mattress*, why, you'll want to lay out a hundred dollars! Won't he, girls?"

Carried away, she leaned forward and laid her ringed hand on Slim's lean thigh. His eyes went wide. He let out a groan that rose to a howl. She looked alarmed. "Son, you better get inside quick!" But he wheeled his horse around and rode off, yelling, "Too late, too late, too late!"

Mary watched him go with a trace of bitterness. "I didn't like that smirk on his face. He looked like somebody that's just saved himself a dollar." She looked back at Cimarron. "Well, young feller, you dug up your dollar yet?"

The one named Patsy called out, "Mary, this is all he's got. So Tina and I'll pay for him ourselfs. He's too beautiful to let get away."

Mary Derrydimple threw up her hands. "Girls like that make a bad name for the business. I tell you, Phoebe, if there's anything that makes me madder'n a wet hen, it's a whore without no business sense."

Black Charlie Nightlinger came riding up with the exertion of a man who doesn't like to ride. Charlie Schwartz rode easily beside him.

Mary rolled her eyes to heaven. "Gawd, the only man in the outfit's black with white hair! Phoebe, we're covering the wrong territory."

They took off their hats, and Black Charlie spoke with a certain grandeur: "Pardon me, ma'am, but may I inquire if what Slim *re*port happens to be a true *re*port?"

"And just what did Slim *re*port?"

"He, hm, hint that your trip out west, ma'am, kindly mixes business and pleasure like business and pleasure ain't usually mixed."

She nodded at Phoebe. "Not bad. Maybe we better send this Slim on ahead of us for the rest of the trip."

"Then you is business ladies?"

"You talk mighty blunt for a nigger."

"Ma'am, when you calls a nigger a nigger, don't be surprise if he call a whore a whore."

Her eyes went wide. "And don't you be surprised if none of us wants your damn money."

"Ma'am, I ain't come as a customer. All four you nice ladies put together couldn't accommodate Black Charlie Nightlinger. What I do come to say is, this here's a cattle drive. And this herd's gotta keep going. Already you knocked off both our lead men that's supposed to tell them critters where to go. Now, you

may not give a little bitty hoot if this herd scatter itself all over the territory, but you should. We don't
interfere with your business, and I don't think you
oughtta interfere with ours."

"Look, black boy, we just been run out of Fort Smith
by a nasty passel of Army wives. Don't tell me you're
running us off the whole range."

"I ain't running you nowheres, ma'am. All I asks is
a little organ-i-zation around here. We got things to
do, and you got things to do, so let's fix it so we can
both do what we got to. Now, what we got to do is
keep the herd going that way."

"All right, I'll keep that in mind. Phoebe, try not to
rustle while you hustle."

"And the only way we can keep the cows going that
way is to let off just one man at a time. Young Charlie
here think we oughtta handle the whole thing just like
night guard. One man come off, and 'nother man
go on."

"Keep talking."

"And you do your part, ma'am, by not letting a man
stay on after he been relieve. Just the same as guard.
Now, they's something else got to be discussed. A
cowhand don't get paid till after the drive's done."

Mary's face set. "Look, if you want to mail us the
money from Belle Fourche, you got another think
a-coming. This is a cash business, my friend."

"No, no, that ain't what I'm getting at, ma'am. All
these boys got is what they left home with, and that's
closer to nothing than something. If they each pays
a dollar, half of them's gotta loan the other half every
cent they got. Now, it bad enough to loan another
man money, but to do it so he can get himself some of
that little old tickly stuff without getting none yourself
is a crying sin and shame. That kind of thing ain't
good for no outfit. We have ourselfs another Civil War
before we goes another mile on down the road."

"Oh, no. Whatever kind of house I run, it ain't a
Poor House."

"Ma'am, we ain't asking nothing free! All I say is,

if I rounds up the whole entire outfit and herds them here, seem to me like we's entitle to something off the going price."

Embarrassed by business, young Charlie and Cimarron walked their horses off a ways. Both hooked a knee around their saddlehorns, and Cimarron leaned back with a hand on his horse's rump. They looked back and studied the little caravan.

Only one of Miss Derrydimple's wagons was a Conestoga. It was half again bigger than the one behind, and scooped way down in the middle. Not only the white canvas curved down; the wagon bed itself dipped deep at the center, so that things wouldn't slide out either end going up and down hills. In spite of the heavy wheels, the whole thing had a kind of graceful look. With the customary bright red paint on the upper sides and the bright blue underneath, it was positively pretty.

Miss Derrydimple seemed awfully little up there in the driver's seat until you heard her. To the team, that booming voice carried more weight than her whip. To Charlie Nightlinger, it was nothing but a challenge.

"Ma'am, you got to give us a rate. Ain't no more than fair."

"A rate! Why, dammit, man, if these boys are all green as I think they are, we ought to charge double for educating them! This ain't no little red-light schoolhouse!"

Black Charlie made an orator's gesture. "Man, I guess you never give no thought to how important these here premises of yours is. Why, these ain't just a couple wagons way out in the middle of the prairie! They is nothing less than Man Factories! You and your gals is turning out presidents and generals and philofficers. Great men! And them that ain't is gonna be the fathers of fine sons and the builders of big famblies. Why, ma'am, when you gets right down to it, you ain't one bit different from Mr. Lewis and Mr. Clark! You's opening up a great big new territory in the life of these boys! My Gawd, woman, ain't you got no pride?"

Mary Derrydimple was gazing misty-eyed out over the plain. Phoebe sniffed softly. Mary gave her handkerchief to the girl and said, "All right, friend, what's your offer?"

"Two bits a head."

The mist vanished instantly. "Good Gawd in the morning! I ain't put my price that low since I was twelve! Get outta here! You're wasting our time!"

"You ain't gonna run accrost a single man in the next hundred miles except Injuns, and they raise your dress with one hand and your hair with the other."

"Phoebe, you ever heard of such a thing? Two bits! This is turning out to be quite a day. First them two bitches in the back wagon pays for that pretty boy themselves, and then this nigger wants a group rate for a bunch of greeners in diapers! Whose idea was it coming out west, anyway?"

"Yours."

"That'll be enough outta you, my girl! Black boy, I don't know whether to ride on outta here or take what's better'n nothing. Don't smile. I ain't said yes yet. All right, you guarantee us twelve boys, pay in advance, and don't cause no trouble, and we'll undertake their education."

"That include the bath thing and one little bitty taste of whiskey?"

"*What the hell is this? A holdup?*"

"No, ma'am, it's a cattle drive being held up by a woman that can't remember how important that first time is. I recolleck mine like yesterday. You recolleck yours? And how you kept saying over and over five thousand times I gotta do that again real soon to see if it really was such a big letdown? Don't you remember, hm?"

Mary almost screamed: "All right, all right! All the fixings! Only shut up! Go away and send your boys, and don't come back! My Gawd, Phoebe, we gotta get this over or this black devil's gonna talk us outta the wagons and both teams!"

*   *   *

Each boy rode up in his own individual way. Each left feeling immensely changed and never guessed that he was only more now of what he'd been before.

Horny Jim was nervous and embarrassed and seemed about to giggle. He rode up slowly, took a long time tying his horse to the wagon, and crawled inside cautiously as if afraid that all of his riotous illusions were about to be laid low by reality. Not long after, he jumped to the ground, vaulted onto his horse with a howl, got back down to untie the reins, and galloped off yipping joyously.

Four Eyes loped up and sat looking at the wagons. He ran the tip of his tongue over dry lips eleven times, then tapped tentatively on the side of the wagon. A soft, white female hand reached out to him. He allowed himself to be drawn inside. He left looking pleasantly stunned.

Singing Fats rode up smiling, went in smiling, and came out smiling.

Shorty rode up like a little man, hitched his horse, and strode to the front wagon as if he had a duty to do. Coming out, he mounted and rode off with no expression on his face that might hint something unusual had happened. Yet he seemed to sit a fraction straighter in the saddle.

Weedy chose to feel ecstatically guilty about the whole thing. He slunk coming and he slunk going, and for days examined his parts for signs of punishment for his sin.

Stuttering Bob seemed most unwilling to take advantage of the group rate. He hung around outside the wagon until Mary and Phoebe dragged him in almost by force. He came out with a secret smile on his face as if he'd made a shrewd discovery, whistled as he mounted, and looked back as if to memorize the address.

Tall, young Slim was docile. He blushed and wouldn't look at either of them until they got him out of his things. Then he seemed abruptly in his element and enthusiastically entered into the spirit of things.

Dressed, the shyness returned. He gave a little half-bow, said, "Thank you, ladies," and left without a smile.

Sweet Nose was covered with confusion from start to finish. Undressing, bathing, and reclining, he was disgraced by three separate prematurities. But he ended up amazing both women with a sketch of Phoebe nude that was her spitting image. They gave him back his money in exchange for it, and everybody parted feeling they'd gotten the best of the deal.

Young Charlie Schwartz rode up, uncovered his glowing tow head, and gave Mary Derrydimple two quarters without getting off his horse. One was for Hardy Fimps, who was asleep because he worked nights, and one for himself. He made neither apology nor explanation for not coming in. When he turned his horse around, Mary said, "But why!" He shook his head and said, "Another time," and rode away. Not knowing about his game leg, she was deeply offended.

Cimarron was the last to leave. He didn't look overly impressed. It was gratifying to know that he could provide diversion for two of them for the better part of a day—at their expense. But then, he'd never doubted that he could. Now it was good to ride away and be alone again and watch his handsome shadow moving over the ground.

Wil Andersen thundered into camp late that afternoon and asked Black Charlie if a pair of wagons had passed the herd.

"Sure."

The Old Woman was stirring a pot of beans with his .45 and periodically shooting out the ones that got stuck in the barrel.

Fimps slept on undisturbed inside the wagon.

"They didn't stop, did they?"

"Mr. Andersen," the Old Woman beamed, "everything fine."

"They *stopped*?"

"Sure, they stop, and like I say, everything just fine."

"Fine, with two wagonloads of cheap whores dosing up my boys?"

"Nobody gonna get anything, Mr. Andersen. I seen to that with my double-strength eucalyptus rinse."

"But you can't be sure!"

"You can't, but you didn't see them. I can, because I saw the way they talked. They got nothing to hide. They's all just nice, pretty little working girls. I don't know how long they stay that way, but they was clean today."

"I hope you're right. I promised their folks—"

"Mr. Andersen, no man could promise to bring them boys back anything but a little older. And that's what they is today. A little older. And the herd's in apple-pie order."

Wil finally said, "All right," sort of hopelessly, then, "Got any coffee?"

And the Old Woman said, "You know where it is. Nobody gonna wait on you."

24

Fort Smith had been in a stew that only a military mind could ken. It was Little Big Horn country, yet regular patrols had taken second place to something else. Two of the officers' wives had arrived. Wil squinted around him watching U.S. cavalrymen spading a garden out on the parade ground. All the bachelors on the post were red-eyed with anger and readier to bury the brass than turn the soil.

Back with Charlie, Wil blew on his coffee. "That fort's in such a state, half a dozen squaws could take it with no trouble at all."

The white-haired man sliced beef in cubes. "Any been seen?"

"No, not a one, Charlie. Not a single solitary one, and that's something to think about, my friend."

Then he looked off at the sky and began figuring days and time and weather. He hunkered and drew in the dust with a twig, pursed his lips at the map, and thought out loud.

"Day after tomorrow we'll be crossing the Little Big Horn and leaving the Bozeman Trail. That's just about halfway. In miles, not trouble. There's gonna be damn little grass till we cross the Powder River. This next hundred miles is gonna be hot and dry, and the last hundred miles cold and wet. By the time we get to the Black Hills, winter'll be starting up. This time we'll be going home in snow, Charlie."

He stood up and smoothed the map out with the sole of his boot. The Old Woman pushed the cubed beef into a pan with the knife. "Take one day at a time. If we got trouble coming, it'll be waiting for us no matter how long we take to get there."

The next hundred miles were hot and dry, and there was little grass. The day after they crossed the Powder River, the sun stopped shining. There was nothing but wind and angry little showers that lasted longer every day. Slickers came out of the war bags and stayed out. And day after day the boys watched the southward flights of geese with awe and a strange little touch of panic at being left behind.

It started with a real goose-drowner. The downpour began just after sundown and kept up till dawn. Depending on where they'd spread their bedrolls, the boys were either soaked and up all night or snug and warm with their tarps over their heads. Slim and Charlie Schwartz spread their bedroll on a little rise and came out dry as toast and twice as warm. Alone, Cimarron got soaked. Wil took all this in and wondered when the switch had taken place.

The Old Woman's wood got wet, and the fire was so smoky you couldn't go near it. He muttered bitterly, "This'd be a fine day to die. You'd never know the difference." On his way to take over for the night hawk, Hardy Fimps slurped coffee through a mouthful of biscuit. He said, "When do you sleep, Mr. Nightlinger?" The black man answered, "In the winter, same as you." Yet, two hours later, the breakfast was as good as ever.

Wil didn't let them dawdle at it, though. The herd had stood where it was put all night, but on toward morning, the critters decided to look for drier country. Old Bull Durham had taken them several miles before the boys caught up and began bending them back toward the trail. The rattle of the rain on their slickers made a little confusion at first, but after a while every critter was back in the place it had chosen for the drive, and plodding solemnly ahead.

Hardy Fimps helped the Old Woman pack in the rain. He was little, but he got a great deal done. In return, Black Charlie let him sleep in the wagon during the day and kept him stuffed with delicious little treats that made the boy's eyes bulge out as far as his cheeks did. Even in the rain he slipped Hardy the last of the doughnuts before starting up.

He'd hardly bullied his four-mule team fifty yards before the wagon started sliding sideways down a muddy slope. The horses strained to stop it. The Old Woman howled. Then suddenly the wagon righted itself, lurched forward, and grazed a rock. Every spoke on one wheel broke off.

Little Fimps went for help. In no time Mr. Andersen and four of the boys were hard at work fixing it. While two unloaded the wagon, Wil took the others back down the trail to a thicket of lodge-pole pines they'd passed late yesterday. In less than an hour they came back with two dozen smoothly trimmed poles. The Old Woman said, "I don't believe it." Then he looked up at the inexhaustible sky and added, "But then, I don't believe that neither."

The rain had slacked off. Now it began again hard. They replaced the broken spokes in a real downpour. The Old Woman supervised the repair and cursed in variations on the theme, "This weather out here gets plumb wholesale." But he conceded the fact that the new wheel was better than the old, and that accidents can be strokes of luck.

While the boys reloaded the wagon, Wil said, "Now, for God's sake, go easy, Charlie. If you think you can't manage that wagon, I'll get one of the boys to drive it."

The Old Woman's eyes widened dangerously. "I can tend this wagon without no more help from you. Jes leave me *be*, my friend."

Wil and the boys rode off to catch up with the herd. Hardy Fimps watched them go, like he'd watched the geese. Black Charlie got up on the driver's seat, grabbed the reins, and howled at the dripping team to hop to it.

For some reason they did. They lunged forward. The wagon leaped after them, tried to straddle a boulder, and broke the front axle clean in two.

Man and boy stared unbelieving at the splinters. Then Hardy started off for help again. The Old Woman said, "No. You and me can fix this thing in no time. We don't need that man to stand around bellering at us."

Later on in the morning Wil wondered why the chuck wagon hadn't passed them yet; then he remembered how slow the Old Woman always drove in the rain. He decided to send Sweet Nose back around noon if the wagon hadn't made an appearance.

But before then the visitors appeared. The instant Wil saw them he smelled trouble. Without waiting any longer he sent the boy back. "Tell the Old Woman to get a hustle on. I think we're gonna need them guns. But don't let 'em see you go."

The visitors wore strange clothes and traveled alongside the herd a quarter of a mile away. There looked to be fifteen or twenty of them, and they watched everything that was going on. Wil passed the word along to keep going and act like nobody was worried in the slightest.

Two hours passed. Wil wondered where the hell that wagon and that boy were. And the Old Woman, Fimps, and Sweet Nose wondered where the herd was now as they cut and trimmed a new axle ten miles back in the heavy rain.

Hoping that the wagon would show up soon, Wil pushed on past a good place to bed down the herd—and then another. The visitors rode steadily alongside without coming in any closer. Then Wil knew. They were waiting for the chuck wagon, too. Only they probably expected it up ahead where it belonged. They wanted everybody together where they could account for them. The rain continued steadily. Darkness came on early. The strangers were silhouetted against the dying western sky.

Wil called in Slim and told him to slip away and go back and find out what had happened to Sweet Nose and what the hell was keeping the wagon. "Light out fast while the gate's still open. Only go easy. They think the wagon's up ahead, and that's fine by me. It keeps them out and away."

Wil pushed the herd on until it was pitch dark and foolish to take another step. He sent out the order to bed down the herd and look for dry wood. He wanted a big fire to guide the Old Woman in.

When it was blazing high, Wil got the boys together. "Whoever they are, they'll be coming in now. But before they do, you listen to me like you never listened before. I'm gonna give you orders that'll be hard to carry out, but, by God, you're going to. Because this time it means life or death."

The boys stood close around him in their shining slickers and listened to every word.

"I don't know what they want. Probly the herd. By now they know there's only one growed man on the drive. They can see you're young and not going to put up a fight. That's good. Leave it just like that. Be boys. When they finally come drifting in here, don't act mad or brave or anything like that. *Just act like boys*. Be quiet and look as scared as you can. Don't talk to them unless you have to, then don't say any more than you have to."

They looked up at him with still faces. There was no sign they felt a thing.

"That understood? Do what they tell you to. Look scared. And if anybody's got boy-tears left, shed them now. Here's a chance to cry for the last time in your life. It may help some of you to stay among the living."

His eyes sought out Cimarron.

"I don't want nobody being brave. You're all boys, you hear? Scared little boys with wet pants, hear?"

He moved away from them as if he couldn't stand their eyes.

"God, now I hope the Old Woman don't show up. It's too late for help, and that wagon's the ace up our sleeve."

There were sounds out there.

"Here they come. Remember what I said, and remember this. I'm proud of you. In my book, everyone of you's a man. All right, now, let's see what's in store for the Double-O."

The strangers came in from all sides. They walked their horses easy, as if they didn't want to startle anybody. Then they stopped and stood in a big circle while one of them said, "Hello, friends," then with great surprise, "Why, bless my soul if it ain't Mr. Wil Andersen of Shields Valley!"

Wil looked at the figure coming in to the fire. It was the little one with the long hair that had come into Anse's place looking for a job. Behind him were the other two, the tall one on the right and the young one with the oddly new-looking Stetson on the left. All three looked as dirty as ever, stank like buffalo skinners, and looked stupidly pleased with themselves. The rest were only dim shapes in the darkness.

The little one had obviously looked forward to this moment for a long time. He played it up big, and everything he said sounded planned way far ahead.

"Now, ain't this the biggest surprise you ever had in your whole long life? I never thought I'd ever see you again—at least so soon. In fact, the boys and me thought if we ever did meet up with you again it would be closer to Belle Fourche, with most of the hard part of the drive all done. None of us is much good at driving. But our plans got changed. Along the way we met up with some experienced waddies that said they'd be more than glad to help us out. So we thought, why wait any longer? Let's close in! They're good men, in case you want to know. Got a good name around Bozeman. Maybe you already met up. Come on closer to the fire, boys."

There was a movement. A voice spoke out of the darkness: "Hi, there, Mr. Andersen." Wil looked over his shoulder. It was Smiley and the Boys. All three looked dirty and worn, but somehow out of place with this bunch, like pure-breds among curs.

Smiley's voice was harsh with resentment: "You didn't believe us when we said we'd be back for the drive. It sure ain't the way we planned it, but here we are! And, Mr. Andersen, I promise you on my range word, every single head of them critters is going to get to Belle Fourche."

Long Hair spoke up, "That's right! Whatever might happen, you can be dead sure we'll get 'em there for you! You know, I think we'd all feel better with some eats under our belts. Where's this famous chuck wagon of yours, anyway? I understand your nigra makes a real good meal. I just hope he ain't uppity. Almost all of us boys served the glorious cause of the Confederacy, and we don't like nigras that takes their freedom serious."

There was a pause.

"Mr. Andersen, I ast you a question."

Wil seemed lost in thought. "Well, I don't honestly know where the wagon is. She broke a wheel this morning, and we fixed it maybe fifteen miles back. But she never did catch up with us. I sent the boy back to see what the trouble was, but I ain't seen hide nor hair of him neither."

"You sent *two* boys back, old friend." He snapped his fingers, and one of his men led Slim's horse forward. The boy lay over the saddle, tied hand and foot.

Wil said loud, "*What'd you do to him?*"

"Oh, now, don't you fret. He's all right. Untie him, boys."

Slim joined them, rubbing his wrists and looking ashamed of himself. There were bruises on his face.

Wil said softly, "You all right, boy?"

"Sure. They only slapped me around a little."

Long Hair said, "Lordy, I hope nothing happened to that nigra. I sure counted on a nice supper tonight. Well, I guess all we can do is cool our saddles and sit around the fire friendly-like and wait for him to show up, huh? I just hope we don't have to wait too long. Might make me so mad I'll settle his hash for him before he gets a chance to fix us some. Oh, Mr. Andersen, would you kindly drop your gun, if you don't mind?"

Wil dropped it, and the circle of men came walking in. They had the look of the retarded, and the stink of animals.

The boys moved closer to Wil.

25

The Old Woman had never fixed an axle in his life. He knew and understood them perfectly, but making one was a new experience. Fimps and Sweet Nose were very little help. They were both in such awe of the black man that they did absolutely nothing but what they were told. The three spent the middle of the day finding a tree straight enough, then proceeded to trim it too much in the middle, and had to go back out in the rain and find another.

It was late in the afternoon by the time the job was done to the Old Woman's satisfaction. He had no intention of going cross-country on anything but the best. For his first axle, it was a very good job.

When everything was back in the wagon, he poured three cups of cold coffee and said, "Now, the next thing we gotta do's the hardest yet. That's stay put."

The boys looked startled. Sweet Nose said, "But Mr. Andersen said for you to hurry up!"

"That was hours ago, child. Things has got to change since then. By now them strangers has played they hand, and Mr. Andersen just has to be praying we won't show up. Because we's the ace up his sleeve. So we ain't going nowheres, and, what's more, we gonna do it in the dark and the rain. We eats cold biscuits and drinks cold coffee and sits in the cold wagon and waits."

Then he loaded his rifle and his Colt and laid them handy on the wagon floor, and they sat close together in the dark, listening to all the odd sounds within the storm.

Wil should have known that Black Charlie would figure the way he figured. Yet he worried that somebody would get it into his head to be a hero and get himself hurt. He just wanted to sit tight and wait. He had a funny hunch that with Smiley and the boys around, things would work themselves out. They didn't really mix with any of these throwbacks, and they never once looked directly at him. That was a good sign.

In fact, when they heard that these rustlers were after the Double-O herd, they'd probably joined up with them just to scotch the whole thing. You could see they were good boys at heart. When this was all over, he resolved to humble himself and apologize for the whole thing. He'd say frankly in just these words, "Boys, it was all my fault." Picturing the scene, he felt very good. Everything would come out all right, and they'd all get home in one piece, and he'd stop being such a proud old son of a bitch.

Wil and the boys were herded close together by the fire. The dark visitors were all around them in a great circle. They seemed real happy with themselves, and lolled against their saddles and scratched like dirty animals. Almost without individuality, they talked and laughed and stank. Smiley especially acted like he was real pleased with the way things were. Wil saw through it right away. How else could the boy act if he had something up his sleeve?

Smiley began telling about the day Wil had thrown him and the boys off the Double-O. The animals began to listen and look hard at Wil.

"You never thought the tables would be turned like this, did you, Mr. Andersen? You never thought you'd need us again, so you slammed the door. Now, here you are in real bad trouble, and you know damn well us three won't lift one little finger to help you. And, if you want to know, when our gold fever cooled off, we never once thought of crawling back to you. We druther be saddle bums. And when we met up with Long Hair and his bunch and they showed a hankering for stock, the first outfit we thought of was yours. It was our idea! Take the herd into Belle Fourche. Sell it in your name and scatter. Our idea!"

Wil's hard nails were tearing a green twig to shreds. The boys looked steadily at Smiley and took in every word. Wil was thinking: *Why not rob me on the way back? It would be much easier. No, Smiley's just got to have something up his sleeve.*

"So here you are saying good-bye to your whole damn herd and everything you worked for all these years, just because you had to get all frothy that day we come in and ast for a little time to sniff for gold. Makes you wonder if maybe for once you wasn't wrong about something, don't it, hm? Chew on it, Mr. Andersen. But you'll have plenty of time to chew it fine going back to Bozeman in the morning with nothing to show for your whole life but a empty belly. And you brought it all on yourself."

Wil didn't bother to look at him as he spoke: "You

better set out a guard, or you won't have a herd in the morning either."

Long Hair complained immediately: "What's this about a guard, Smiley? We never said we'd stay up all night nursing cows. That's your job, you and your boys. You know all about that kind of thing, so go right ahead and get on guard. And we'll do our share right here by the fire guarding your Mr. Andersen and all his nice bright little schoolboys."

"Hell, there's gotta be more than just three of us riding guard all night."

Long Hair laughed and shrugged. "Who cares if a couple head strays off!"

"When the hell are we supposed to get some sleep? We'll be riding all day and standing guard all night for a week without no rest!"

Long Hair patted the air with his palms. "Easy, now. We'll figure all that out when the time comes, friend."

"We'll figure it out right now."

Long Hair smiled and said softly, "The hell we will."

"That ain't no answer!"

"How about this, then?"

Long Hair raised his rifle and aimed it right at Smiley's gut. In the silence, he cocked the piece and held it a long moment. Suddenly he yelled, "BANG! You're dead!"

The animals all laughed at the way Smiley jumped. Long Hair turned to the boys and said, "By rights, he oughtta fall down, oughtn' he?"

The boys looked at him gravely. There wasn't a trace of fear in their faces. Long Hair's smile began to fade. Wil said quickly, "That's all right, boys. He ain't gonna hurt you." Their faces didn't change, but they did two good things. Slim Honeycutt put his arm around Charlie Schwartz's shoulder, and little Four Eyes stepped behind Weedy and peered out at the man with the rifle. Long Hair took it to be terror and was delighted. His simple companions laughed with him.

Smiley and the Boys rode off without another word.

Long Hair said, "Mr. Andersen, sir, how much you reckon I'm gonna get for your herd?"

Wil thought a moment and shook his head. "The prevailing price is between eight and twelve dollars a head, the last I heard."

Long Hair blinked and said, "How many head you got?"

Wil said, "Fourteen hundred and eighty-seven by the last count yesterday."

Long Hair blinked several times and whistled. "Man, man, that's nice! That's even better'n Smiley promised! Boys, we're rich! And here I am so hungry I could eat a horse, saddle and all. That nigra of yours better show up by morning, or we're going back after him, and he's gonna wish he was somewheres back in Africa. Where I come from, a nigra's on *time* no matter *what* happens."

His eyes fell on Four Eyes. He said, "You. Come here." The boy obeyed slowly.

"How old are you?"

The boy mumbled something.

"Speak up, Gawdammit."

The boy spoke out: "Almost fifteen," and his voice cracked. Long Hair imitated him, and his friends laughed loudly. He glanced at Wil, who looked away in irritation.

"What's your name?"

"Four Eyes."

"Now, whoever, gave you a name like that?"

"The Old Woman."

"You mean you got your name from a nigra? Oh, what that Lincoln did to our poor country! Hey, come here closer. Boy, you ain't got no glass in them glasses!"

"They broke, but the rims is still good."

Long Hair whipped them off the boy's nose and put them on. He opened his mouth and stared. His men laughed. He said, "Hey, I can see real good now!" They laughed again. "In fact, I can see where a stupid nigra off over in there somewhere's gonna be in real trouble come morning!"

When the laughter fell, Four Eyes said timidly, "I'd like 'em back when you're through."

Long Hair looked down on him like a judge. "You know I'm a dirty old thief, and yet you say you want your glasses back?"

"They been in our fambly I don't know how long."

"But they ain't worth nothing now."

The boy's voice quivered. "All the same—I can't go home without them."

"Well, let me tell you something, little snot-nose. That's just exactly what you're gonna do."

And he slowly crumpled the delicate rims in his hand until they were nothing but golden haywire. Long Hair looked over at Wil, who sat glaring at him. The boys watched with cold eyes, and Four Eyes stared in a kind of horror.

Somebody said, "Aw, Long Hair, if you ain't one mean old son of a bitch."

"Oh, you think I oughtta give him back his glasses? All right. There. Now, am I such a mean old son of a bitch?"

The boy didn't reach for the crumpled rims in the man's hand. He just stood looking at them, and a tear rolled down his cheek. Long Hair looked uncomfortable. He didn't seem to know what to do with the rims. He finally tucked them in the boy's pocket along with a shining fifty-cent piece.

"There, boy, that's my lucky piece. It's one of the first things I ever stole, and I'm giving it to you. There now, am I so bad, huh? You gonna shake hands?"

After a long moment, the boy shook with him, as if he had no bones in his arm. Then he went back to the others. Long Hair called out, "Hey, let's have a look at the dirty-face one there beside Mr. Andersen! Come on out here, boy!"

Horny Jim obeyed very timidly and stood looking at the ground.

"Look at me, boy."

After a moment the boy looked at him. Long Hair began to laugh. "By grab, if that ain't the ugliest damn child I ever laid eyes on in my whole gol-dang life!"

The tall man agreed with a choking sort of laugh. "He's no bigger'n a turd—and he sure smells like one!"

While the others roared, the boy looked steadily at the tall man.

Suddenly Long Hair noticed Cimarron. "Hey, you boys notice the little spik? Step out here in the light, boy!"

Cimarron obeyed as if walking on hot coals.

"Say, now, anybody ever seen such a neat little gimlet end? Now, that boy's as pretty as any señorita I ever laid eyes on!"

Somebody whistled and started a storm of foolish lewdity. Cimarron stood looking at the ground. His fingers fluttered slightly. Long Hair noticed and smiled to himself.

"Yes indeedy, and the nicest pair of lips I seen all summer."

Wil Andersen was staring at him. Long Hair pretended not to notice.

"This must be the one them gals in the wagon said was such a lover. Oh, how they carried on! How about letting us take a look, hm, boy?"

Cimarron neither answered nor looked up. His fingers had stopped quivering. He seemed to have made up his mind.

Wil's stare had taken on a fury. Ignoring him, Long Hair moved his rifle around to aim at the boy's belt. "Come on. We're all friends."

A moment later the rifle jabbed forward. Cimarron swallowed and raised his hands to his belt.

With a roar of rage, Wil threw himself on the rifle. Before he could bring it around to fire, Long Hair's whole camp was on him.

They held him while Long Hair looked the big man up and down. There was a smile of glittering delight on his face. His fine white teeth shone through the whispered words, "*At last!*" Then he braced his feet, clenched his fists, and hit the big man in the gut as hard as he could. Wil grunted, and the small man hit him again and again until his knees buckled. Once down, they all joined in the beating with fists and feet and gun butts. Even after he lay still, some went on until bored or winded.

The boys watched with still faces.

Long Hair said, "Land sakes, Mr. Andersen, that sets a bad example for the boys! You should know better that that, old coot. Stand up and say you're sorry."

Wil stirred painfully.

"Old man, I said stand up, or you'll get a lot worse than you already got."

Wil slowly rolled over onto his hands and knees and stood up in pain.

"Now, you're gonna say you're sorry, understand?"

Wil's face was a mess. He looked at Long Hair through blood and said thickly, "Don't hurt the boys. They're little and never been away from home."

"Goddammit, man, I'm gonna ask you just once more."

Wil's eyes stared at him and finally looked down. Suddenly the smaller man jammed a knee hard up between his legs. Wil cried out and sank to his knees. The smaller man took him by the hair and shouted in his face: "Say it, proud old man, say you're sorry!"

Wil mumbled in pain. The little man twisted his hair sharply.

"Say it louder!" He kicked sharply into the big man's groin. "Everybody's got to hear!"

In agony, Wil Andersen said, "I'm . . . sorry."

Long Hair let go. He stepped away, threw back his head, and laughed in a terrible joy. His friends joined him. They'd heard a hundred times about that day in Anse's Golden Eagle.

Wil remained kneeling and spent. Then he began to raise his head slowly and look at the tumult. Through pain-glazed eyes he saw Long Hair hopping around in a victory dance. He was lithe and young. His hair was golden banners in the firelight, and his teeth radiant as he laughed.

Wil's eyes moved by degrees to the boys. They stood in a close little group looking at him. Their eyes were intent, their faces expressionless. Eph Wormwood's voice was saying, "A growed man understands, but kids just stare at you and think."

Suddenly Wil knew that they, too, were lithe and young, and dancing a victory dance inside. *Old Iron Nuts is getting his.* They seemed fascinated at the spectacle of his pain.

Wil did not know them, and his heart died.

With a tremendous effort Wil Andersen got up and stood swaying. Then he turned his back on the boys. He took a shuffling step toward the darkness, then another.

Long Hair called out behind him: "Hey, just where do you think you're going, old friend?"

Wil slid his foot forward in another step.

"You deef? I said, where *are* you going!"

Wil stopped a moment to answer, and the tumult faded. His voice was thick, but everyone heard his words. "Away. I got nothing here to stay for now."

Then faintly as a whisper on the wind: "*I failed again.*"

He took another step, and Long Hair called out irritably, "Now, you ain't going nowhere, hear? You stop right where you are, or I'm gonna get a little riled, old friend."

Wil went on a step at a time. He was tall in the darkness.

"Gawdammit, I said stop!"

Wil went on. Long Hair fired. Wil's left arm jerked. He went on another step. Long Hair fired again. Wil's right arm jerked, but he continued into the darkness.

The tall one got up and drew. "No fair you having all the fun. Lemme wing him."

He fired, missed, and fired again. Wil half-turned with the impact of the bullet. As the others stood up with their guns drawn, Long Hair said, "Now, wait a minute! If everybody's gonna get in a shot, we can't

no more than just nick him, hear? Nobody finish him
off, you hear? That's for me!"

He began calling their names, and each stepped
forward to fire at the stumbling figure in the dark.
Each hit made him turn and twist, but he went on into
the night with a terrible determination.

The boys watched.

The target fell, then got up on its hands and knees
and began to crawl.

Smiley rode up and said, "What the hell's the shooting all about? You want to start a stampede?"

Long Hair shrugged, "Your Mr. Andersen just tried
to get away. You know that old boy's got something
like fifteen bullets in him?"

Smiley stared, grabbed the rifle, and fired at the
crawling figure again and again. It lay still at last.

Smiley pushed the rifle back into Long Hair's hands
and said, "That ain't a very smart thing you did. Wil
Andersen's got lots of friends that'd ride clear to hell
for him when they hear about it. We better get out of
here."

"You mean that white-haired old darky'll take out
after us? Mercy me. Friend, nobody's coming after us
fast enough to get here before we scatter. Don't let
your weak bladder make you forget we're way out in
the middle of nowhere and the only law there is, I'm
holding right here in my hands."

"All the same, *we're* starting the herd out of here
right tonight. You can tag along if and when you want.
Just remember, we're the ones that sells the beef when
we get to Belle Fourche! Not you prairie dogs!"

"Now? At night? You scared, or crazy?"

Smiley almost shouted, "I ain't staying with *him*
laying out there like that!" The young man seemed
near tears. "I *knew* him!"

"Well, then, let's bury him!"

Smiley glared down at the shorter man. "That's for
his friends to do."

Uneasy voices said, "Sure, let's go. He's right." Long
Hair shrugged. As Smiley started away, Slim called

out, "Mr. Smiley? We can't walk all the way home.
Don't we get our personal horses back?"

As if he were boss, Smiley said, "The saddle band's
right here. Go get 'em."

Long Hair whirled. "You crazy? First thing they'll
do is go for help!"

"Long Hair, old girl, you scared, or crazy? You forgot we're way out in the middle of nowhere? What
help they gonna get?"

Long Hair mounted and rode off. The rustlers followed him. Cimarron ran to get his horse and rode off
after the rustlers. His voice came back to the boys out
of the darkness: "Hey, let me come with you, huh? I
can help Smiley and the boys. Honest. I ain't just a
kid like *them.*"

His voice faded as he kept begging, and at last Long
Hair said out of the distance, "All right, sonny, but
you're on your own. Eat from your own greasy sack.
Nobody shares a bite with *no*body in my bunch."

The boys hustled out after their own horses. By the
time they'd brought them back to the fire, all the
sounds of the drive had vanished in the darkness. It
was the first time since leaving home that they'd
known complete silence on the prairie.

They were on their own.

26

He was pretty full of holes, but not quite dead.
They brought him up beside the fire. Young Charlie
Schwartz said, "I'm going back and find out what
happened to the Old Woman. I think he's been waiting for them to go, but you can't tell."

Slim said, "I'll come, too," but Charlie shook his head. "No, you're the leader. You belong here with him. I'll take Shorty."

It seemed like they were gone forever. The wagon didn't come creaking up until almost dawn. By then Mr. Andersen had begun to get terribly thirsty and strangely restless. The boys were deeply relieved to see the Old Woman take over, order water to be heated, bandages to be torn, and the medicine drawer to be brought up to the fire. He kept very busy for a long time. Then he slowed, stopped, and murmured, "Who'm I fooling?" Then he sat down beside the dying man and gently wiped the sweat off his forehead.

Wil came back to consciousness when they started to put him in the wagon. He said, "Leave me by the fire. It's cold out there." Then he opened his eyes and looked up at the circle of boys, frowned, and said sternly, "Go home." He closed his eyes, lay for several moments, then said, "Do what I say. Go home."

Young Charlie Schwartz said, "Mr. Andersen?"

"What?"

"You telling us we don't work for you no more?"

"Featherhead. No herd. No outfit. Nothing. Go home."

The boy cleared his throat and said, "Then I guess we better get our things."

One by one the boys looked up at him. Wil Andersen suddenly opened his eyes. He looked desperately afraid. "*No!*"

The Old Woman said, "Boy, we all go home together just the way we come."

The boy was patient with the man. "No, sir, if we're not working for the Double-O no more, we got to have our things."

Wil opened his eyes again and looked at the boy, and the boy said to him, "We've got to have *all* our things."

Black Charlie said, "Well, for your information,

mister, you ain't getting *all* your things, and that's that. Ain't that right, Mr. Andersen?"

"That's right."

The boy looked at Black Charlie quietly and said, "I don't mean no disrespect, but the thing is, we want our things, and if you don't give us our things, we're gonna take 'em."

"Simmer down, li'l boy. The growed-ups is still in charge here."

"Mr. Nightlinger, we like you a lot, but there's more of us than there is of you."

The Old Woman's eyes flashed in anger. "You trying to threaten me, you uppity li'l piss-ant you?"

"Yes, we are."

"Well, all I can say is, you just try!"

"We will."

Wil sighed. Everybody looked at him. As if embarrassed by all this attention, he closed his eyes and said, "Charlie Nightlinger, you there?"

"Where else would I be, Mr. Andersen?"

"I think I begin to see what I did wrong. I tried too hard. I held on too tight, and I can't no more. For Pete's sake, I ain't everybody's father. I ain't fate. I ain't God. I'm just a ordinary man bleeding in a lot of places."

The Old Woman seemed to be running out of air. He moved his head from side to side and breathed through an open mouth. Then he got up suddenly and said, "I get you some coffee."

Wil's eyes opened. "Then I am dying, after all."

"Why, what make you say a thing like that?"

"You've never went to get me coffee before. Not in twenty years. I didn't think I was hurt that bad. It sure don't feel good, but it felt much worse the day I took the wagon and went to get my boys."

"Mr. Andersen, you was a *good* father."

"Hold on, Charlie. Funeral's not till morning. Now, listen, boys. You all there? Get around here where I can see you."

They gathered in a little still-faced bunch before him.

"I'm gonna tell you one last thing. Stay alive. You boys got something that's got to be handed on. You're a special little bunch. So forget everything else I've said and *just take care*. It's the easiest thing in the world for a good man to get himself killed, and hard as anything to stay alive. Everybody got that?"

The boys murmured, just like they'd said "good morning" that first morning at the ranch a thousand years ago last spring.

"Charlie? Charlie Nightlinger, you there?" It took great effort for him to raise his voice.

Black Charlie answered soft as velvet, "Yes."

"Give them the key."

The black man froze. The boys became very still. "You raving?"

"Not no more. I'm calm as anything. Give them what's theirs. They're all men now."

"You's raving for sure."

"No, I'm just curious to see what kind of a job I did on them. Get the key and open the box."

The Old Woman was aghast. He obeyed in muttering outrage. Each boy walked up to the open box and took out his guns and ammunition. They stood around girding themselves in silence.

Then young Charlie Schwartz said, "First we got to find out where they are, then we'll come back here for breakfast and figure out how to go at it."

Wil asked almost gently, "How to go at what, boy?"

Young Charlie looked down at him and said matter-of-factly, "Getting the herd back so we can take it on in to Belle Fourche, sir."

"Think you can?"

"Ain't nothing in the world can stop us."

Wil closed his eyes and kind of smiled, then he lay listening to the boys ride off.

He opened his eyes one more time and said

anxiously, "Charlie? Tell them to be nice to Smiley and the Boys. They're not really bad. It wasn't their fault. It was mine. I could have stopped this whole thing with just a word."

"I tell 'em, Mr. Andersen."

"And there's something else that bothers me more than all the rest. One time I said a terrible thing to those boys. I said 'Look on no man as your father, no woman your mother, nobody your brother. And if you're asked is that your son, say I do not know him.' It was true, but not the kind of truth you tell a boy. Now I wish I'd said *I am your father. I am your mother. And you're the best of all my sons.* Does that sound like anything that they'd believe?"

The Old Woman didn't think so, but he said, "Sure, Mr. Andersen. I tell 'em. Oh, I never did get your coffee."

When he came back with the steaming cup, the man had died. The Old Woman sat down and looked at the still face for a long, long while.

Then he lifted his head to the gray dawn and began to cry. It was more in terrible anger than in grief. He said loud to the sky as if They were a little deaf up there, *"Nobody could of stopped all this!"*

27

They wrapped him in a tarp, lowered him into the hole, and covered it over so that even an Indian wouldn't guess it was a grave. Then each of them sighted on several landmarks so they'd be able to find the spot again.

While they stood around gulping hot coffee, young Charlie Schwartz started talking as if taking up a discussion that had been momentarily interrupted.

"One thing we can't forget. They got it over us in a lot of ways. They're bigger'n we are, for one thing, and they all been in and out of plenty of trouble, so they got experience, too. So we got to go at them just as light and easy as a raw finger on a hair trigger. Okay?"

Their silence was assent.

"And there's something else. We gotta keep it looking like accidents just as long as we can. The minute they guess one of them got himself bush-whacked, they'll know who did it. And when they get the wind up, they're gonna come at us like mad dogs. And if they catch anybody, they'll finish him slow, just for the fun of it. You saw the game they made outta Mr. Andersen, so hold your water and do it like we plan, okay? We'll pick our man, cut him out of the herd, and blow out his lamp. And everybody'll get a turn. Each time, we'll decide ahead whose man it is, okay? So the big thing is to go quiet and *take it real easy*."

For a moment it was Mr. Andersen saying the words. Only now he talked quiet and was almost enjoying himself.

Smiley spoke loud and angry to Long Hair and his bunch. "I and my two partners can't keep this whole damn herd going all by ourselfs. Sure, the bean-eater helps, but he only makes four. We gotta have real help, not just when somebody feels like it, and not just the *way* he feels like. If I put a man on the right swing, by God, he's gotta stay on the right swing till somebody comes and takes his place. God-amighty, we spend half our time going after strays. By the time we get to Belle Fourche, everybody in town'll know how we got this herd. We got to go fast, make a deal fast, and get out fast. Them buyers ain't stupid, but you sure are. You just fork off and horse around like this was a big old picnic. By grab, if us four's gonna do all the work, we oughta get all the money!"

That was not well received. Cold eyes began looking on Smiley in a new light. There were mumbled threats. Long Hair calmed everybody down. This was no time to get riled. He said those political things that would half-please everybody and upset none.

"Look, Smiley don't mean it like it sounds. Everybody's gonna get his fair share. There's plenty. But he's right. We got to get to the end of the line before we can collect our loot, don't we? So let's all pitch in and get there! Hell, I'm willing to let Smiley be trail boss with me until the end of the drive. I want to get this damn job done. I didn't turn to a life of crime to *work*, for Chrissake."

No one was amused. When Smiley assigned positions, he got only scowls and vague threats. When he put the tall man in the rear riding drag, he got a flat refusal.

"I ain't trailing back behind everybody and eating dust all day long, and that's final."

"Somebody's got to. Anyways, we're taking turns. Get somebody to take your place."

"You get somebody to take my place. Wasn't my idea. What about the kid?"

"The bean-eater? He's too good to waste back there!"

"But I ain't?"

"You ain't anxious to work like he is. He's always everywhere doing everything. Are you?"

Long Hair sighed and said, "Do what the man says, Snoots. This drive ain't forever. Anyways, you ain't took a bath in so long, a little more dust won't hurt you none. *Skedaddle*."

He somehow got hot lead into the word. The tall man rode off grumbling but cowed.

Snoots had to fall way back behind to avoid the dust. It was lonely back here. He liked to hear the fellers talk. He liked best lolling around the fire

laughing and the fellers jobbing each other and trad-
ing tales. Hell, he wasn't no damn waddy. He was
a useless hunk of nothing, and he knew it, and
wished vaguely that he could change. He wished
that he could settle down and learn a trade of some
kind. He didn't like life in a greasy sack outfit like
this, eating old food out of a dirty bag, keeping to
the coulees and never going over the top of a hill
without your hand on your gun. He did it only because he couldn't do anything else.

With his share of the money, he'd settle down
somewhere and learn a nice trade, maybe, like bar-
dogging. He pictured himself shaved and clean in a
white apron yawning on the glasses and making them
shine. And everybody liking him and looking up to
him. Drinkers always seem to like bartenders, and
he was just the man to be everybody's friend. After
this job was done.

Snoots never knew how long the other horse had
been walking alongside him before he actually noticed
it.

He looked up and got a big surprise. It was this
kid that called himself Horny Jim. He was riding easy
and looking over this way.

The tall man returned the impersonal gaze and
said, "What you doing here, kid? You lost? You can't
come along with us."

The boy only rode and looked at him steadily.

"Damn if Long Hair wasn't surely right. You're the
ugliest child in all creation. Now, git. We don't need
no more kids."

The boy paid no attention, and his eyes didn't
falter.

"What the hell you staring at, boy? You git, or I'll
kick your ass for you."

The boy just looked at him. The tall man pointed
his quirt and said, "I 'ain't gonna tell you again, you
hear?"

The boy didn't seem to. The man swung his quirt.
He didn't mean to hit the boy, but somehow he did,
right across the face.

The rest was a nightmare. The kid, this little tiny boy, didn't do a single thing that a normal person is supposed to when they're hurt. He didn't bring his hands up to his face. He didn't make a sound. He hadn't even ducked. He just rode on, looking at the tall man, and let the trickle of blood come out his nose without so much as a sniff.

The man stared. Then the worst thing happened. The boy grinned. It was a terrible, knowing grin, and the blood made it worse. Then he finally spoke. It was only one word, but it was enough. In his high, clear little voice, he said, "*Turd*."

With a roar, the tall man wheeled his horse. The boy turned on the instant and started off. The man rode low, ramming his rowels in his horse's ribs. He was cursing. He was furious for letting himself be afraid of a baby for a minute there.

Then he noticed that the boy didn't seem to be trying too hard to get away. With misgivings, the man closed the gap between them.

He sensed rather than saw this other boy standing in the brush. He was holding a rope ready. It flung out and formed a figure eight around his horse's legs and head. The horse pitched forward. The tall man went over its head, landed on his shoulder, and lay groaning.

Then there was a high young voice: "Don't get down. You'll leave footprints."

"But he's still alive, Bob. You said you'd break his neck."

"Well, I didn't. But I *seen* necks broke like this. Well, now I got to find me a big rock."

"Right behind you."

The boy they called Stuttering Bob turned and lifted it. It was heavy. He grunted carrying it over to the man on the ground. He stood with a foot on either side of the man's head, took aim, and dropped it into the staring face.

All of Long Hair's boys were expert trackers. If there'd been anything out of place, they'd have seen

it right off. As it was, not a man but assumed the
horse had bolted, stumbled, and flung its rider at the
rock. They just went through his pockets, covered
him over with brush, and stood gloomily for the
funeral oration. It was brief. Long Hair said, "Good-
bye, old friend, too bad you won't be sharing with
us at the end of the drive."

The sentiment brightened everybody's spirits considerably.

28

They were only five days out of Belle Fourche. Already they kept an eye peeled for Devil's Tower. The
spirits of the rustlers had lifted so high they took
Smiley's orders in crossing the Little Missouri with a
certain complacency. He shouted all of the wrong
things and rubbed everybody the wrong way, but it
was something that had to be done.

None of them liked bodies of water from bathtub
size on up to a river. Few could swim, and some
were frankly terrified by the idea of having to.
Peachy Cox had been known to ride miles to avoid
crossing deep water. He was one of the older men,
almost thirty, and held in a certain veneration. It
was said he'd killed nigh onto a dozen men, yet he
never talked about it. The rare modesty impressed
his present associates. It never occurred to them that
he'd never killed anything but lice.

Peachy was an ugly man and impossible to love on
sight. So he'd made the most of it and worked at this
perfect excuse for not being loved. *You think I'm
ugly? All right, let me show you how ugly acts.* He
played the part perfectly. They all said of him,

"He's got the look of a real killer." He was always gratified to hear that.

But the man with the look of a real killer hated water. Lagging farther and farther behind, he found himself among the last to enter the water. Even the cattle went before him, and Plummer yelled from the other side, "Dammit, Peachy, you coming or not?"

He said, "Go on and mind your knitting. I'll catch up."

They did, and he watched them appalled. For the first time in his adult life he felt the terror of being left behind. The feeling can make even a strong man falter, and Peachy wasn't strong. He'd gone through life avoiding all such situations, and hadn't the average man's experience facing familiar fears. Out of practice, and alone, he stood on the bank with a sinking heart and watched them go.

He finally took a deep breath, gave his horse a mild kick, and walked it into the water. When the cold hit his feet, he gasped. Icy water and death were one to him, so he was helpless from the beginning.

All he could do was stare as the boy's hand reached up out of the water, grabbed his ankle, and pulled.

He made no sound as it pulled him slowly down into the water. But once in, he exploded in terror, thrashed insanely, and tried to scream. As if to soothe and reassure him, the boy's naked body wrapped itself around him, held his arms firmly to his sides, locked its legs around his, and sank with him down to terrible silence and deadly peace.

They rolled over and over in a firm embrace. The river took them around a bend and into shallows. The body was limp now. Shorty let him go and surfaced cautiously.

The bend hid him. He waded out of the water dragging the body face down by the ankles. He stopped on a sand spit, crouched, and began tugging the man's gun out of its holster. While he examined it, the man groaned.

Instantly, the naked boy flung himself full length on

the man and held his face under the surface, until no more spasms shuddered through the body.

When it was over, Shorty rolled the body back into the current, splashed water on his foot-prints, and walked up into the grove of water trees, where Four Eyes waited with his clothes and horse.

Four Eyes watched him whisk the water off. Shorty panted briskly, making no attempt to hide his excitement. Four Eyes looked out at the river and said, "Well, that's two." Shorty dressed deliberately, then reached for the reins.

Four Eyes squinted up at him and said, "Don't this seem a little easy?" Shorty said, "Yup."

They took a good look before walking their horses out of the grove.

The boys didn't have anything to do with the third man's death. It was apparently an accident. Sometime in the heat of the day, and hidden by dust, the man's horse shied at something, then bucked sharply. He was thrown and dragged to death by one stirrup. His remains were pretty much of a mess.

Long Hair looked at it and said, "Mitch was one hell of a horseman. Don't seem reasonable he'd let something like that happen to him. Look how his boot heel's off and his foot's pushed clear through the stirrup. Damned thing's clear up around his ankle. Know what? I don't think this was no accident. Not on top of Snoots getting his head bashed in and Peachy getting drownded."

They looked at him with dull eyes. Somebody said, "Who you think? Them kids back there?"

Long Hair's eyes flashed with a strange intensity.

"Talk sense. Them babies? No, it's got to be one of us. I think somebody wanted a bigger share and maybe still does. Bigger and bigger. Keep your eyes peeled, boys. This is bad medicine, and I say this: the shares of the dead goes to the man that finds out who's doing this. That all right with everybody?"

A couple said yup, and he let it go at that. The men began stealing little glances at each other.

"Before we cover him up, let's take a look at what he's got in his pockets."

"He ain't got a cent, Long Hair. He's been borrowing on his saddle to play poker nights."

"What about that funny-looking gold ring of his?"

Long Hair looked at the hands. There was only a band of pale skin where the ring had been. He held the hand up. "*Now's* there anybody that think this is a accident?"

Kitten Craig looked up alarmed. "Hold on there, boy. Maybe he sold it or lost it or something."

"Kitten, that ring was gave him by his *mother*. I say it couldn't be no accident."

The ring turned up by acident, too. Kitten was rolling up his soogans the next morning when it fell out. Everybody seemed to notice but him. They gradually stopped what they were doing and stood looking down at the golden ring in the dust.

Long Hair picked it up and said, "Hey, Kitten, you dropped something. Here, catch!"

Kitten caught it, frowned, and said, "Ain't mine. You know, this looks like . . ." He looked up. Everybody was staring at him. He swallowed and said, "Mitch's ring."

Long Hair tilted his head. "How d'you suppose it got in your bedroll, Kitten?"

"I donno. Somebody must of put it there. There's no other way. What are you bastards all staring at? You think I'd kill a friend just for a stinking little old ring?"

They just stood. Somebody's hand moved, and Kitten whipped out his gun. He started backing toward his horse.

"Looks like it don't take much to make you coyotes think you caught a fox. Well, I ain't hanging around here to try to prove you're wrong. All you boys want is to cut down the population so the split'll be bigger. Well, you can take mine and be damned. None of you ain't gonna get to Belle Fourche anyway. Not the way you're going."

Behind him they saw the little bean-eater from the waist down on the other side of Kitten's horse. He was loosening the cinch. Long Hair took the cue and yelled, "*Get* him, boys!"

Nobody moved but Kitten. He took a flying mount, and the saddle and everything came right down on top of him. Everybody was laughing so hard they could hardly catch him. He almost got away a couple of times, gun and all. But they finally sat on him, trussed him up, and stood around trying to decide what to do with a man so low he'd kill his own friends.

That was when he started begging and talking. "Look, boys, I admit holding out on you about the ring. I loaned Mitch five dollars on it to play poker with. I didn't steal it, 'fore God, I didn't! Jesus Christ, would I kill him for a little thing like that?"

Long Hair said, "No, for a bigger share. Like you drownded Peachy Cox and bashed in Snoots's head."

Kitten could only stare. Then Long Hair thought of the anthill. "Cut some stakes, boys." Kitten gasped, "But I'm your friend! I saved your life twice! Every cent I had was yours!" Long Hair looked at him like a stranger.

They stripped and staked him face up on the biggest anthill they could find. It was a burning hot day. The sun was blinding, and the ants were busy.

A mile away they could still hear him screaming.

29

It was Weedy who gave the whole thing away. He was afraid. Weedy feared for his soul. The boy felt he was faced with a terrible dilemma when he stumbled on one of the rustlers. He knew what would happen if he didn't fire, and he remembered Wil Andersen's words as if the big man were alive and shouting them in his ear: *It's the easiest thing in the world for a good man to get himself killed, and hard as anything to stay alive*. But the boy just couldn't pull the trigger.

It was because this whole thing was Wrong. In there in the Good Book among tales of universal slaughter to survive, it said you shouldn't ought to Kill. The contradiction disarmed him. Weedy just stood there numb while the rustler reached out, took his gun, and hit him across the face with it.

Weedy told the rustlers everything they wanted to know, and some things they didn't. They were stunned at who'd killed the first two men. Long Hair's eyes seemed to go blank in outrage and fury. He almost screamed.

"Them other two was bad enough! But Kitten was my friend! My God in heaven, he saved my life twice! Every cent he had was mine for the asking! *And they made me kill him!*"

He grabbed Weedy and shook him by the throat until the boy's face was purple and the gun cuts began to bleed again. The others pulled him off because they'd already agreed to do a real slow job on the boy altogether. Something that would take at least as long as the ants had.

Long Hair calmed down after a while and got to thinking. "We can't just rush out there and grab those kids. They're spread out all over, in pairs, according to this one. God knows how long it would take to go around beating the brush and flushing them out. So what we're going to do is sit right here and let them come to us. When they find out we got Weedy here, they'll come for him. All we got to do is make him howl like Kitten did. And I mean howl. I want everybody in Montana territory to know this boy's in trouble."

They decided on the hot-foot to start off with. Invented by rustlers for calves so they couldn't follow their mothers, it was a simple burning between the toes with a hot iron. It was effective. Weedy's agony reached every corner of the prairie. The stink of his burning flesh filled the still night. Used to bad smells, the rustlers joked by the fire about what they'd do to the others.

But nothing happened. None of the guard they'd posted reported a thing.

With Weedy, much happened. With each fresh roar of pain that rushed through his body, he relived the moment in which he'd faced that other creature made by his same God—and hadn't fired. This was his strange reward. For the first time it struck Weedy that maybe He overdid His "mysterious ways" thing.

It was far deep in the hollow hours of the night. Long Hair had said he'd watch the prisoner because he was sure he wouldn't sleep. Like a deadly catechism, his thoughts repeated that Kitten had been his friend, had saved his life twice, and every cent he owned was his. Over and over and over until he woke with a start.

Everything was still as death. You'd never know a big herd of cattle stood just a short distance away. He reached over and threw a couple pieces of wood on the fire. The coals sent up little feelers to probe the wood. They became arms and embraced it, and light spread in a silent circle.

Long Hair became very still. Weedy and his fried feet were gone.

He leaned over. There were prints. He followed them to the edge of darkness, then went back to the fire. He should wake up everybody and admit what had happened and order them out to beat the brush. Or he could wait till it was lighter and follow those tracks himself. Nothing that walks the earth can hide its tracks for long. And when you know something's been this way, you can always find out how he came and how he went. Tracks stop only with the person making them.

Long Hair sat weaving back and forth the rest of the night, chewing strands of his long hair with bright white teeth. He felt a savage impatience to follow those tracks. He wanted to come back with bloody hands. He wanted to bathe in blood for Kitten.

In the first faint light he was half-walking, half-running in the brush and devouring the ground with his eyes. The tracks were plain. The earth screamed. It was only gradually that he realized the tracks were familiar. He frowned as he followed them around the east edge of the herd. Then there were rocks, and they stopped. He looked all around him in the gray light. Stillness.

Then a faint whisper: "Hey, come on! They're here!"

Not six feet away was the bean-eater, smiling his good-looking smile, and till then invisible because he was lying flat on his belly on a ledge above. He was looking at something down the far side. His hand motioned silence. The soles of his feet showed that the tracks had been his.

The lean little man crept up on the ledge and flattened out beside him. It was dark down there. At first he could see nothing. Then a familiar white design began to appear many feet below. It was the face marking of his own horse.

The long-haired man stared into the gloom. He didn't understand. He looked at Cimarron, then back down. Now he saw that there was somebody on his horse. Somebody young. It was Weedy, and his feet hung bloody outside the stirrups. He sat on the horse as if waiting.

Long Hair started to rise. Cimarron touched his arm and whispered, "Wait. They'll show up in a minute." And when Long Hair flattened out again on his stomach to stare into the dark gulch, the boy leaned close and again whispered in his ear.

Long Hair didn't catch what he was saying. He whispered, "What?" Cimarron again leaned close and said, "I pried the heel half-off. I made his foot catch in the stirrup. I made the horse throw him."

Long Hair stared at the boy. Cimarron smiled back, his face just inches away. Wholly unafraid.

Then the man realized that something had been happening while they whispered. Someone was squatting over the small of his back, a foot on either side. But before he could turn to look over his shoulder, hands grabbed his long, fine hair and pulled his head back.

In the half-light, he saw a grubby little hand holding first a mangled pair of glasses rims and then a fifty-cent piece. And then he saw a knife.

A moment later it cut his throat from ear to ear.

Four Eyes remained squatting while he wiped the blade on the dead man's shirt. Then deftly, as if rippling a scale on his guitar, his fingers unbuckled the man's gun and belt and pulled it off. He asked, "Cimarron, you gonna keep on here with them?"

Cimarron shrugged in the gloom. "You got to know what their plans are, don't you?"

"But you could get yourself kilt."

"I'm all right. I do better by myself."

"Look, Charlie says two things. He says remember what Mr. Andersen said about going easy on Smiley and the Boys. But he says not to trust them too far. He says not to tell them anything, okay?"

"I won't. They think that I am just a handy little boy."

Four Eyes started down the rock and stopped. "Take care of yourself, you hear? Charlie Schwartz says that, too."

Cimarron nodded and went trotting back to camp. Four Eyes hurried down to where Weedy was waiting.

30

There had been seventeen. Now there were twelve, and Smiley and the Boys. But a leader had appeared among them. There's always a sucker for command.

Itchy Jake was an angry man, and one you had to listen to, because he shouted his anger round the clock. As a subordinate he had been respectful of better minds. Now he saw them all disgraced by children, and he screamed his outrage. He was for going out there and setting fire to the brush and burning the little bastards out.

Smiley stopped that fast. Did he want a stampede ending with nothing but a barbeque? The others listened to Smiley and wished he'd show a little fight. Snapped at, they knew that Jake would back down and let Smiley become Long Hair's heir.

Smiley didn't. His modesty was appalling. As long as Jake didn't do anything that would hurt the herd, he was willing to take whatever orders were given him.

The men got disgusted and worried. They weren't really scared, but the whole thing was getting to be a whirly mess. They disagreed on everything. Every damn day somebody came up with a new idea and everybody else blasted it to hell. Everything was touch and go.

Then Jake showed his genius. He brought them all back together with a line of thought they took to right off. He declared that this damn nigra they'd never seen was behind the whole thing. Them kids couldn't have figured all this out alone. There had to be a grown-up mind behind it. And it had to be this cook of theirs.

Jake said positively, "Get him, and you've got 'em all. Come on. A chuck wagon's the easiest thing in the world to find."

He took half the men and rode back down the trail. An hour out, they began to see dust up ahead, a nice solid little cloud of it. It was the chuck wagon going as fast as it could.

They laughed for the first time all day and rode up on either side. When he saw them, the black man pulled in the reins, then he just sat up there and looked them over as if he were hiring.

They pulled him down and searched the wagon. No little boys.

"All right, nigra, where you got them hid?"

"My boys? They ain't hid nowheres. They's all up with the herd where they belongs. And by now I wouldn't be the least surprised if they hasn't took care of at least one more of you. Maybe two."

One of the Deeper Southerners got so mad he took a shot at the black man but missed. Black Charlie had winced, but he didn't look as scared as some thought he should.

Jake said, "I can see you think you're a brave man, black boy."

Black Charlie shook his head. "No, I ain't brave so much as bored. You go through all this foolishness as much as I have, and pretty soon you figure maybe you's gonna die from pneumonia after all. And that ain't no better'n lead poisoning."

Jake drew away and lowered his voice. "Look, if this black old bastard's telling the truth, some of us better get back to the herd. There's a dozen of these damn kids, and only six of us back there. Let's split up. You four hightail it back, and the rest of us'll see what we can get out of the nigra besides blood."

There was silence after they rode off. Jake got down.

"You been behind all this, ain't you, nigra?"

"A couple miles. Growing boys got to eat."

"You ain't gonna die from no pneumonia."

"I got a feeling you might be right."

"You put the boys up to this. Why?"

"Do me any good to say I dint?"

"No."

"I dint think so."

"This is one cool damn nigra. I guess he's too stupid to know what's coming next."

"I may not be the brightest nigra that ever live, but I ain't so stupid I think you rid all this way just for me to cook you up a batch of tasty bear-signs."

They looked at him intently for a long moment. One of them swallowed. Another looked at the rest and down at the ground. As at a signal, everybody shifted weight to the other foot—then they were all putting their guns away. Jake, their big bad leader, was the first to lick his chops.

If there is a hell, it is a quiet, comfortable place where there is nothing whatever for a man to do but endlessly reflect on those things that he did to bring about his own ruin.

This applies to little boys as well. Young Charlie Schwartz saw the eight men stop the wagon, search it, then four ride back to the herd. Those that stayed had their guns out. The Old Woman was in trouble.

Young Charlie was alone with Horny Jim. They must do something fast, but he had no illusions about being able to create more than a diversion. They'd made it a rule never to attack a man unless he was alone and outnumbered, so this would have to be nothing but diversion.

He saw a tree and had an idea. It was risky, and contrary to their plan, but the Old Woman was helpless, and something desperate had to be done. He gave Horny instructions, hid his own horse, and climbed the tree. It was in full leaf and made a good hiding place, but he had the impression that Mr. Andersen wouldn't have approved.

Horny Jim rode straight to the wagon, hauled up short, looked surprised, and took off fast as he could go. The men jammed cold biscuits in their mouths, mounted, and followed, making dust. Horny Jim kicked Miss Minnie's sides hard and took out for the tree. All four followed him directly under it.

The loop of rope dropped around the neck of the last man. He swung off his horse and dangled in the air, silently fighting death. Pieces of biscuit splattered from his mouth into the dust below.

When he was dead, young Charlie began sliding down the other end of the rope. When he was half-way down, the first riders came back. They fired again and again. He fell the rest of the way. They'd have come up to make sure he was dead, but Horny Jim came back to see what the shooting was about, and they took off after him again.

Young Charlie didn't die until after Slim brought him to the wagon. The Old Woman was stunned. He moved about mechanically and finally sat down beside the dying boy to wait. The boy took his hand, and Black Charlie held it tight. He said, "Damn, I just wish you wasn't so far from home."

The boy said, "Oh, no, Mr. Nightlinger. I like the wagon. It's a whole lot better than a house with doors. This is just exactly where I want to be. I hurt all over, but I druther hurt out here than be well at home."

A shudder went through him. When he could speak again, he said, "I wish Four Eyes was here. I'd sure like to work on that song some more."

The boys were drifting in. They stood away and watched him in silence. Suddenly he flared up just like he used to: "I don't want none of you sons of bitches feeling sorry for me, hear? It was my own fault. It sure takes a real smart man to do a real dumb thing."

Then his fist smoothed out, and the Old Woman took it in both hands. He kept sitting there beside the boy, and never let go.

When it began to get dark, young Charlie seemed to wake up. He frowned and ran a dirty hand through his white-gold hair. He spoke in a very young boy's thin voice. "You know something? I'm the only one that never got a nickname."

Then he died.

It wasn't so much work digging his grave as Mr. Andersen's. He was just a little boy. But the odd part was all their faces. The Old Woman stood there with honest tears glistening on his cheeks, yet not one of the boys cried. They just stood there eating cold biscuits and looking a bit impatient to get on with it.

31

Sometime in the night, Jake and the two men who'd killed young Charlie Schwartz vanished. Their friends scoured the territory and couldn't find a trace. When Smiley and the Boys went on with the herd, they gave up and followed.

On toward afternoon, when the herd came in sight of Devil's Tower, the missing men were found. They'd been impaled beside the trail. Jake was still a bit alive. He kept whispering, "Kill me, kill me, kill me!"

The rustlers stared in horror. Nothing in their cruel lives quite equaled this. They granted Jake's favor and felt comparatively kind.

A sort of dull panic took them then. They tried to push the herd all night, and only brought confusion. They argued furiously and jumped at the smallest sound. Each withdrew from the others, staying with the drive only because of a few last remaining shreds of greed.

Smiley and the Boys did all the work. They went without sleep keeping the herd together and the men apart. They weren't sure exactly why. All they knew was they had to get the beef to Belle Fourche.

The only real help they had besides the bean-eater was a fellow with a soft golden beard, blue eyes, and a broken nose. Zeke wasn't very smart, but he was faithful. All he wanted was to buy his parents beautiful tombstones—marble if his share of the drive allowed; if not, granite would have to do. The only trouble was, he didn't know where they were buried. All he had was this one letter from somebody who'd talked to them once before Shiloh. It was all mixed up, but he'd get the money for those markers if it was the last thing he ever did. And he seemed to sense it would be.

Then one day even he turned and rode back down the trail. The Old Woman was alone when golden-bearded Zeke rode up. He got down with the awkwardness of fatigue, stood before the black man, and said simply, "I'm hungry."

The Old Woman looked at him a long moment, then pointed to the cups and the coffeepot. While the musky visitor sat on the ground slurping in the boiling brew, the Old Woman dug up the last of the raisin rolls and some beans in black molasses he'd planned on eating himself if he ever got hungry again. The visitor ate like an animal. The Old Woman didn't watch. He felt completely numb these days.

While he was soaking up the last of the syrup with the last of the bread, the visitor became conscious of someone else. Without lifting his head, he looked up ahead and saw feet. Small feet. Boy's feet. It was the tiny one called Fimps.

He ate the last mouthful, laid the plate aside, and suddenly lunged forward. Hardy Fimps instantly whirled and ran as fast as his short little legs would take him. The Old Woman felt around inside the wagon for his rifle.

The little boy dodged in and out of brush, but

the man caught up with him without much effort. He was just about to touch his prey when the little fellow whirled around and drove the Old Woman's butcher knife into his stomach up to the handle. Then he pulled it out and drove it in again.

Black Charlie leaned against the wagon, groaned, "Oh, my God!" and vomited all over his own toes. He knew he'd never be able to use that knife again and that the sweetest little white boy he'd ever known was no longer a being that he could understand.

When he was alone, he said to the air, "Mr. Andersen? Is *this* what you wanted?"

There was no Wil to answer. Black Charlie's attention drifted back to the present. There was coffee to be made, and water to fetch from the stream. He took a couple buckets on down there. He filled them. Before he'd gone ten yards back, the whole bunch of rustlers rode up for his blood.

He was so sick and tired of the whole thing, he didn't even look up. Even when the lead man dropped the noose around his neck, he kept right on walking back toward camp with the splashing buckets.

Now, breathe in, hold it, and just squeeze ever so easy.

The shot came from the trees. The man with the noose fell off his horse. Half his face was gone. Everybody hauled up and drew, but they didn't know where the shot had come from.

Rest the barrel there in the crotch and sight just a hair above your target, Good, boy, good.

Another shot, and the nearest man grabbed his belly, slid slowly from his horse, and knelt in the dust.

Hold your pistol with both hands, boy. Makes no difference what it looks like. Steady, steady.

A third man just leaned forward and sat dead in his saddle.

The Old Woman kept going with his water buckets, the rope dragging along behind.

The rustlers fired in panic, but there was nothing to see. You can't fire at a puff of gunsmoke. Their horses whirled and kicked up dust in the confusion. A wounded man was trampled. He screamed something awful.

Except for the four shots and the frightened horses, there hadn't been much noise. Now the screaming seemed to crack open the sky and bring it right down on them. A rider broke and left the bunch. The others followed. The last man got it in the back and fell off into the stream. He floated on down, struggling weakly, with only his hand showing above the surface.

Without changing pace, the Old Woman went on with the buckets into camp.

Slim came out of the trees and put a stop to the screaming. He called out, "Come on, boys! Let's clean up on the rest while they're running scared!" The boys rode after him fast. The Old Woman noticed how calm their faces were.

The thunder of the rustlers coming up started the herd. The brown mass started running. Smiley and the Boys yelled and beat at the leaders. A rustler passed, screaming, "We're done for! They got us all!"

Smiley and the Boys stared after him.

"Let's get the hell out of here, Smiley!"

"Leave the herd?"

"*You know how kids are! They won't let up till there's nobody left!*"

Smiley couldn't believe it, but he decided not to hang around and sift exaggeration. Jamming the breeze, he led the three off for some northern nowhere.

The one that had yelled found himself up at the head of the run with panicked cattle all around him. His arm jumped. He felt it and stared at the blood on his hand. Pain plowed through his shoulder. He cried out. Then it felt like his whole side had been blasted out. He rode on in terror, screaming, "No, no, no, no!" at the crest of the tide. He leaned forward clutching his horse's mane and sobbing that one word over and over. As weakness took him, he slid off into the brown flood, still protesting.

Slim Honeycutt and two of the boys took out after another rustler headed for the hills. Slim gave orders by pointing, and the three began to herd the fugitive like any critter. Bending him a little here and a little there, they kept him headed toward the river. He was so busy peering over his shoulder he didn't realize what was happening until too late. He tried wildly to break away, but the three had him hemmed in. All he could do was go on ahead as fast as his horse would take him.

Then there was the cliff. He and his horse went right on over into a bottomless darkness. The three boys pulled up at the edge and watched him go.

The last man crawled up to Weedy on his hands and knees crying and begging and making promises. He'd have hugged the boy's feet if they hadn't been covered with bloody bandages. Weedy sat looking at him and listening as if it were all in some foreign language. Then he emptied all five chambers into the writhing, twisting man.

That night around the fire Slim announced that they'd have to be taking a count first thing in the morning.

By afternoon the herd was moving at its regular plodding pace. The boys were again at its edges, and the chuck wagon was on up ahead where Slim had picked tonight's bedground. The whole world was still. Larks sang.

That night Slim assigned new positions. Then he added, "Cimarron wants to take off a couple days and see what happened to Smiley and the Boys. I think we need him with the herd, but it's up to you boys."

Everybody but the Old Woman thought he ought to go, so Slim gave in. Without good-bye, the dark, handsome boy mounted and walked his horse off into the darkness. That was the last they saw of him.

Eating industriously, some of them didn't even watch him go.

32

Smiley and the Boys headed due east until they hit
the Texas Trail, then hightailed it north as fast as
they could go. They wanted to get to Miles Town,
one hundred and fifty miles north and west. Once
there, everything would be all right. Howdy had a
brother there. He'd put them up, and maybe even
stake them until they got in with another outfit. If
not, the inevitable would happen. They'd have to
split up after three years of hardly being out of one
another's sight.

Miles Town was the biggest, liveliest town any of
them had ever seen. There must be at least six
saloons running full blast, two pleasure parlors, and
a wide street with all sorts of stores on both sides.
The boys' spirits rose, then fairly soared after they'd
had a bath and put on clean clothes and jingled a
little cash in their pockets borrowed from Howdy's
brother.

The first thing they did was go in Big Nose Levitt's
for a drink. Glasses in hand, they roamed around
and looked at all the games going on: roulette, faro,
blackjack, keno, and every kind of poker you could
think of. Then they sat down off to one side and
listened to the old piano player in his long-tailed
coat, and they speculated about the men and watched
the women. Howdy leaned forward and said softly,
"We oughtn't stare." He was serious, and they took
him seriously. In this world of drinking, gambling,
and prostitution, manners were prime. You don't ask
a man's name or business, and you treat all women

like ladies. A breach of this etiquette could cost a man his life, and Smiley and the Boys had begun to cheer up so much that living forever in Miles Town seemed the only wish a man could have.

Smiley tilted back his head and held the glass over his open mouth until the last drop rolled out. Then he rocked back and forth on the back legs of his chair and thought out loud: "I knew the minute we ran into that prairie scum they'd all end up in bad trouble. I just can't understand why we didn't turn right around right at the start and go the other way. I guess I was hungry. I get plumb discouraged when I'm hungry. Still, after we told them about the Double-O drive, they wouldn't of let us go if we wanted to. Oh, that was a bad lot. They sure deserved everything they got."

Howdy was thoughtful. "Hey, Smiley, what about us? What you think we deserve, hm?"

"Don't think I ain't been thinking about that, mister. I been thinking hard. Ever since we began riding alongside the herd and I saw Mr. Andersen way off there in the distance."

"Me, too. I tell you, it was plumb wrong of us to tell them scabby bastards about the Double-O. I know we was still mad at Mr. Andersen, but we didn't have no call to go around talking about his herd like that and telling everybody all he had for hands was little boys."

"Dammit, I know that, Howdy. I knew it the minute I said it. It was my own fault, and I nearly got us all kilt for it."

He filled the glasses all the way around and sat and looked at his. "But I'll tell you what sticks in my craw worse than anything. You know how I stood there and said to Mr. Andersen the whole thing was his fault? I said if he hadn't kicked us out none of all that would of happened. Remember? Well, I was wrong. I was dead wrong. You want to know God's honest truth? We was the ones that started that whole thing. We quit him right smack when he

needed us most. He had every right in the world to
be mad. What gets me is why he didn't up and whip
our asses right there on the spot."

"I bet he could of."

"He should of."

"Hey, wouldn't it of been nice if he'd of said right
there, 'No, you boys forget all this dad-burned gold
business and get on in the stable and get to work,
or I'll tan your hides!' I'd of said yes *sir* and hustled
off to do anything he wanted!"

"Oh, *I* wanted to. You heard me say let's forget it."

"You did, Howdy, you sure did. That's a fact.
Say, you know what I'd like to do? I'd like to get up
from this table right now and saddle up and ride
back to the Double-O and tell Mrs. Andersen it was
our fault what happened. And I'd like to say, 'Ma'am,
because of what we did, we want to work for you
as long as you'll have us and take no pay. Just
food and somewheres to sleep. Sincerely.' "

"Wonder what she'd say."

"Well, I know she wouldn't cry. That's for sure."

"Everybody knows she wouldn't cry, but I wonder what she'd say. You don't spose she'd grab down
the rifle from over the door and run us off the
place, do you?"

"Not her. She wouldn't do a thing like that. But I
sure don't know what she'd say. Maybe just 'No,
thank you, boys.' "

"Hell, let's go and find out. I think the least we
can do is offer. And if she won't have nothing to do
with us, well, we can head on out to Californy."

"You know what? I bet a dollar to a doughnut
she says, 'Wash up, boys. Eats'll be ready soon as
you are!' *Wouldn't that be just fine?*"

"I'd feel like a new man! All right, boys, let's earn
us a few dollars here in Miles Town and head on
back to the Double-O!"

By now they were feeling better than they had in
weeks. They loved everybody.

There was a bunch gathered over at the end of

the bar. They went over to see what the fun was all about.

At the center of the crowd was Dulcy Drew, Big Nose Levitt's biggest drawing card. She was no bigger than a minute, sharp as a needle, and cute as a bug's ear. And she had a quick little tongue that drew howls of laughter when she began jobbing somebody. Dulcy charged more than any gal in Miles Town, but she was mighty choosy. The few she took upstairs each day had to scrub down from top to toe right in front of her and then behave like it was Sunday school. But once they'd paid her a visit, they wouldn't settle for anyone else.

Tonight she was all dressed up, in girlish high spirits, and real skittish about telling why. This made the boys herd around her more than ever to banter guesses back and forth.

"Dulcy, I swear you're acting like a girl that's just about to do something mighty foolish."

"You ain't gonna get married, are you, Dulcy?"

"Me married? Rip Wybow, you know me better'n that! Here's one filly that'd get unbroke all over again if she had to put up with the same man in the saddle all the time!"

"All the same, I bet you're a one-feller filly underneath it all!"

"No feller's gonna get *that* far underneath Dulcy Drew!"

"Look at the way she's laughing! I tell you, boys, some fodder-forker's asked her to marry him!"

"Better a farmer smelling of hay going in the north end than a waddy smelling the way it comes out the south!"

"Now, Dulcy, that ain't fair! They ain't a man in fifteen feet of you right now that didn't wash out the canyon real good 'fore coming here tonight! And on top of that, after he's borrowed on his saddle to go up and sit with you a spell, he's gotta go through the whole thing all over again. I swear, that much soap ain't good for a man, and more'n one of your

admirers has got a chill from being rigged out in
nothing but his birthday suit."

Dulcy laughed and said, "Somebody told you! I bet
it was Nell, wasn't it?"

"Told me what?"

"Oh, you're an awful liar, Jim Pym! She told you
to say something about a birthday suit, didn't she,
hm?"

"I swear she didn't."

"Hey, Dulcy, that why you're all rigged out in
your Sunday best? This your birthday?"

"No, it ain't!"

"You're not such a good liar neither. I bet it is!"

"No, it ain't! I swear!"

"When is your birthday, Dulcy?"

"Yesterday, and I plumb forgot about it!"

When they'd stopped laughing, they all turned to
the bar for drinks to toast her. When somebody
pushed a glass in her hand, she said, "You crazy ga-
loot, you know I don't use tonsil paint!"

"But you got to join in the toast! That's the way
it's done!"

"A person don't drink to herself."

"Sure, a sip. It's like saying thanks."

"Well, all right, if it's manners, but I sure don't
like the taste."

By the time there'd been a dozen boisterous salutes
to her youth and beauty, she began to get alarmed.

"Land sake, you crazy things, you'll have me thinking you right down from the bottom of my glass!
Now, no more, you hear, or I'll have to learn to
walk all over again!"

Big, deep-voiced Omaha Jack said, "One more,
Dulcy, just one more. Now, listen, everybody:

> Here's to the gal named Dulcy Drew,
> Most modest woman I ever knew.
> All dressed up she looks real cute,
> But I druther see her in her birthday suit!"

She laughed with them, then yelled, "Not half so

modest as you, Andy Adams! Boys, you should of seen where he hung his hat the last time I got him to take a bath!"

Andy blushed. "Dulcy, how come I don't notice you jumping in that tub when I come up to pass the time of day?"

"Looks to me like she's more modester than all of us put together."

"That's extra, cowboy! Nobody here's well heeled enough to see Dulcy Drew in her birthday suit!"

"Why, Dulcy, ain't we all your friends?"

"Hey, boys, let's call her hand! Everybody put up a silver dollar!" Silver rang on the bar. "There, now, Dulcy girl, that enough to get us just a peek?"

The dollars kept ringing. She blushed and laughed and said, "Now, you stop it! People'll think I'm the worst thing that ever come to town, letting you carry on like this!"

Omaha said, "You started it, Dulcy! All right, boys, looks like that ain't enough. Everybody put up another dollar."

Dollars rang again on the mahogany bar. Men came over to see what was going on. The more novel the bet, the bigger the crowd. Dulcy kept glancing from the silver pile to the other people in the room. She lowered her voice and spoke in the tense tones of delicious fear.

"Boys, I declare, you're gonna have me run right out of this town, joking like this! Put that money away!"

More dollars rang on the bar and shone in the lamplight. Except for the serious poker players, everybody in the place was gathered around, including Big Nose himself.

Dulcy was trying to act angry, but there was uncontrolled laughter in her voice: "I swear, don't a girl's name mean anything to you boys? Wait'll everybody hears what you tried to make me do! It ain't fair to tease a girl like this! You *know* what a liking I got for silver dollars!"

"Not enough, huh? Well, boys, once more around!"

The money rang. Dew stood on Dulcy's forehead, yet she squared her little shoulders and bravely shook her head. Nobody expected her to do otherwise.

"Well, sir, I never thought I'd live to see the day that Dulcy Drew would back out on her own bet. Looks to me like our favorite little old gal's got cold feet."

Her eyes flashed. One of her hands rolled a dollar around and around on the bar. "You hold on there, old friend. Nobody ever called Dulcy Drew a coward. It ain't that. It's just there's some things a gal don't do. Even if there was twice that much money on the bar!"

"All right, boys, shell out! Twice that says the little lady's scared!"

The money rang out, and Dulcy stared at it in a trembling terror. In the silence somebody whispered, "My *Gawd*!" and Dulcy lashed out: "You needn't swear, Frank Rohner. I may be considering this terrible thing, but you needn't curse right out in front of me!" Several men snarled at Frank until he mumbled, "Dulcy, I'm damn sorry," and she patted his hand absently.

The girl was mighty upset. This was more money than she'd ever seen at one time in her life, and it was hers if she just said the word. As if sympathizing with her deeply, somebody put a glass of whiskey in her hand. She threw it down in one swallow without seeming to taste it. Her trembling subsided. She cleared her throat.

"Boys, I like you. I sure appreciate the compliment. I guess some of you's put down everything he's earned this year. But you gotta realize it's—well, it's one thing to be a whoor and something else again to act like one. And if there's one thing I've always prided myself in, it's behaving myself like I was well brought up."

The deep voice said, "We know that, Dulcy. Ain't

a gal so well behaved in the whole Montana territory. And we wouldn't have you any other way. We ain't aiming to make you look foolish or get you in trouble. But the whole thing is, you started all this, saying what you did, and any man that's a man would just *have* to take you up on it. Any man that ain't put his last dollar on this bar there just ain't no man! And every man that did's ready to take on anybody that says the least thing bad about you. Right, boys?"

An assenting grunt vibrated through the room. Every man was solemn as a judge. The room was quiet as a court.

"So there it is. The money's on the bar, and it's all yours for the taking. If you got the gumption."

"It ain't that, Omaha. You know it ain't."

There was a moment of nonplus, then the tempter played his trump card.

"Dulcy, Big Nose here says there's three hundred and twenty-three good American dollars stacked up there on the bar. Every single one of them says *Dulcy Drew ain't got the nerve.*"

Dulcy looked almost grateful for the challenge. All of her hesitation fell away. Her eyes flashed. Her voice rang.

"I ain't no coward, Omaha, never was, never will be! All right, I'll make a deal with you job-simple saddle-thumpers. Make it an even *four*, and I'll walk right down the middle of the street nekkid as the day I was born! *Now* let's see who's got the nerve! Boys, you can put up or shut up!"

She walked away proudly. There was a stunned silence. Then two more dollars rang on the bar. Men began feeling deep in their pockets. Loans were made. Dulcy stood over across the room talking earnestly to two of the girls. They kept patting her arm sympathetically. It was a cruel challenge, and just exactly the kind of thing a man would think up.

"Boys, we need thirty-one more. Come on, it's the chance of a lifetime. Beautiful little Dulcy Drew walking right down the middle of the street from one end of town to the other—nekkid! That's a boy. We need twenty-seven more. Twenty-five. Keep it coming. Twenty, nineteen. It'll be whole generations before men get a chance like this again! Thirteen more, boys. Don't let's be stingy."

When Dulcy had checked the count, she said, "All right, boys, what are your conditions?"

"Conditions? We're gents, we ain't got none. You just do what you said, and we'll be satisfied."

"That's all you ask?"

"That's all. Who'd want more? Right, boys?"

They all agreed. The atmosphere was dead serious. Long ago the last note of jollity had gone out of it. There was a bet on.

"All right, then. I'll do just exactly what you say, only in my own way at my own time. Any objections?"

There was silence.

"I'll walk down the middle of the street from one end of the town to the other nekkid, *but . . .*"

The crowd grew tense.

"I'll be carrying a six-shooter in each hand, and if I see as much as one hair of the head of a man peeking, I'll shoot his eye out. And I can, too. You know I can."

Out of the silence, deep-voiced Omaha said, "Then how'll we know you done it?"

"That should of been one of your conditions. So as long as it wasn't, you'll just have to take my word for it. Anybody that thinks I'm a liar on top of being afraid can just gather up his money right now."

Nobody moved. He'd have been a dead man.

"Then it's a bet?"

Everybody said a gusty "yes" and "sure" and "aye." Some shrugged and smiled wryly. *They ain't got the vote, but as long as men are men, women got the country.*

33

The crowd in Big Nose Levitt's stayed and stayed
and played and drank and waited all night long.
The news spread, and everybody in the other saloons
stayed at his post and waited for the event to begin.
Everybody but Dulcy glanced over at the stacks of
silver dollars on the bar now and again, and then at
the clock. She went about her business as if it were
just another night. Then around five in the morning
somebody noticed that she was gone. The news
spread like wildfire. A hush came over the place.

All of a sudden Big Nose had a good idea. He
decided to close up and call it a day. He said, "You
boys can stay if you want to, but I'm blowing out
the lights and getting to bed."

The serious poker players complained bitterly as
he went around puffing out the lights, but he assured
them all he needed was a short little nap and he'd
open up again in no more than half an hour, on his
range word. He sent word to the other saloons to this
effect. They agreed that a bit of rest was called for,
and began puffing out their lamps, too.

Big Nose still had a half a dozen lamps to go when
the swinging doors swung and this young kid walked
in. He was maybe fifteen, dark, and as good-looking
as they come, but everybody looked on him as wholly
irrelevant. And he looked at them as if they'd done
something. He walked around peering hard at each
face as the lights went down. Pretty soon he was almost touching noses with everybody, and getting
pretty tart reactions.

When the last lamp went out, Smiley and the Boys got up one at a time and walked casually out the back door. All three were appalled. Smiley was trembling. The sight of Cimarron had brought the bright world crashing down about their heads.

The boy sensed the movement toward the back door but took no real notice until the third man had left. He followed immediately and found himself in the darkest part of the night. Dulcy had picked her time shrewdly.

Cimarron stood very still. The whole city seemed dead—or holding its breath. Then he heard rather than felt a movement between the buildings up the street. As he started in that direction, he bumped into somebody that whispered, "Sorry, partner," then into somebody else that growled, "Watch where you're going!" The night was filled with quiet men who stood or crept in every shadow. The boy peered up at each of them and went his way.

Dulcy dropped her wrapper and stood gorgeously bare in the middle of the street at the far end of town. It seemed a miracle that a little tiny thing so feminine could even lift a pair of big old forty-fives. But she did, and in a way that showed practice.

Before taking her first step, she looked around at the utterly dead town and was satisfied that she was the focus of almost universal attention. She was not angry. Big Nose had asked her if it was all right to close up, and she'd assented generously. Nor was she overly pleased that the night was so dark nothing but a cat could see twenty-five feet away. It was true she was ready for anything on two feet or four, but utterly unwilling to fire. That would give the whole shooting works away.

Dulcy had worded her conditions with considerable care: she was determined to retain her respectability and also satisfy the boys for putting up all that money. She said she'd shoot any man that she *caught* peeking. And anyway, she had no intention of waking up the respectable minority to what was going on. What she'd do was just put one foot in front of the other and keep her eyes on the ground for ruts. And pray God no drunk old fool forced her attention on him.

Yet even with her eyes glued to the ground she was aware of many things going on. The shadows were alive, and there were movements behind the buildings as if a tiptoeing crowd were following her down the street from shadow to shadow.

And worst was the short figure of a boy that crossed the street way down ahead, then crossed again, closer. Each time she raised her guns to threaten him, but neither time did he so much as give her a glance.

From what she could see with her head demurely lowered, he was pretty as he could be, sturdily built, and looking for somebody. He went boldly into every shadow, stirred up a whispered fuss, and passed on to the next. He crossed in front and behind her and a couple of times walked along with her some feet away—yet never once paid her the slightest attention.

Dulcy Drew, for the first time in her professional life, began to blush.

When he walked into Big Annie's, voices slapped out at him from the dark.

"What's got into you, boy, You want to get yourself all shot up?"

"I look for somebody."

"But Dulcy's gonna shoot the first man she catches peeking."

"I do not peek. I got nothing in this bet."

"She don't care. She's gonna shoot anybody she sees."

"I make no bet with no whore."

"Watch who you call that, boy."

"That is not no preacher's wife out there!"

"But she don't know you *didn't* bet."

"If she don't by now, she is not so very bright. I

think she know if she shoot at me, I shoot right back."

By then he'd stuck his face into everybody else's, found nothing, and left.

By now Dulcy's only concern was her good name, and that dadratted boy was trying his best to spoil the whole thing. It was getting to the point where she'd have to be deaf, dumb, and blind not to notice him, yet she just couldn't lift her guns and begin shooting up the town.

It was a choice between letting all the boys in the shadows know she knew and losing their respect, and standing up for her conditions and letting the whole territory know.

Dulcy moved straight ahead like a penitent sleepwalker, utterly undecided on which was the lesser of the evils. The guns weighed a thousand pounds.

Had the boy simply looked right at her, everything would have been fine. She'd have shot him, to unanimous applause, and sprinted down to where Nellie waited with her wrapper. She'd staunchly deny having been that pink blur in the night, attend the funeral, and invest her silver dollars in something safe like a millinery shop with a couple bedrooms upstairs. But that handsome little devil wouldn't look! Not one single, tiny peek!

Smiley and the Boys didn't peek either. They spent their time keeping out of the bean-eater's way. They'd never have thought of shooting it out with him, not a fifteen-year-old boy. Nor did it occur to them to split up and each go his separate way. They moved from building to building, shadow to shadow, arguing in whispers about where they should go next and what they should do.

Their horses were clear down at the other end of town, outside Big Nose Levitt's. Yet even mounted they had nowhere to go now that they knew they were followed. Surely not back to the Double-O. You don't lead the Devil home. You try to get him off the track. But it wasn't possible. It was terrifying how the

boy kept on coming without actually seeing them.
He seemed to sense where they were. Each time
they thought they'd found a good place, here he
came stalking as sure as death. The Devil sees best
in the dark, and the dark was closing in on them.

Instead of going for their horses, they ducked
into a big stable set back from the street. It was
pitch black and silent. A few minutes later the boy
came in by the other door. He stood looking around
until his eyes got accustomed to the dark. Then he
began peering into each stall.

Cimarron saw them at last and walked over to
where they cowered in the hay. They stared up at
him, and he looked down at them.

Then the boy drew his guns and fired again and
again and again.

When the stable was still, he walked out. Avoiding
the silly game still going on in the street, he found
his horse and swung up into the saddle.

Cimarron sat thinking a moment, then pulled his
hat down snug, and started home to Texas. He'd
fulfilled his obligation.

34

The entrance of the herd down the main street of
Belle Fourche was something few would forget. At
first the good citizens were riled that these cowmen
hadn't taken the usual route outside of town to get
to the cow pens. Then they saw the brand and all
these strange young faces. Godamighty, they were
hardly more than boys! And they rode almost solemnly.
The tall, auburn-haired boy riding Wil Andersen's Sad

Sarah looked like he was coming home from Appo-
mattox.

Slim wasn't worried about selling the herd. Knowing
he didn't know a damned thing about it was a start.
He went from there into John Tingle's office and told
the quietly stunned man about everything from Miss
Fanny Zook's schoolhouse down to the prairie fire
they almost ran into yesterday.

John Tingle was an imposing man in his tie, shirt,
and vest, and the heavy gold watch chain looping
from left to right. You had to look that way to get
business off on the proper foot. The man sitting across
the room in the visitor's chair had to feel at a slight
disadvantage. Today John Tingle forgot to smoke his
cigar, and from the boy's manner, he himself felt the
disadvantage. The youngster had the serene air of a
man who's done his job, and God help you if you
tried to mess it up.

Tingle never took his eyes off the boy, and the boy
never took his eyes off the man.

When the story was told, John Tingle slid open a
drawer. "You may be fifteen by the book, but let's
start off our business like two men, because that is
what we are."

He poured them each a shot of whiskey. Slim drank
his down like Mr. Tingle did and sat back to feel it
burn. Mr. Tingle belched a fine, deep, rumbling belch
and wrote out a draft on the Bozeman National Bank
for thirty-six thousand dollars, twice the going price.
He pushed it toward the boy, who didn't move. The
burning had spread all through Slim Honeycutt, and
he felt gravely grand.

"Ain't you gonna look at them?"

"If they're Wil Andersen's, no. My boys took a
count, and that's enough for me."

"What's the paper?"

"It's a draft."

"Only draft I ever heard of had to do with a chill."

The man took a chaw of Climax and replied in the
same vein, "I take it this draft leaves you cold."

"Mr. Tingle, I don't know nothing about you except what I see. I like what I see, but then, I liked Smiley and the Boys, too. So after all that work and worry, I just can't see going back to Mrs. Andersen with only that little old slip of paper."

"Well, Judas Priest, boy, you're not going to carry thirty-six thousand dollars in silver four hundred miles back across the most lawless country in the West!"

"Mr. Tingle, we *got* here."

The man chewed and looked at him and finally made a small hopeless gesture.

The boy said, "And there's something else."

The man slapped the desk top with the flats of both hands and said, "What?"

"Bull Durham's not for sale. He led all the way here, and we decided to take him back home."

The man shrugged.

Black Charlie drove around to the back door of the bank and helped them carry the sacks to the wagon. They put them in the big wooden box that the guns had been in, put flour and cornmeal and beans in on top, and everybody wrote receipts for fifty dollars and put them in, too. Then Hardy Fimps collected all his gambling debts.

The boys had grown. They'd hardly be recognized when they got home. So, like all hands, the first thing they bought was clothes. It was gratifying to hear the clerk say, "Well, young men, and what can I do for you?" and to see what the mirror answered when they stood before it.

Next they began filling their war bags with gewgaws and necessities for their families. They remembered the girls and women first. The fathers were a little harder to buy something for, and the only thing they could think of for the younger boys was a drive of their own when they got between hay and grass, and the juices of manhood began seeping into every little crevice of the boy.

Belle Fourche was not unaware of them. Eyes widened when word got around about how much money was in that wagon that two younkers guarded all the time. John Tingle heard the talk and began reciting the story of the seventeen dead rustlers and how they got that way. If there'd been plans, they were temporarily set aside. When witnesses came in describing all the bodies along the trail, the deferment was made permanent. All the stern vigilance on the way home wasn't necessary. Nobody came within miles of them.

In the last cold winds of autumn, the boys rode gravely and talked little except around the fire. The hundred horses grazed in the oncoming night, their manes antic in the wind. Bull Durham kept to himself, a leader now of nothing. Now and again the Old Woman heard them all swept up in some little boyish gust of foolishness. But it soon passed, and they were quiet again. "All of which prove," Black Charlie murmured to himself, "that still water ain't necessarily deep."

Bathing in the river, they again compared the jewelry of their groins and that peculiarly male thing, their hair: how dark in the crotch, how thick on the chest, how bristly on the chin.

The Old Woman looked at them and wondered: *Don't none of you realize what happen this summer? I don't see it in your eyes. You's still just boys adventuring. How long will it take to hit each one of you and leave you staring at the dark?*

When they came to where the graves should be, nobody could find them. None of the sightings was any use, and they stared at the ground wondering, *Charlie Schwartz, are you there—or there—or there?* and crying silently, *Mr. Andersen, give us a sign!* They spent most of one day crossing and recrossing the square mile where they knew the sleepers had to be. But not a trace. They rode on, incredulous.

*   *   *

The smoke of the October fire went straight up into the cold evening air. Four Eyes asked a question that had been bothering everybody. "Hey, somebody's gotta tell Mrs. Andersen. Who's it gonna be?"

No one answered. No one guessed. Not until the words were spoken back at the Double-O would any of them realize which of them it had to be. But most of them felt that if Wil Andersen were here, he'd say, "There's nothing much to say to Annie that ain't already clear. She knew, or she wouldn't of said come back."

Singing Fats smiled suddenly and surprised everybody by saying, "I can just see him right now saying to Charlie Schwartz, 'There's one good thing to be said for all this. Now I won't have to face that mother of yours.' "

Then, because ghosts are as natural to the prairie as wind, they saw the two as clear as day.

Being as how no cowman would go footermans to heaven or to hell, the man and boy swung up on strange horses, and rode off together without dust or sound or looking back.

The Old Woman placidly served up a nice dessert of hound-ears and whirlups. Tonight he added dried fruit to the syrup, and a secret combination of spices to the grease-fried sourdough. The boys ate as if supper had been last year.

But when they'd finished and lolled around the fire, the silence came again. Here and there a boy glanced up at the darkness as if he were expecting somebody. Four Eyes plucked his guitar earnestly, but nobody listened. There were too many sounds *out there*.

Suddenly Stuttering Bob burst out, "But what are we going to say to them about coming home *alone*!"

There was a long silence; then the Old Woman offered this suggestion: "Say? Ain't nothing to say, and the less said the better. All that happen was we all got ourselfs swept up in life. Me as much as anybody. Maybe more, because I kep' you fed."

Four Eyes' fingers came to a certain phrase and stopped. He frowned down at the strings as if one of them had broken and said, "He never did teach me the end of that song."

One by one they looked up at him, and the first cold wind of winter tore at the fire.

A Word About Time

Like the zenith of ancient Greece, the golden years of the American West lasted less than a generation and then were gone. Yet in those few years much happened, and great names were made that seldom connote a cattle drive.

While Lincoln, Grant, and Hayes were President, Victoria reigned as queen, and Disraeli and Gladstone played leapfrog with the office of prime minister. While the Texas Trail became packed with steers, and Czar Alexander freed the Russian slaves a shade too late, Mexico found itself with a European emperor briefly, and Bismarck prepared to become chancellor of the German empire. As Montana territory filled with fattening cattle, the telegraph became a platitude. It was the coming of the telephone that momentarily took the breath away. Emile Zola and Charles Dickens wrote copiously. Lewis Carroll and Mark Twain were more entertaining. It was the thunder of Brahms, Liszt, and Wagner that drew more rapt attention.

Even a brief list of contemporary events looks a little strange viewed in relation to beef, brands, and broncs:

1858 Juarez in Mexico and the first National Association of Baseball Players in the United States

1861–63 Russian serfs and U.S. slaves freed; Winslow Homer becomes a war correspondent for *Harper's Weekly*

1862 "Battle Hymn of the Republic" and invention of machine gun

1863 Red Cross founded, and French take over Cambodia

1864 Montana territory organized, and Karl Marx founds first Communist International

1865 Publication of *Alice in Wonderland, Hans Brinker,* and *The Celebrated Jumping Frog*

1869 Opening of Suez Canal and U.S. transcontinental railway

1871   The Franco-Prussian war, Chicago fire, first football game, and Whistler paints his mother

1876   Custer's death, *Tom Sawyer*, and invention of telephone

1877   Nez Percé defeated, *Anna Karenina*, and Queen Victoria becomes Empress of India

1878   Invention of phonograph, and manufacture of first U.S. bicycle

1879   Invention of electric light, *Doll's House*, and beginning of Panama Canal

1880   There is a gold strike in Alaska, and Stanley explores the Congo

1881   Pasteur tackles anthrax, and *Leaves of Grass* is banned in Boston

1882   Wagner's *Parsifal*, banning of Chinese labor, and John L. Sullivan is world heavyweight champion

1883   *Treasure Island*, and first steel vessels in Navy

1886   Geronimo captured, and Electoral Count Act passed

1890   United States agrees to suppress African slave trade, census shows sixty-two million, and Census Bureau announces end of Western frontier

A Western Glossary

These definitions of words used in the story have been culled from years of reading—especially those books listed in the Bibliography. Yet many come from memory, although I was born a few years after the heyday of the West; even today, the most cosmopolitan city-dweller still uses range words and expressions. For a full listing of them, go to the unique Ramon F. Adams, whose *Western Words* (University of Oklahoma Press) will be both valuable and enjoyable to lovers of language. Because he is actually unique, you'll find yourself consulting him more than any other source.

Yet even this excellent book is at times incomplete, at variance with others, and tantalizingly reticent. However much real westerners may deplore the cowman's image as manufactured by literary dudes, they themselves have been traditionally guilty of whitewashing that image.

As far back as the 1870's, it was inexcusable for the cowman to use the term "bull" in front of a woman. All women were "ladies" and all bulls were "animals" in polite conversation, and I'm told that quite recently in Nevada the male was called "Mr. Cow." Even Mr. Adams' excellent dictionary does not include a term as generally used and noncommittal as "bunky" for "bedmate"—although it bravely mentions "split a blanket" for "sharing a bed." Most of the western terms that have come down to us are euphemisms. It is tantalizing to think of how many instances of such ridiculous subterfuge have been lost to us because of an almost imbecilic sense of propriety in the West.

Because omissions are always more intriguing than candid confessions, the western buff is impelled to wonder why the West's literature seldom if ever mentions relief from tension in a situation where normal outlets were unavailable most of the time. Most old authorities make not the slightest mention of variation on the range. They do not even record slang words for it that might have been used in joking among men who had an unlimited capacity for kidding. It seems unwarranted to assume that no such thing existed. Men do not cease to be men

simply because there are no women around. Yet western his-
torians and Hollywood would have us believe that erectile
tissue was completely missing in the metabolism of the West.

The writer complains only for the loss of fascinating fact.
There was a time when no book about the hallowed West
would include an incident like the one happening here to
Miss Dulcy Drew. But it did happen, and survives only because it is part of the *spoken* history of the West, and printed
perhaps just once before.

But to regret the loss of other such delicious moments is to
burn daylight. We'd do better to get where the horses are and
listen for all we're worth. The old-timers have much to say
and are glad to say it—if we'll give the smallest sign. We must
not let them go silently into history.

—W.D.J.
1971

Alder Gulch	Site of one of the biggest gold strikes in history; June 1862 saw the start of a hundred-million-dollar bonanza.
Ankle Express	Other than a hearse, the least palatable means of transportation on the range—the feet.
Anxious Seat	A place as close to the front as possible at a revival meeting.
Appaloosa	A breed of horse credited to the Nez Percé Indians in the Pelouse River Country; he has a scant tail, spotted rump, much white in the eye—and a certain greatness.
Arbuckle	Perhaps *the* brand of coffee in the West; used here a shade anachronistically.
Ate Grass	One of thirty-one terms that Ramon Adams lists for being thrown from a horse.
Baaaaal	The cowman's way of dismissing the whole subject of sheep or somebody he'd just as soon start a fight with.
Back Arched	Ready to fight.
Bad Medicine	Bad thinking, advice, news, or men.
Bake a Horse	To overheat a mount.

Bar Dog	A bartender.
Bean-eater	A Mexican.
Bear Signs	What we in Colorado called "sinkers," a word the cowman used for doughnuts.
Belle Fourche	A little town in what is now South Dakota, the farthest west that the railway had come in the 1870's.
Belly Cheater	An epithet for "cook," and usually unjust; Adams' comments on the high quality of cooks and cooking on the range make very good sense.
Between Hay and Grass	Neither man nor boy.
Bible	The little folder of cigarette tissues.
Blow Out His Lamp	To kill him.
Bone Orchard	A cemetery.
Borrowing on His Saddle	The ultimate in western bankruptcy; doing work that depended wholly on his saddle, to borrow on it was to put the cowman's livelihood in doubt, and *to sell your saddle* was the end of everything.
Breaking Patter	The sweet nothings that horse breakers murmur to beguile the horse while saddling and mounting; while dulcet as a wind from the south, the actual sentiments expressed during this patter are enough to curl the horse's mane.
Brockled	A splotched hide of varying colors; similar to "brindle," usually describing a cow.
Broomtail	An unbroken range horse with a full, long tail; when broken in the Northwest, its tail was pulled or shortened to distinguish it from the unbroken horses, and called a "shavetail." Second lieutenants, please note.
Buffalo Skinners	Hide-hunters, according to Theodore Roosevelt, comprised a distinct class that was on the lowest rungs of the range's social ladder; rough, tough, and filthy, many drifted into criminal occupations.
Bug Juice	Hard liquor.

Bunkie, or Bunky	Bedmate; possibly related to "bunky," a horse that pitches, though which came first is a question.
Burning Daylight	Wasting time.
Burning Shucks	To leave in a hurry; from burning a corn shuck to see by, when going off into the night on urgent business.
Bushwhacked	Shot from ambush.
Calf Roundup	The spring roundup, when the calves born during the winter were branded.
California Vest	Like other California-style clothes, it was of durable wool, roomy in the pockets, and neutral brown; leather edging on the pockets was preferred.
Cavvy	The saddle band of horses not in use; when each man had between six and eight or more horses on his own string, the saddle band got pretty big at times; "cavvy" is a typical distortion of the Spanish *caballada*, like a host of other gringo mispronunciations of Spanish, such as lariat, hoosegow, hackamore, cinch, wrangler.
Charlie	Such a frequent name in the Old West that qualifying nicknames to go with it appear to be required.
Chew It Fine	From "chew it over," or "think it over," and, in this case, think it over thoroughly; also means to explain at greater length or put in simpler terms.
Chouse	To stir up the cattle unnecessarily with rough handling or loud noise.
Chuck Box	This was bolted to the back end of the wagon facing south and consisted of perhaps a dozen drawers for foods and necessaries pertaining to food; there was a door or flap covering it that was hinged at the bottom and opened down into a table with a single leg, on which Cookie performed the mysteries of his art; a yard square, it was the seat of his government, not to be trespassed.

Chuckle-headed	Once meant "contrary," or "slow to understand," but now suggests plain, unadorned "dumbness."
Cimarron	A Mexican term for an animal that runs alone or a man who is wanted; in combining the sense of being both wild and solitary, it is one of the beautiful words in the language.
Cinch	Goes way back; we still use the word frequently, although few know what the darned thing is; a cinch is that woven or canvas band which goes under the horse's stomach and attaches to the saddle on either side; it holds the saddle on the horse and must be constantly attended to: unloosed to rest the horse while standing, and tightened upon starting up again; so when we say, "That cinched it," or "That's a cinch," our meaning is quite clear, even to somebody who has never come closer to a horse than a John Wayne movie.
Cinch Up	Let's get going.
Coffin Varnish	Whiskey, of course, and the wryness of the term "hard liquor" suggests that it also came in off the range to embellish our slang.
Coosie	See "Cradle."
Cowpuncher, or Cowpoke	A term of derision coming from the lowly job of poking or punching the cows through the chutes to get them into the boxcars for shipment; hard-bitten cowmen shunned any such work that required dismounting.
Cradle	A rawhide sling or hammock under the chuckwagon that was never used for a siesta because it was either full of firewood or being filled. Ramon Adams has it coming from *cocinero* and boiled down to "coosie," while Andy Adams shortens it further to "cusi," both of which suggest that there's more to the term than meets the eye.
Critter	Any bovine.

Croon

The soft, reassuringly monotonous way that cowhands sang to the cattle at night; it had to be in lullaby sadness or the blues—however shocking the libretto. Don't take the *American College Dictionary* too seriously on this one.

Cut the Deck Deeper

Comes from gambling (like a multitude of other western terms) and means "explain further," with a suggestion that something was wrong with the first explanation.

Cut His Picket Pin

Derived from the pin itself which the rider pounded into the ground with his heel and staked his night horse to; he carried it with him as part of his equipment, or simply knotted the end of the reins, buried it, and stomped down the earth; it held the horse more by the brain than anything else, but worked, more often than not; so when you cut your picket pin, you up and leave, usually for parts unknown.

Cutting the Dust

As even Aunt Mary knows, is the pleasant act of wetting one's whistle.

Desperado Flag

Although explained in the story, this had a background that deserves your digging. Simply a red sash, it was kept in the war bag of the old-time cowman for those times when he wanted to show the flamboyance that threatens violence and promises brave deeds.

Drag

Was the position at the rear of the drive, where the poor rider covered his mouth and nose with his bandanna like a bandit and squinted through dust for strays; in dry spells, everyone took turns at this miserable position.

The Dreamers

Were the followers of a hunchbacked priest of the Nez Percé tribe named Smohalla; he demanded that his people resist the "progress" of the white man and return to the Old Ways, which were based on a reverence for the earth; it was utopian, and he and his followers

were called Dreamers by the whites, as
if it were some secret religious plot to
overthrow the government; the moving
story is given fully in *The Nez Percé
Indians*, by Alvin M. Josephy, Jr.

Druthers
: Seems to mean "preference," as if it
were a country mispronunciation of "I'd
rather" into "I'd ruther."

Dusted
: Another term for being thrown from a
horse.

Dutch Oven
: Ramon Adams describes it as a three-
legged skillet that squatted low over the
fire, with a heavy lid.

Featherhead
: Indicates the lightness of the contents of
the subject's cranium.

Fimps
: Suggests the melting pot that was the
West; German, of course, it is a gambling
term, this time dice, but a little puzzling,
as it describes ten as two fives.

Firehole
: The more important of two campfires
was built in a hole to facilitate cooking
over it; the other fire that the men sat
around at night was larger and on the
surface of the ground.

Fish
: Came from the picture on the trademark
of the most popular slicker in the West;
this yellow oilskin lifesaver was carried
in the saddle roll at all times and put
to a variety of uses other than shelter
from the wet.

Five Beans in the Wheel
: Was simply five bullets in the chamber,
which accommodated six; one was left
empty to give the firing pin a safe place
to rest between shootings; only fools and
very desperate desperadoes rested their
pins on a live cartridge in order to have
an extra shot in an emergency; doing so,
they risked shooting themselves, their
horses, and anybody else around when
they accidentally jarred their six-guns.

Flank
: One of the side positions in a drive. See
"Positions in Drive," below.

Flapboard
: See "Chuck Box."

Flaps

Were the leather loincloths worn by warriors "stripped for action," and consisted of a flap in back and front that was pouched between; more for decoration than modesty; it could be dispensed with to show utter derision for the enemy; the original "g-string" (another western term) was not primarily utilitarian; today's male is advertised as requiring "much-needed support," yet Indians, cowmen, and bronc busters had no equivalent of the athletic supporter.

Flying Mount

A spontaneous shortcut in a crisis or showing off in which the rider swung himself up into the saddle without touching the stirrups. Also called "pony-express mount."

Fodder Forker

A farmer.

Footermans

Was one of the most western terms in the West: to go afoot.

Frothy

Another self-descriptive term for anger.

Frying Size

Meaning either short or young, and one more incentive for the boy to grow up fast or compensate; unlike today, boyishness and childishness were states to get out of at the earliest, so that the individual could make his own decisions and "be his own man," a viewpoint almost unheard of today.

Ganted

Was probably related to "gaunt," meaning thin, and, by connotation, poor; many of the new pronunciations of old words came especially from the southern cowman, who had a language all his own and a viewpoint not to be influenced by anything like books.

Gather

The cattle or horses rounded up.

Getting Up the Horses

Rounding up the saddle horses from "out yonder," preparatory to the critter roundup.

Gimlet-ended

Usually a man with small hips, but this wasn't necessarily a compliment; to gimlet your horse was to ride him so that he got a sore back; however, this range comparison of a shaft for boring holes with a man's rump seems to leave something unsaid; the cowman was usually more precise and apt.

Godown	A dip in a river bank where cattle could go in and out of the stream conveniently.
Goose-drowner	One of those joys of western speech, it suggests our "cloudburst."
Grassed	To be thrown from a horse.
Greaser	A Mexican.
Greasy Sack	In the absence of a chuck wagon, the cowman carried his food in a cotton bag; this could be in an emergency or customarily because the outfit was too poor to afford a chuck wagon; a "greasy-sack outfit" was your last resort; good cowmen would have nothing to do with them.
Greener	Greenhorn.
Guest Food	In the early days, and later among families of only moderate income, the guest customarily brought something as his contribution to the eats; if not previously decided upon between guest and hostess, the visitor played it safe—as we do—and brought something sweet or liquid.
Gunny	A gunslinger or hired killer who sometimes wore a burlap sack for a mask, with holes for eyes, hence "gunny sack," a disguise used extensively during the trouble between cattlemen and sheepmen. This explanation, however, suggests an ignorance of Hindustani in our Western scholars.
Gun Shark	A man skilled in the use of a shooting iron.
Hay Shaker	A farmer.
Haywire	When the wire was taken off bales of hay, it was all twisted up into a ball so you wouldn't be stumbling all over it; the image is perfect for a situation that's

	all fouled up; the term is used a bit anachronistically here.
Haze	Adams says "to drive cattle slowly," yet other sources say it refers only to horses; and Buzz Henry declares the term isn't favored in either sense.
Hazer	The bronc buster's assistant.
Hear the Owl Hoot	To live an eventful life; to get royally drunk.
Heated Up	In reference to "baking" a horse; and of course, to become angry.
Hen Wrangler	Another name for a farmer.
Hollow Horn	When cattle got rundown, the condition was often diagnosed as due to hollow horns.
Honky Tonk	One of those palaces of pleasure at the end of the drive where the cowman sought the society of bar dogs, card sharks, and the sisterhood.
Honyock	A homesteader, farmer; later it came to mean a green youngster—male; I don't remember anyone ever referring to a girl as a honyock; sometimes spelled "hon yocker," this calls for further research.
Hook	The verb describes an unfriendly tendency of the cow to impale enemies on its horns.
Hotfoot	Originally the burning of a calf's feet by rustlers so that it couldn't join its mother and slow down the flight.
Hungrier Than a Woodpecker with a Headache	Comes from Ramon Adams, too. It was too good to let lie sleeping in a dictionary.
Hunker	A squatting on the heels; the dismounted cowman can maintain this position for hours.
Individual Horse	A cowman's personal horse; oddly enough, all cowmen didn't have their own horses, although everyone had a saddle.
Irons in the Fire	Reference to branding, with many outfits participating.

Jamboree	A joyously wild event, like a drinking party, a dance, shoot-out, or even a stampede, depending on how it all turned out; because the job of cow nurse was actually quite monotonous and required infinite grit and patience, the cowman welcomed excitement; as a memorable character remarked when his drive was lost in a storm, "I can't help the weather, boys. And as long as I have chuck, I'd as soon be lost as found." (Andy Adams' classic, *Log of a Cowboy*.)
Jamming the Breeze	Riding at full speed.
Jewelry Chest	A box on the outside of the chuck wagon containing all those gewgaws that might be needed in an emergency—latigos, cartridges, pickets, hobbles, and so on.
Jiggle	The normal gait of a horse, about five miles an hour.
Jingle Your Spurs	A better way of demanding speed than Teddy Roosevelt's famous, "Hasten forward quickly there!" which almost got him laughed out of the Dakotas.
Jobbing	Joshing, joking, kidding; Andy Adams makes it "codding," as the Old English did.
Job-simple	A logging term that got into the West; a man afraid of losing his job, or someone just plain stupid.
Jockey Box	The oblong box under the chuck wagon driver's seat; Cookie might keep in it a variety of things from his Sharps to a selection of small rocks to pelt his mules into greater effort.
Keno!	A happy exclamation from an Old English gambling game called lotto; means "I've won!" or "Everything's fine and dandy!"
Kitchen String	What Cookie threw the small rocks out of the jockey box at.
Knot and Dip Bandanna	A bit of western redundance, because the Hindu word for knotting and dipping is

bandhnu; this type of dyeing was replaced by white floral designs against a dark background when commercially manufactured and sold in vast quantities in the West, where it became a necessity rather than decoration; the list of uses the bandanna was put to is almost ludicrously long: one of them accounts for the fact that they almost always came in only two colors, red and blue. Tied around a man's arm, it indicated whether he was dancing the man's or woman's part at a party short on women.

Live on Jawbone	To live on credit.
Monkey Ward Wife Sent on Approval	A long way of saying homely; it refers to something ordered from the Montgomery Ward catalog and kept whether you liked it or not.
Montana Bedroll	Larger and thicker than those used in the southern states.
Moonlight, or a Falling Star	On good authority, we are assured that such minor things as these actually did start serious stampedes.
Mustard	To stir up or get the cattle excited.
Near Side	The left side, on which the white man mounted; the Indian side was the right side; not to be confused with *near* side as opposed to *far* side, which Wil complains about in the first chapter.
Nester	The early squatters could not afford to build fences as protection against the cattle, so they piled up brush around their ramshackle houses; it looked like an immense bird's nest and earned the despised occupants the name; from the number of insults built around the occupation of farmer, we might incorrectly conclude that the cowman was blindly prejudiced; this was not wholly the case; the coming of the farmer began the decline of the West—and the cattlemen knew it.
Nigger Horse	A black horse; dictionaries incorrectly call the term offensive without reference to its use.

Night Blind	After staring at the fire for some time, the blackness beyond is impenetrable. See the fascinating corollary under "Burning Shucks."
Night Hawk	The man taking care of the saddle band at night. Sometimes he was spelled by others, like the night guard, and at others he was also the day wrangler and never slept long at a time.
Night Horse	One especially good at finding his way in the dark.
On Tick	On credit.
Opera Seat, or Opera House	The top rail of the corral where everybody sat to watch the show and comment, or just talk.
Pepper Gut	A Mexican.
Picket Pin	See "Cut His Picket Pin."
Point the Herd	Aim the herd in a certain direction.
Positions in Drive	*The Pilot* went ahead of the herd and picked out where to skirt hills or cross a river, and where to bed down the cattle for the night; he knew the country. *The Point Positions* were just slightly behind the first cattle, because you don't lead a cow, you nudge it; it took two good men that knew their job. *The Swing* was a third of the way down the march on either side; like the other positions, consisted of one or more men according to the size of the herd. *The Flank* was where the flank should be, between the belly and the hip of the herd, or about two-thirds of the way back. *Drag* brought up the dusty rear.
Prairie Oyster	Bull's balls that were eaten fried or roasted, making an excellent meal.
Pulling Leather	Holding on to the horn to stay on a bucking horse.
Pulling Tails	Shortening the horse's tail by pulling until it only reached the hocks.
Quirt	A short whip with a long handle.

Rancid Old Parallelogram	Comes from Ramon Adams in the great introduction to his *Western Words*.
Range Word	A cowman's solemn word of honor.
Remuda	The saddle band, those horses not being used at the time; from the Spanish *remonta*, or "replacement"; generally used in the South, while *cavvy* was preferred in the North; but "saddle band" seems to be preferred over both.
Rep	The representative sent from another outfit to cut its stock out of the roundup; he was highly respected and trusted.
Riata	Spanish for "rope," from which the gringo cowman got "lariat"; incidentally, while *gringo* is given as Spanish for "gibberish," most dictionaries neglect to indicate it as offensive.
Rim Rocker	A horse that will go as far as necessary, is sturdy, tireless; the territory to be covered in a roundup was indicated by the rocks or other landmarks on the far rim of the horizon.
Rope	Is the northern term; only much later did the Montana cowman use "lariat," and by then the West was declining.
Rope Corral	The line of rope drawn around the saddle band so that the hands can pick their first mount of the day; frisky as they are and unwilling to be picked, the horses stay inside the rope more often than not.
Rowels	The wheel of a spur; the more the points, the less it hurts the horse; the fewer points, the more. The meanest had only four points.
Runt	Said of a cow or calf when it is small and puny.
Saddle Band	Those horses that are not being used at the moment on a drive; consists of each man's string of six to a dozen head; each man changes horses twice a day at the very least; in various emergencies, more.

Saddle Bums

Drifters or unemployed cowhands who ride from ranch to ranch to get free eats; they *rode the grub line* and were seldom refused in the early West, just as there were seldom locks on the doors; if nobody was home, you went right on in and ate what you needed; this survival hospitality didn't last long with the expanding western population, and the Yale people began to make a mint.

Scattering the Riders

Sending men out to assigned sections in a roundup; the range boss sent them in pairs to complement one another.

Scratching

To move the feet in a kicking motion, or to rake the bronc's ribs with your heels in rodeo competition.

Sharps

The "Old Reliable" rifle of the West, either .45-120 or .50-130 and weighing eighteen to twenty pounds.

Shavetail

See "Broomtail."

Shebang

A way station; to a miner, any structure.

Shed

To get rid of.

Sodbuster

A farmer.

Soogans

Blankets. It could also be spelled sougans, sugans, soogins, or suggans; actually, it's one of those good words that shouldn't have a "correct" spelling; but however variously spelled, they were all heavy, averaging four pounds, usually patchwork, and very serviceable.

Spik

A Mexican.

Split the Blankets

To share your soogans with a bunkie.

Steer

A castrated bull.

Stetson

A part of the West that transcends commercialism, just like Levi's, the Colt, Arbuckle coffee, and Justins, the boots that symbolize the West. Ramon Adams' tribute to the Stetson is one of the longest sections of his impartial dictionary and reads wonderfully.

String

A small bunch of horses assigned to each man and numbering between six and a dozen; among them he had a good cutting horse, a night horse, a rim rocker, a circle horse, a roping horse, one that swam well, and a couple broncs that were learning cow work. Once chosen or given to him, the string was his as long as he stayed with the outfit; not even the boss touched his string without permission.

Sucamagrowl   A sweet pudding or pie.

Summer Name   Nobody asked into anybody else's business in the West; you didn't even ask a man his name; he told it to you, and if it happened to be George Washington, you called him George Washington. Some men had something to hide or just didn't feel their private affairs—however honest—were anybody's business but their own. So they almost welcomed random, quixotic nicknames, even if they were, by our standards, insulting; for instance, a white man named Nigger Levitt who ran a Montana saloon. Because there was little work in the winter, a man had a summer name that might change from year to year—even if everybody remembered last year's and found it hard to get used to the new one. This was the last great flaring up of human individuality just before it died, possibly to be heard of no more.

Sunned his Moccasins   To get thrown from a horse.

Tick (On Tick)   Credit.

Tonsil Paint   Hard liquor, namely whiskey, also commonly known as stagger soup, conversation fluid, and scamper juice. It may or may not be significant that there were at least sixty-five such synonyms for wet goods in the West.

Vivaldi   Of course, it doesn't belong here, but the "prettiest little old song you ever heard" (p. 79) is the theme of the second movement of Vivaldi's Concerto in D

THE COWBOYS

239

Major for guitar and orchestra. It puts the West into melody like no Yankee ever could or will.

Waddy

The name for a cowhand who fills in around the ranch, just as wadding fills in an empty space; apparently later used to include just about everybody but the boss.

Wagon Manners

Good behavior, because the cook would allow nothing else; a desirable woman exacts the same punctiliousness.

War Bag

A sack for personal belongings containing those particular gewgaws that each man feels are necessary to his well-being; Adams mentions a variety of possibilities from bible to Bible, but does not mention shaving things; since most were beardless, though moustached, how and when did these men shave, and what tools did they use?

Wash Out the Canyon

To bathe; one of the few expressions that got by the image-makers.

Whacked the Cork

The gesture that the bar dog made when a man's credit ran out; used in the story with a shade of difference, but nevertheless indicating the bartender's prerogative then as now.

When School Kept

Here must come a confession: not until this story was finished and sold did the writer discover that most schools a century ago in Montana territory did business in the summer but not the winter; only later did the reverse become custom; by then the publisher, film producer, and writer were quite unwilling to scrap the whole project just because this one point made the story impossible; chalk one up for sublime ignorance.

While the Gate's Still Open

While you have the chance.

Working Ahead of the Roundup

Another term that shows an interesting tolerance for the irregular; this is what an ambitious rancher or cowhand did to increase his herd; he moved his cattle onto the range ahead of the big outfits and claimed a quantity of unbranded stock. This same tolerance for expediency shows up again in *to steal a start,* the practice of stealing enough cattle to start a subsequently honest spread with.

Wrangler

The man who took care of the horses during the day; apparently a diddling with the Spanish *caverango.*

Wreck Pan

What you put your dirty dishes in if you knew what was good for you.

Wrench

I knew several old-timers who "wrenched" the dishes or the mouth, and were amused at my effete "rinse."

Yack

Someone stupid.

Younker

A young one, usually a boy.

Western Words in Present-Day Use

Here is a sampling of modern terms used over a century ago on the range. Some of the meanings have changed somewhat, but not very much. Incidentally, a host of card and gambling terms have come down to us almost completely unchanged; apparently gamblers are more precise about language than grammarians. As suggested above, this is only a small fraction of our unexpected heritage from the West.

ace in the hole
bandwagon
to batch (like a bachelor)
the blues
boilermaker (drink)
brand (product name in the saddle)
to be buffaloed
busted (to throw)
that's a cinch
to croon
earmark
g-string
get a kick out of
gunny sack
hang up
haywire
a lowdown heel
well-heeled
hell for leather
hell on wheels
in hock
honky tonk
I got hooked
hoosegow
horsing around
hotfoot

hotheaded
irons in the fire
keep an ear to the ground
keep an eye peeled
Kenol
kitty (gambling)
knothead
lone ranger (unmarried man)
lone wolf
neither hide nor hair
pass the buck
to pull up in front of
ride herd
to ride somebody
round up your friends
screw (boss)
shavetail
shebang
small fry
spooning
stop riding me!
tail dragging
trot that by again
whang
what you're driving at
whing ding
yack

241

Bibliography

Before Barbed Wire, Mark H. Brown and W. R. Felton, Bramhall House.

The Frontier Years, Mark H. Brown and W. R. Felton, Bramhall House.

Western Words, Ramon F. Adams, University of Oklahoma Press.

Trail Driving Days, Dee Brown and Martin F. Schmitt, Scribner's.

The Nez Percé Indians and the Opening of the Northwest, Alvin M. Josephy, Jr., Yale University Press.

From the Pecos to the Powder, Ramon F. Adams, University of Oklahoma Press.

Back Trailing on the Open Range, Luke Sweetman, Caxton Printers.

The Log of a Cowboy, Andy Adams, Houghton, Mifflin.

The American Cowboy, Joe B. Frantz and Julian Ernest Choate, Jr., University of Oklahoma Press.

The Great North Trail, Dan Cushman, McGraw-Hill.

Cowhands, Cow Horses and Cows, Owen C. Ulph, American West.

The Story of the Cowboy, Emerson Hough, Grosset and Dunlap, 1897.

The Cowboy at Work, Fay E. Ward, Hastings House.

Forty Years on the Frontier, Granville Stuart, Arthur H. Clark Company, 1925.

Tread of the Longhorns, Walter Gann, Naylor.

The Longhorns, J. Frank Dobie, Bramhall House.

The Union Sundered, T. Harry Williams, Time Inc.

The Union Restored, T. Harry Williams, Time Inc.

The Age of Steel and Steam, Bernard A. Weisberger, Time Inc.

. . . and extended cud-chewing with Buzz Henry, one of today's authorities on the Western horse. The son of a cattleman and rancher, his information comes straight from the horse's mouth.

243

ABOUT THE AUTHOR

WILLIAM DALE JENNINGS was born in Amarillo, Texas, in 1917. He served during World War II as a sergeant in the U.S. Army at Guadalcanal and Leyte. Upon his discharge, he intensively studied literature and published his first short stories. Most recently he has written exclusively for films. He also makes his own films. *THE COWBOYS* is his second novel. His first, *The Ronin*, was published in 1968 and has been bought by Sterling Silliphant, who hopes to bring it to the screen in 1972. Mr. Jennings lives in Hollywood, California, and is at work on his third novel, *Ninety Miles from Home*.